Also by Gin Phillips

A Little Bit of Spectacular
The Hidden Summer
Come In and Cover Me
The Well and the Mine

FIERCE

Gin Phillips

BLACK SWAN

TRANSWORLD PUBLISHERS
61–63 Uxbridge Road, London W5 5SA
www.penguin.co.uk

Transworld is part of the Penguin Random House group of companies
whose addresses can be found at global.penguinrandomhouse.com

First published in Great Britain in 2017 by Doubleday as *Fierce Kingdom*
an imprint of Transworld Publishers
Black Swan edition published as *Fierce* in 2018

Excerpt on p. vii from 'Questions for Emily' from *Guest Host* (National Poetry
Review Press), © 2012, used by permission of Elizabeth Hughey.

Quotations on p. 100 from *Jaws*, written by Carl Gottlieb, and *Star Wars:
Episode IV – A New Hope*, written by George Lucas.

Quotations on p. 136 from 'The Highwayman' by Alfred Noyes, 1906,
and *Goodnight Moon* by Margaret Wise Brown and illustrated by
Clement Hurd, published by Harper & Row, 1947.

Lyrics on p. 165 from 'Monster Mash', released 1962 by Bobby 'Boris'
Pickett and The Crypt Kickers.

A CIP catalogue record for this book is available from the British Library.

ISBN
9781784162870 (B format)
9781784164041 (A format)

Typeset in 11.83/14.51pt Adobe Garamond Pro by Jouve (UK), Milton Keynes.
Printed and bound in Great Britain by Clays Ltd, Bungay, Suffolk

Penguin Random House is committed to a sustainable future
for our business, our readers and our planet. This book is made
from Forest Stewardship Council® certified paper.

1 3 5 7 9 10 8 6 4 2

To Eli,
who has entire worlds inside him

I just want to know if a sound can create a boy. Or, if a woman becomes a mother when she thinks she hears a baby crying for her.

'Questions for Emily', Elizabeth Hughey

FIERCE

4:55 p.m.

For a long while Joan has managed to balance on the balls of her bare feet, knees bent, skirt skimming the dirt. But now her thighs are giving out, so she puts a hand down and eases onto the sand.

Something jabs at her hip bone. She reaches underneath her leg and fishes out a small plastic spear – no longer than a finger – and it is no surprise, because she is always finding tiny weapons in unexpected places.

'Did you lose a spear?' she asks. 'Or is this one a scepter?'

Lincoln does not answer her, although he takes the piece of plastic from her open hand. He apparently has been waiting for her lap to become available – he backs up, settling himself comfortably on her thighs, not a speck of sand on him. He has a fastidiousness about him; he never did like finger painting.

'Do you want a nose, Mommy?' he asks.

'I have a nose,' she says.

'Do you want an extra one?'

'Who wouldn't?'

1

His dark curls need to be cut again, and he swipes them off his forehead. The leaves float down around them. The wooden roof, propped up on rough, round timber, shades them completely, but beyond it, the gray gravel is patterned with sunlight and shadows, shifting as the wind blows through the trees.

'Where are you getting these extra noses?' she asks.

'The nose store.'

She laughs, settling back on her hands, giving in to the feel of the clinging dirt. She flicks a few wettish grains from under her fingernails. The Dinosaur Discovery Pit is always damp and cold, never touched by the sun, but despite the sand on her skirt and the leaves stuck to her sweater, this is perhaps her favorite part of the zoo – off the main paths, past the merry-go-round and the petting barn and the rooster cages, back through the weedy, wooded area labeled only WOODLANDS. It is mostly trees and rocks and a few lonely animals back here along the narrow gravel paths: There is a vulture that lives in a pen with, for some reason, a rusted-out pickup truck. An owl that glares at a hanging chew toy. Wild turkeys that are always sitting, unmoving; she is not positive that they actually have legs. She imagines some cruel hunter's prank, some sweat-stained necklace strung with turkey feet.

She likes the haphazard strangeness of these woods, which are always shifting into some half-hearted try at an actual attraction. Currently a zip line is strung through the trees, although she never sees anyone zip-lining. She remembers animatronic dinosaurs here a couple of years earlier, and once there was a haunted ghost trail. There are hints at

2

more distant incarnations: large boulders that she assumes are real but possibly are not, plus split-log fences and a pioneer cabin. No obvious purpose to any of it. Empty cement pools might have been watering holes for large mammals. There are occasional efforts at a nature trail, random signage that makes a walk feel less anchored rather than more – one tree labeled SASSAFRAS while the twenty trees around it go nameless.

'Now, let me tell you something,' Lincoln begins, his hand landing on her knee. 'Do you know what Odin could use?'

She does, in fact, know a great deal about Norse gods lately.

'An eye store?' she says.

'Yes, actually. Because then he could stop wearing his eye patch.'

'Unless he likes his eye patch.'

'Unless that,' Lincoln agrees.

The sand around them is scattered with small plastic heroes and villains – Thor and Loki, Captain America, Green Lantern, and Iron Man. Everything comes back to superheroes lately. Pretend skeletons lurk beneath them in this sand pit – the vertebrae of some extinct animal protrude from the sand behind them, and there is a bucket of worn-down paintbrushes for brushing off the sand. She and Lincoln used to come here and dig for dinosaur bones, back in his former life as a three-year-old. But now, two months after his fourth birthday, he is several incarnations past his old archaeologist self.

The dinosaur pit is currently the Isle of Silence, the prison where Loki, Thor's trickster brother, has been imprisoned, and – when questions of extra noses don't arise – the air has been echoing with the sounds of an epic battle as Thor tries to make Loki confess to creating a fire demon.

Lincoln leans forward, and his epic resumes.

'The vile villain cackled,' Lincoln narrates. 'But then Thor had an idea!'

He calls them his stories, and they can last for hours if she lets them. She prefers the ones where he invents his own characters. He's concocted a villain named Horse Man, who turns people into horses. His nemesis is Horse Von, who turns those horses back into people. A vicious cycle.

Joan is half aware of Lincoln's voice changing tones and inflections as he takes his different characters through their paces. But she is pleasantly drifting. In the mornings these paths would be crowded with strollers and mothers in yoga pants, but by late afternoon most visitors have cleared out. She and Lincoln come here sometimes after she picks him up from school – they alternate between the zoo and the library and the parks and the science museum – and she steers him to the woods when she can. Here there are crickets, or something that sounds like crickets, and birds calling and leaves rustling but no human sounds except for Lincoln calling out his dialogue. He has absorbed the patter of superhero talk, and he can regurgitate it and make it his own.

'There was a secret weapon on his belt!'

'His evil plan had failed!'

He is vibrating with excitement. Every part of him is shaking, from the balls of his feet to his chuffy fists. Thor bobs through the air, and Lincoln bounces, and she wonders if he loves the idea of good conquering evil or simply an exciting battle, and she wonders when she should start making it clear that there is a middle ground between good and evil that most people occupy, but he is so happy that she does not want to complicate things.

'Do you know what happens then, Mommy?' he asks. 'After Thor punches him?'

'What?' she says.

She has perfected the art of being able to listen with half of herself while the other half spins and whirls.

'Loki has actually been mind-controlling Thor. And the punch makes him lose his powers!'

'Oh,' she says. 'And then what?'

'Thor saves the day!'

He keeps talking – 'But there's a new villain in town, boys!' – as she curls and straightens her toes. She thinks.

She thinks that she still needs to come up with a wedding present for her friend Murray – there is that artist who does dog paintings, and one of those seems like a thoughtful choice, so she should send an e-mail and see about placing the order, although 'order' is probably an insulting sort of word to an artist. She remembers that she meant to call her great-aunt this morning, and she thinks that maybe instead – she is solving problems left and right here, having a burst of mental efficiency as Loki gets buried in sand – maybe instead she will mail her great-aunt that hilarious paper-bag monkey that Lincoln made in school. Surely the artwork is better than a phone call, although there's a certain selfishness to it, since she hates to talk on the phone, and, all right, it is a cop-out – she knows it – but she settles on the paper-bag monkey regardless. She thinks of the squash dressing her great-aunt makes. She thinks of the left-over plantain chips in the kitchen cabinet. She thinks of Bruce Boxleitner. Back in junior high she was slightly obsessed with him in *Scarecrow and Mrs King*, and she has discovered that the show is available in its entirety online, so she has been rewatching it, episode by episode – it holds up well for a 1980s show, with its Cold War spies and bad hair – and she can't remember whether Lee and Amanda finally kiss at the end of the second season or the third season, and she has six more episodes to go in the second season, but she could always skip to the third.

A woodpecker hammers somewhere nearby, and she is pulled back to here and now. She notices that the wart on Lincoln's hand is getting bigger. It looks like an anemone. There is that beautiful shifting of shadows on the gravel, and Lincoln is doing his evil-villain laugh, and it strikes her that these afternoons, with her son's weight on her legs, the woods around them, are something like euphoric.

Thor falls against her foot, his plastic head landing on her toe.

'Mommy?'

'Yes?'

'Why doesn't Thor wear his helmet in the movie?'

'I think it's harder to see with a helmet on.'

'But doesn't he want his head protected?'

'I suppose sometimes he wears it and sometimes he doesn't. Depending on his mood.'

'I think he should protect his head all the time,' he says.

6

'It's dangerous to battle without a helmet. Why do you think Captain America only wears a hood? It's not good protection, is it?'

Paul gets bored with this superhero chatter – her husband would much rather talk football formations and NBA line-ups – but Joan doesn't mind it. She was once obsessed with Wonder Woman. *Super Friends.* The Incredible Hulk. *Who would win in a fight,* she once asked her uncle, *Superman or the Incredible Hulk?* He'd said, *Well, if he was losing, Superman could always fly away,* and she'd thought that a blindingly brilliant answer.

'Captain America has his shield,' she tells Lincoln. 'That's what he uses for protection.'

'What if he can't get it over his head in time?'

'He's very fast.'

'But still,' he says, unconvinced.

'You know, you're right,' she says, because he is. 'He really should wear a helmet.'

Some sort of man-made rock forms the back wall of the pit, beige and bulging, and a small animal is rooting around behind it. She hopes it is not a rat. She imagines a squirrel but makes a point not to turn her head.

She opens her purse to peer at her phone. 'We probably need to start heading toward the gate in around five minutes,' she says.

As he often does when she says it's time to stop playing, Lincoln acts as if she has not spoken at all.

'Does Dr Doom always wear a mask?' he asks.

'Did you hear me?' she asks.

'Yes.'

7

'What did I say?'

'That we're about to leave.'

'Okay,' she says. 'Yes, Dr Doom always wears a mask. Because of his scars.'

'Scars?'

'Yeah, the scars he got in the lab experiment.'

'Why would he wear a mask because of them?'

'Because he wants to cover them up,' she says. 'He thinks they're ugly.'

'Why would he think they're ugly?'

She watches a bright-orange leaf land. 'Well, they made him look different,' she says. 'Sometimes people don't want to look different.'

'I don't think scars are ugly.'

As he's speaking, a sharp, loud sound carries through the woods. Two cracks, then several more. Pops, like balloons bursting. Or fireworks. She tries to imagine what anyone could be doing in a zoo that would sound like small explosions. Something related to the Halloween festivities? They've strung up lights all over the place – not here in the Woodlands but all over the more popular pathways – so maybe a transformer blew? Is there construction going on, a jackhammer?

There is another bang. Another and another. It sounds too loud to be balloons, too infrequent to be a jackhammer.

The birds are silent, but the leaves keep skittering down.

Lincoln is unbothered.

'Could I use my Batman for Dr Doom?' he asks. 'He wears black. And if I use him, can you make him the right kind of mask?'

'Sure,' she says.

'What will you make it with?'

'Tinfoil,' she suggests.

A squirrel scrabbles across the roof of the dirt pit, and she hears the soft *whoosh* of its impact when it leaps to a tree.

'And what will we use for the scarves?' Lincoln asks.

She looks down at him.

'Scarves?' she repeats.

He nods. She nods back, considering and replaying. She gives herself over to deciphering the workings of his brain: it is one of the bits of mothering that has delighted her all the more because she did not know it existed. His mind is complicated and unique, weaving worlds of its own. In his sleep sometimes he will cry out entire sentences – 'Not down the stairs!' – and there are windows to his inner machinery, glimpses, but she will never really know it all, and that is the thrill. He is a whole separate being, as real as she is.

Scarves. She works the puzzle of it.

'Do you mean the scarves on his face?' she asks.

'Yes. The ones he thinks are ugly.'

She laughs. 'Oh. I was saying "scars" – you know, like the one on Daddy's arm where the water burned him when he was little? Or the one on my knee from when I fell down?'

'Oh,' he says, sheepish. He laughs, too. He is quick to get a joke. 'Scars, not scarves. So he doesn't think scarves are ugly?'

'I don't really know how Dr Doom feels about scarves,' she says.

'He doesn't have them on his face.'

'No. Those are scars.'

She listens, half considering whether she could have handled the idea of scars more tactfully, half wondering about gunshots. But they could not have been gunshots. And if they had been, she would have heard something else by now. Screams or sirens or a voice coming over a loudspeaker making some kind of announcement.

There is nothing.

She has been watching too many battles.

She checks her phone. They only have a few minutes until the zoo closes, and it is entirely possible that they might be overlooked back here in the woods. She has imagined the scenario more than once: camping in the zoo overnight, maybe even intentionally hiding back here, going to visit the animals in the pitch-black of midnight – children's books are written about such situations. It's ridiculous, of course, because there surely would be security guards. Not that she has ever noticed a security guard here.

They should get moving.

'We need to go, sweet,' she says, lifting him from her lap, waiting until he takes his weight on his own feet, which he does reluctantly. She thinks he should be wearing a jacket, but he swore he wasn't cold, so she let him leave it in the car.

'Do we have a little more time?' he asks.

She gets up from the sand and slides on her sandals. This preference for sandals is the reason she lacks the moral authority to tell him to wear a jacket.

'No,' she says. 'It's nearly five thirty. Closing time. Sorry. We need to get out of here fast, or they might lock us in.'

She is now starting to get nervous about that possibility – she's waited too long, and they have the whole walk out of the woods and then the long way through the children's area, and they really are going to be cutting it close.

'Can we stop at the playground and go across the bridge?' Lincoln asks.

'Not today. We can come back tomorrow.'

He nods and steps from the sand onto the sparse grass. He does not like to break rules. If the zoo people say it is time to go home, then he will go home.

'Can you help me with my shoes?' he asks. 'And put my guys in your purse?'

She bends down, brushes the sand from his feet, then pulls his socks over his pale toes and his wide, stubby feet. She tears open the Velcro straps of his tennis shoes and looks up to see a cardinal land an arm's length away. The animals have no fear in them at all here. She can sometimes spot half a dozen sparrows or chipmunks or squirrels within a few feet, eyeing whatever battle Lincoln is staging.

She drops his plastic figures into her purse.

'All done,' she says.

5:23 p.m.

Joan scans the sand pit for any forgotten plastic men, and then she takes Lincoln's hand and heads down the path leading out of the woods. She wonders when he will stop wanting to hold her hand, but for now they seem equally happy with the arrangement. In less than twenty steps the trees have opened up – it's only an illusion, the seclusion of this place – and there's the sound of the waterfall splattering on the rocks in front of the otter exhibit.

The otter is one of their favorite animals, one of the few that will still pull Lincoln from his stories. The two otters have a huge cavern-styled enclosure with faux-rock overhangs, and the animals curve and flip and dive in a greenish pool behind a wide glass wall. The rocks jut over the walkway, and a waterfall rushes over visitors' heads and spills down to a turtle pond thick with lily pads and reeds and some sort of purple-flowered stalk. The wooden footpath that winds over the pond has always struck her as the prettiest part of the Woodlands – but now it seems only empty.

Lincoln laughs next to her. 'Look at the otter. Look how he swims.'

He still struggles with words ending in *-er*. 'Ott-o,' he says, instead of 'otter'. Lex Luth-o. Score a goal in socc-o.

'I like his paws,' she says.

'He has paws? Not fins? Real paws like a dog or finger paws like a monkey?'

She is tempted to stop and point out the anatomy of otters. This is what she wants most for him, maybe, to see that life is full of astonishing things, to know that you should pay attention – *Look, it's beautiful*, he said, staring into a puddle of gasoline in the zoo parking lot – but they don't have time. She gives his hand a tug, and he comes easily enough, though his head is slow to turn away from the otter. As they step onto the wooden bridge, lily pads to either side of them, she wishes that they would see someone else, some other chattering family also running late. Not that it's unusual to have the path to themselves. They often see no one else all the way to the exit in the afternoon, and they are pushing it closer than usual to closing time. She picks up her pace.

'Want to race?' she asks.

'No.'

'You want to skip?'

'No, thank you.'

He plods along.

She sometimes wonders if his determination not to do a thing is in direct proportion to the amount of enthusiasm she shows for it. He continues meandering along the bridge, pausing to shrink back from a gnat or to stare down at a speckled koi. He comes to a complete stop to scratch his chin. When she asks him to hurry, he frowns, and she knows by the look on his face what he will ask for.

13

'I want you to carry me,' he says.

'I can't carry you all the way to the car,' she says. 'You're getting too big.'

She watches his lip slide out.

'Here's my compromise,' she says, before this escalates and slows them down further. 'I'll pick you up when we get to the scarecrows, and I'll carry you from there. If you can do a good job of walking to the scarecrows.'

'Okay,' he says, although his voice is wobbly and his lip is extending more, and he is starting to wail even as he moves his feet in time with hers.

She did not, it occurs to her, specify that he could not cry as he walks. He is technically meeting her terms. It is possible that he will cry himself out in a few seconds and get distracted by some passing thought of Thor's helmet or Odin's eye patch. It is possible that he will only cry more loudly, and she will give in and pick him up because he has actually walked quite a long way, uncomplainingly, on his small legs. It is possible that he will keep crying and she will stand firm and make him walk all the way to the car because she does not want him to turn into one of those children who throw tantrums.

Such a system of checks and balances – parenting – of projections and guesswork and cost–benefit ratios.

A dragonfly hovers and darts. A heron picks its way along the edge of the water. The wooden path cuts back and forth through trees and wild grass.

Lincoln has stopped crying, and she's fairly sure he's humming the Georgia Bulldogs' fight song – 'Glory, glory to old Georgia! / Glory, glory to old Georgia!' – although as soon as she finishes the thought, he switches to the Texas Long-horns. No one in their family is a fan of either team, but he soaks up fight-song lyrics as he soaks up superheroes and villains.

He is a collector. He accumulates.

Through the trees she can see the tent-like top of the merry-go-round. It shines white against the dishwater sky. They pass a chicken-wire-enclosed exhibit for a one-legged eagle and a near-invisible enclosure for a pair of egrets. There are dead logs and monkey grass and lime-green weeds. She walks toward an overhanging branch, and one of its leaves detaches, turning into a yellow butterfly and weaving up to the sky.

Finally they are back on the concrete sidewalks, which are as wide as roads. Jack-o'-lanterns perch on the fence posts.

They take a few steps into civilization, and she glances over at the merry-go-round. It is still and silent; the painted giraffes and zebras and bears and gorillas and ostriches are frozen. Lincoln used to love the merry-go-round, although he would only ride a zebra. Now the carousel animals have rubber bats and tiny Kleenex ghosts floating around them, hanging from the wooden framework. She and Lincoln are close enough that the white canvas top covering the carousel spreads over them, bright and calm.

'Mommy,' he says. 'Carry me.'

'When we get to the scarecrows,' she says, ignoring his arms stretched toward her. 'Just a little farther.'

He doesn't protest this time. They hurry past the merry-go-round, toward the food court and the Kid Zone

Splash Park, with the fountains of shoulder-high water still arcing onto the blue-raspberry-colored splash pads.

'Medusa's been here,' Lincoln announces, and she looks beyond the spraying water to the shaded spot with the stone statues of a turtle, a frog and a lizard. These days, anytime they see stone figures it is a sign that Medusa has passed by. *Spider-Man has been here*, he says to spiderwebs.

'Those poor guys,' she says, because it is what she says every time they pass Medusa's victims.

'They should have kept their eyes closed,' he says, because it is what he says every time.

She glances at the darkened glass of the Koala Café, with its shelves of plastic-wrapped sandwiches and Jell-O and hard-boiled eggs, but she sees no sign of movement inside. The plastic chairs are upside down on the square tables. The staff usually close down the restaurants and lock the buildings fifteen minutes before closing time, so she's not surprised.

Off to their right is the playground with the rock mountains and swinging bridge. Once upon a time, Lincoln was interested in Antarctica, and the big rocks were icebergs. Then last spring he was playing knights and castles on the swinging bridge, yelling at invisible kings to bring out the cannons and to fill the catapults with rocks. Now that same bridge is always Thor's rainbow-colored pathway to Earth. In a year Lincoln will be in kindergarten and these days of superheroes will fade and be replaced by something she can't guess, and then at some point the zoo itself will be replaced and life will have gone on and this boy holding her hand will have turned into someone else entirely.

They are making good time now, scurrying past the gift shop and the wooden cut-out where a kid can stick his head through a hole and pretend he is a gorilla. They slow down by the algae-clogged aquariums at the edge of the children's area – Lincoln cannot resist looking for the giant turtle – and an older woman appears a few yards in front of them, just around the curve of the aquarium walls, staggering backward slightly. She is holding a shoe.

'The rock's out, Tara,' she says, and there is a certain cheerful desperation in her voice that identifies her as a grandmother. 'Come on, now.'

Two blonde girls, surely sisters, come into view, and the grandmother leans down, holding out the shoe to the smaller girl. Her hair is in pigtails, and she looks a little younger than Lincoln.

'We've got to go,' says the grandmother as she works the rubber sandal onto a small foot. Then she straightens.

The little one says something, too quiet to hear, even though they are all within a few feet of each other now. Several flies tap against the aquarium glass.

'I'll take them off when we get to the car,' says the grandmother, out of breath. She takes an off-balance step, holding the girls by their wrists. The girls blink at Lincoln, but then the woman is propelling them forward.

'That's a grandmother,' Lincoln says, too loudly, stopping suddenly enough that he jerks Joan's arm.

'I think so, too,' she whispers.

Joan glances toward the older woman – there is a flowery chemical smell in the air, perfume that reminds her of Mrs Manning in the sixth grade, who gave her and no one

17

else a copy of *Island of the Blue Dolphins* on the last day of school – but the woman and her grandchildren are gone now, already past the curve of the final aquarium.

'If I had a grandmother, is that what she would look like?' Lincoln asks.

He has been fixated on grandparents lately. She hopes it will pass as quickly as all his other phases.

'You do have a grandmother,' Joan says, tugging him forward again. 'Grandma. Daddy's mommy. She was here at Christmas, remember? She just lives far away. We need to go, sweet.'

'Some people have lots of grandparents. I only have one.'

'No, you have three. Remember? Now we've got to get going or we'll get in trouble.'

The magic words. He nods and speeds up, his face serious and resolute.

There is another popping sound, louder and closer than before, maybe a dozen sharp cracks in the air. She thinks it might be something hydraulic.

They've come to the edge of a pond – the largest one in the zoo, nearly a lake – and she catches a glimpse of swans cutting through the water. The path forks: the right branch would lead them around the far side of the pond, up through the Africa exhibit, but the left will take them to the exit in a few less seconds. She can see the green-and-red flash of the parrots up ahead, unusually quiet. She likes their little island in the middle of all the concrete – a bricked-in pool with a grassy mound and spindly trees – and it is always their first and last stop, the final ritual of every visit.

'Start practicing your parrot caws,' she tells him.

'I don't need to practice,' he says. 'I just want to see the scarecrows.'

'We'll have to look at them while we walk.'

A long row of scarecrows has been propped along the fence that circles the pond. Many of them have pumpkins for heads, and Lincoln is fascinated by them. He loves the Superman one and the astronaut one – with the pumpkin painted like a white space helmet – and especially the Cat in the Hat.

'All right, sweet,' she says.

He drops her hand and lifts his arms.

She glances along the fence, spotting the bright-blue pumpkin head of Pete the Cat. About halfway down the fence several scarecrows have fallen. Blown down by the wind, she assumes, but, no, it hasn't been stormy. Still, the scarecrows have collapsed, half a dozen of them scattered all the way down to the parrot exhibit and beyond.

No, not scarecrows. Not scarecrows.

She sees an arm move. She sees a body way too small to be a scarecrow. A skirt, hiked indecently over a pale hip, legs bent.

She is slow to lift her eyes, but when she looks farther, past the shapes on the ground, past the parrots, toward the long, flat building with public bathrooms and doors marked EMPLOYEES ONLY, she sees a man standing, facing away from her, unmoving. He is by the water fountain. He is in jeans and a dark shirt, no coat. His hair is brown or black, and other than that she cannot see details, but she cannot miss it when he does finally move. He kicks the bathroom door, his elbow coming up to catch it, a gun in his right hand, some sort of rifle, long and black, the narrow end of it stretching like an antenna past his dark head as he disappears into the pale-green walls of the women's bathroom.

She thinks there is another movement around the parrots, someone else still on his feet, but she is turning away by then. She does not see more.

She grabs Lincoln and heaves him up, his legs swinging heavily as he lands against her hip, her right hand grabbing her left wrist underneath his bottom, linking her arms.

She runs.

5:32 p.m.

She goes forward, not toward the bodies, of course, but around the pond, toward Africa. As she's moving, it occurs to her that she could have gone back toward the woods and that she could still turn around and aim for the shade of their sand pit or the tall trees, but she does not want to turn around, because she is not sure if the man – men? – saw them or not, if he might be following them, taking his time, because he is the one with the gun and for him there is no hurry. Also there is a part of her that resists going backward anyway, that thinks forward must be better. Safer.

Go. Go. Go. The word is in her head, repeating. Her feet slam the concrete in time to it.

She imagines the gunman watching them, taking his first steps toward them, rounding the lake, smile spreading. She imagines him picking up speed.

She cannot stand it. She glances over her shoulder and sees no one, but she cannot get a good look, because she does not want to slow down.

Her knit skirt stretches tight against her legs as she runs, and she would like to yank it higher, but she does not have a free hand. *Maybe it will rip*, she thinks hopefully. She can hear the tiny rocks scrape under her shoes. She clenches the thong of her sandal between her toes, hearing her soles flap – one more fear, a shoe falling off.

There are Halloween lights strung all along this path, just above her head, lights glowing cheerfully every step of her way, bright white, like when Lincoln accidentally shines the flashlight in her eyes.

The sky is darkening.

'Why are we running?' Lincoln asks, all forty pounds of him bouncing against her hip bone, and she is amazed that he has been quiet for so long. Maybe he has only now noticed that they are not headed for the parking lot.

Her lungs burn when she tries to take in enough breath to form an answer.

'I'll tell you' – she has to inhale – 'in a minute.'

His arms tighten around her neck. The railroad track is paralleling them, just beyond the bright lights, and what she would not give to see the little red-and-black train pulling up beside them now, ready to whisk them off, although she thinks she might be able to run at a faster speed than the train can manage. Still, she wants the train. Her arms are already starting to ache, and she flashes to last week when they walked to the park – *do ducks have teeth? will they definitely not bite me? do ducks have feet? why didn't I walk when I was a baby? did I have feet? did I have legs?* That afternoon she actually reached a stage on the way back home when she was unable to carry him farther and had to put him down on the grass even though he was crying as she did it.

22

She will not put him down.

'Mommy!' he says, frustrated, a hand on her face. 'Not in a minute.'

'There was a bad man,' Joan says, and surely she would not have said it if she weren't panicked.

'Where?' he asks.

She has lost track. 'What?'

'Where is the bad man?' he asks.

She hops over the railroad crossing in two steps – also, if the train came along, it would mean there was another human being driving it, and she would like to see another human being – and then the lake is behind them and the bodies and the man are on the other side of it, and that is a good thing. The winding, uphill path to Africa is lined with trees – broad-leafed things, rainforest plants – good for blocking anyone's view of them. They are surely harder to see now, if anyone is looking.

'He was back there,' she says, nearly stumbling.

She hears sirens. Impossible to tell how close, but it means the police are coming and they will fix everything, but that does not help her now.

'I didn't see a bad man. How do you know he's bad?' His chin rams into her shoulder.

It upsets him when she won't answer his questions, and she does not want him to start crying, because she does not want noise and also because then he would start fidgeting or, worse, go limp. He is twice as heavy when he goes boneless.

'We need to get away,' she says, panting. 'Right now. So help Mommy and just hold on – wrap your legs a little

23

tighter – and let me get somewhere safe and then I'll answer you.'

She barely gets all the words out. Her lungs are bursting. Her thighs scream. The sun has dropped behind the tree-tops, and the shadows of the plants are long and emaciated under her feet.

Her elbows brush a banana leaf, solid and broad as a wing.

'Where?' he asks, because of course he will not stop asking. 'Where are we going?'

She does not know. Which way? What next? What is she even looking for? Her feet keep their rhythm, and she curls her toes more tightly, and she wishes this way were not uphill.

She cannot do this for much longer.

Hide. They have to hide.

That must be the first thing, and then they can call the police or Paul or both. She thinks she should call the police – just to let them know that she and Lincoln are trapped in here. Surely they need to know who is still inside the zoo? She shifts him from her right hip to her left and readjusts her hold on him.

'Mommy!' he says, still wanting some kind of answer. Always wanting an answer.

Finally they have crested the hill, and the walls of perfectly wildly landscaped plants are past them, and she is staring at the African elephant exhibit, all sandy hills and grassland and flowing creek, and they must either turn left or right. Right would take them to the giraffes and lions and tigers; left would curve around to the rhinos and wild dogs and monkeys.

24

'Mommy!'

She kisses his head and turns left.

'I hit my tooth on your shoulder,' he says.

'Sorry,' she says.

She is glad now that she did not go to the woods and the familiar narrow paths of the dinosaur pit, because even with all the tall trees around, they would not have found much to hide behind, and the few good spots – the log cabin and the butterfly house, maybe – would have been far too obvious. Of course, there would have been room to run and maneuver if they'd been spotted, but how much can she really maneuver with Lincoln attached to her? No, they do not need space to run. If someone spots them, running will get them nowhere.

This strikes her as an important thought. Proof that her brain is pushing through the panic.

Yes. They will get nowhere running. They need to hide so well that they cannot be seen, not even if someone walks right past them. She needs a rabbit hole. A bunker. A secret passage.

He has stopped saying 'Mommy'. Something of her fear must have communicated itself to him, and she is glad as long as it is the right amount of fear – enough to turn him docile but not terrified. She can't really tell now, but she will find out once they are safe.

The elephant exhibit stretches out forever, and as she skirts the railings of it, she hears music playing, and at first it is unintelligible, only a note here and there, but soon she can make out the *Ghostbusters* theme song. The music is cheerful and far too loud by the time she passes the

Coke machine that Lincoln often pretends is the Bat computer.

The Joker is up to his old tricks! To the Batmobile! Mommy, do you think there's a Bat carwash, because the Batmobile gets dirty but it's a convertible, so could they wash it? Her ankle turns slightly, but she does not slow down. There is an actual elephant, sleepy-looking, surprisingly close to the railing on their right, and she is glad for the substantial shape of it. She half sees the gentle tick-tock of its trunk, registers the rhythm of it, but she is turning in the other direction, to her left, scanning the broad building only a few yards away. The Savannah Snack Bar. They've eaten raisins under its giant thatched roof, the ceiling fan blowing on them in the summer air, but they have never sat inside the actual restaurant. She likes to stay outside, watch the elephants, pretend they are in Africa – she will take him there someday, she's always thought – she likes to think of all the places she will show him. *Did you really ride an elephant in Thailand, Mommy? Yes, that was before you were born.* She eyes the bathrooms as she passes them, slowing, but she thinks of doors being kicked in and speeds up again. The restaurant itself, now that might be safer – surely the doors have locks, and there would be more rooms inside, offices and storerooms with better locks, hiding places and closets, maybe chairs or tables or heavy boxes you could pile against a door. The thought is quick and tempting, and she darts under the shade of the thatched roof and shoves the glass doors, but they don't budge, and everything is dark inside.

OPEN, says the sign.

WITCHES' BREW SLUSHY, says another sign, purple and pink. SPOOK-A-LICIOUS!

Joan spins and begins running again, and Lincoln's arms are tight around her neck, which helps take a little of his weight off her arms, but she is spent and off-balance, and she nearly runs into a concrete column.

There is a speaker above her head, she notices. The music is blaring from it, promising that the Ghostbusters can take care of invisible men.

She backs away from the pavilion, away from the speakers, back into the dimming sunlight. The elephant and its graceful trunk are gone and how can anything that big disappear and she whispers *It's okay* into Lincoln's ear, over and over, and she speeds up again even though she is aimless. This is nothing like the steady rhythm of her regular runs around neighborhood streets. She is ill-prepared. She thinks of her big brother, back during his army training, when he was obsessed with something called rucking: strapping a thirty-pound bag to himself and running many miles with it. She hardly knew him by that time, because he had moved to Ohio with her father, had escaped long before she did, and she only saw him for two weeks in the summers and sometimes holidays. He was a grown man visiting her, and he slid his rucksack on her – that was, what, seven years before she ran her first marathon – and she tried to impress him but her back was wet with sweat and she was panting after two blocks. She is panting now, biceps burning, Lincoln's weight listing her to the side, and she'd be so much better off if she'd been rucking all these years.

How long has she been running? Three minutes? Four? No time. Forever.

Behind the '80s synthesizers in the music, she can still hear the sirens. Louder now.

She is nearly at the rhino exhibit. She sees two teenagers, a boy and a girl, running toward her, running as if they know something is wrong, not as if they are only trying to make it to the gate by closing time. She thought she wanted to see people, but now she finds she does not. People only complicate things. They slow down when they see her – the boy grabs at his sunglasses, which are falling from his face – and they both talk at once, asking something, but Joan only steps around them, turning sideways as she moves.

The girl's skirt is orange with a fringe of black lace, so short and tight it barely covers her underwear and what kind of mother does this girl have at home and maybe actually a very good mother who has taught her she is beautiful even in a skirt like a sausage casing.

'Don't go toward the exit,' Joan says, hardly slowing. 'A man is shooting people.'

'Shooting?' says the girl.

The boy lets loose more words, too many of them, lost in the air.

'He'll kill you if he sees you,' Joan calls over her shoulder, but she is long past them. 'Go hide somewhere until the police come.'

She does not look back. The only thing that matters is Lincoln. He cannot wind up bleeding on concrete.

It's good that the restaurant was locked. That would have been stupid. She and Lincoln might have been well hidden

28

there, but the man would check the buildings, wouldn't he? Indoor places would be his first targets. Kicking in doors and smashing windows and knocking things down – it must satisfy him, breaking things, and there is not much to shatter in the open air, not like furniture and doors and bones, so solid.

She can hear her breathing and her footsteps, as soft as she can make them, but she can also hear the wind and the background noise of traffic not so far away and the leaves trembling on branches – all the background noise that she never bothers to listen to. She needs this background noise, because Lincoln will never be perfectly quiet. He is a good boy, but he cannot be expected to stay completely silent, and what if a single whisper slaughters them?

Out in the open.

But hidden. Someplace no one would look.

She glances behind her at the open space of elephant habitat, which has plenty of rocks and entire walls of boulders, but there is a steep drop – not jumpable – down to ground level. And there are elephants, and the whole idea is moronic, but there is a spark there – something – the shooter would not check exhibits, surely?

She has thought this in no more than ten footsteps, so quickly and so slowly – if she turned around, she would likely still see the teenagers – and all this thinking is getting her nowhere. The lion roars, from a distance, and it is not a shocking sound, because they feed the animals right before closing, and the lion is always vocal, anticipating. It roars again, comforting almost. She is surrounded by wild things in boxes. She feels a thrum of solidarity.

A monkey chatters, high-pitched and aggressive, and she wonders whether maybe the keepers never got to the evening feedings. Maybe they were interrupted.

It comes to her then. The porcupine.

The buildings should all be locked, but maybe not? Maybe that last set of keys never made it up this way?

She prays as she has not in a very long time while she spins toward the primate building. She passes the African-themed playground on her left – drums and masks and seesaw and the statue of the dung beetle – and then she darts under the spider monkeys and their complicated rope course, where they are lolling about, oblivious, swinging paw-to-tail, and then she is at the entrance to the Primate Zone, shoving the double doors, which give way immediately. She sprints deeper into the cool, dark halls of the building, passing lemurs with their black-and-white-striped tails, and then she is around a curve, everything shadowed, with tree trunks growing through the floor. As with most of the scenery here, she does not know whether the trees are real or manufactured, but when she puts out one hand to steady herself, the bark feels real.

'A man was shooting people?' asks Lincoln against her collarbone.

'Yes.'

'Is he chasing us?'

'No,' she says.

'Then why are we running?'

She can see natural light in the exhibits, sunlight trapped inside the glass, and she can't help but notice that the animals have boulders and caves to hide in, caves that might even lead into unseen rooms if you could only get through the glass barriers. But she cannot pass through walls – the Invisible Woman? one of the X-Men? – so she keeps jogging through the halls, brushing against smooth glass and cinder-block walls that are rough and tidy.

There will be a point, she knows, when her muscles stop working. When her arms loosen and fall no matter how she fights them. For now, there is only a constant burn – pulsing – from her shoulders to her wrists, from her hips to her ankles.

'Mommy?'

'We're nearly there,' she says, but the words come out barely formed.

There are monkeys and more monkeys, all unconcerned.

Then she sees a glass door, and she rams it with her shoulder and they are outside again, cool air blowing. They're facing a weathered railing that comes up to her chest. Beyond it, there is a small fenced-in wilderness of pine trees and tall grass. She's standing on the wooden planks of a deck – a patio between the exhibit halls. To her left is another glass door that would lead to baboons and orangutans and other glassed-in habitats and open hallways that are no good to her. Here the sign on the brick wall explains the habits of the porcupine, although there is no explanation for why a porcupine was put in the Primate Zone. Months ago a zoo-keeper with a notebook in her hand admitted – quietly, so Lincoln wouldn't hear – that the porcupine had died. Joan and Lincoln have been checking periodically for a new specimen. She told him the truth, since it wasn't as if he hadn't seen dead birds and squirrels and squished roaches and why act like nothing ever dies, and he has been hoping for a baby porcupine. But the pen has stayed empty.

She hopes it has stayed empty.

She steps closer to the railing, scanning the low-growing trees and hollowed-out logs. The bare patches of dirt and gravel overwhelm the few tufts of wild grass. The whole thing is unkempt and neglected. The middle section of the pen is what she's remembered – boulders three or four feet high. The wall of rock stretches maybe a dozen feet across, curving around so there is no clear view of whatever might be behind it. A chain-link fence, half covered in vines, seals in the space. The fence is easily fifteen feet tall, with the top panel angled steeply, prohibitively inward – did they really have any sort of trouble with climbing porcupines? – and pine trees tower along the edges.

It is hidden back here, deep in the twists and turns of the primate house. It does not look fit for humans, and that is what strikes her as perfect about it.

She lowers Lincoln onto the railing and gasps as she surrenders his weight. The railing will be easy enough to climb over, and there is a short ledge on the other side that's nearly as long as her feet. She can get her footing there and then lift Lincoln, and even if something goes wrong, the drop to the ground is no more than a couple of feet, and he wouldn't get hurt, but he might start crying and the noise would be – no, there is no danger of him falling. She can keep a hand on him the entire time.

'This is what we're going to do,' she says. 'I'm going to sit you right here while I climb over—'

He shakes his head and grabs tightly above her elbows.

'Mommy, we can't go in with the animals!'

'There aren't any, remember?' she says, trying to dislodge his fingers. 'This is the porcupine's home. And there's no new porcupine yet.'

'Fences are to keep the animals in and the people out,' he says.

She has never been so sorry that he always follows the rules.

'The rules are different today,' she says. 'There are emergency rules now. The rules are that we hide and do not let the man with the gun find us.'

Lincoln relaxes his hold, peers behind him, and clutches at her again.

'I'll fall,' he says. 'It's too high.'

'Would I let you fall?'

'No,' he says, pressing closer to her. 'Mommy.'

'I'll have my hands around you. I'm just going to climb over now—'

'Mommy,' he whimpers.

'Shhhhh. I've got you.'

She boosts herself and straddles the railing, keeping her hands on either side of his body so that her arms are still bracketing him. It is awkward, but she swings herself the rest of the way over, the balls of her feet fairly stable on the ledge.

He has clasped a hand lightly on each of her wrists. She can hear him breathing, near tears. Because of a man shooting people or because of this complete break from the normal boundaries of things? She has no idea.

'Mommy.'

'I've got you,' Joan says, and she loops an arm around him, pulling him against her chest with the crook of her elbow. His heels thud against the iron mesh.

'I'm going to lift you down,' she tells him, 'and I want you to put your feet on this little step here and hold on to the metal part with your hands. Then I'm going to hop on the ground and scoop you up.'

She lifts him even as she is still speaking, not giving him a chance to think more about it, because he does not usually get braver when he considers things, and she can have this over in two seconds. She holds tight to the railing with one hand and slides him back, bending her waist and holding herself far from the railing to make room for him, and there is one moment when he is in midair, anchored only by her arm and elbow, and she feels his panic, but then she has his feet on the same ledge she is standing on, his tennis shoes tucked between her own leather sandals. She wraps his fingers tightly around the mesh.

'Hold tight,' she says.

She pushes off, landing soft and easy in the dirt beneath them, the grass high enough to tickle her wrists. She pulls him down to her, turning him so that his arms wrap around her neck. His legs clasp her hips, and she is moving again, watching her footing as much as she can with him obscuring her view – she remembers how a pregnant belly made uneven ground an unseen obstacle course – and finally they are behind the tall rocks she had found so tempting.

She lowers herself, sinking down so that her back is against the rock – hard and cold – and her legs are splayed on the ground. He is still curled around her.

34

5:42 p.m.

Lincoln has not loosened his hold on her, so she pulls her phone from her purse with one hand and then holds it in front of her, just past the curve of his skull, her palm brushing his tangled curls, which are always matted in the back, like he has been rubbing syrup into his scalp. She swipes her thumb across the screen, and then she freezes, still not sure whether to call the police or Paul – the police are here already, surely, and maybe they would have questions for her. But it is Paul's voice that she needs to hear.

And then she sees a text from Paul already. She stares at his black-and-gray message, the squared-off bubble of it so familiar.

You didn't go to the zoo this afternoon, did you? Let me know asap.

He has no idea where they've gone, of course. She usually doesn't know their destination until Lincoln declares his choice for the afternoon as she buckles him into his car seat. Paul can only be asking because he knows something.

She types back, and she has a thought of calling him

instead, but her thumbs have automatically begun responding. It is habit.

Yes. At zoo. Do you know what's happening? Hiding in porcupine exhibit right now.

There is no way he will know where the porcupine exhibit is. He does not visit the zoo nearly as often as she does. She adds:

In the Primate Zone.

She presses Send, then immediately begins a second message.

Call police. Saw bodies at the entrance. Man with gun.

Again she presses Send. There's something wrong with the order of her messages – they are jumbled up – but she cannot stop her thumbs from typing. She likes watching them move, likes seeing the letters string themselves together into sentences, likes the light of the screen, and as long as she is typing there is nothing but blue shapes filled with words, stacked one on top of the other.

We are fine. Totally safe, she tells him, and then her thumbs pause, thinking of what can come next.

Lincoln's hair tickles her arm. He is beginning to shift and wriggle. Under her breath she hums 'Edelweiss', the lullaby she and Paul sing to him every night. She is humming too fast, too high, the song on fast-forward.

She needs to type something else. Her fingers tap slightly against the air, twitchy.

'Why are you on your phone?' Lincoln asks, his voice muffled against her shoulder.

'Daddy,' she says, just as Paul sends another message.

Read this. Am calling you now. Love.

There is a link below the message. She glances at the blue string of underlined letters and numbers, and then the phone rings, trilling far too loudly – it has not occurred to her to silence it – and she immediately answers.

'I can't talk,' she says, sounding somehow professional. Like she is in the middle of a meeting. She is not sure where this voice has come from. 'We have to be quiet. I don't know where they are.'

Maybe it was more than habit that had her texting earlier. Maybe some part of her already knew what the rest of her has just realized: the phone is a risk. It makes noise. When she talks on it, she makes noise. Noise will bring the man.

It is simple, almost. If she thinks of it a certain way, it all makes perfect sense.

She starts again. 'We're okay, but—'

Her husband starts speaking before she has finished, and his voice is too loud.

'What's going on?' he says. 'Is anyone with you? Have you seen the police? Is Lincoln okay? What do you mean, you're safe? Can they get to you? God, I'm sorry I'm not there, honey – I'm so sorry—'

She lets him talk. She understands his need to hear her, and she thought she had the same need, but his voice does not make her feel like he's with her – it makes him feel farther away, or, no, it makes her feel farther away. Like a part of her is floating toward him, out of the zoo, into life as she knows it, and she does not want to float anywhere. She cannot. She must be here, completely here. She cannot console him at the moment.

'We're fine,' she whispers, still talking in some lawyer's

voice. Some CEO's voice. If those kinds of people ever whisper. 'We're hiding.'

'What did you see?' he asks.

'I love you,' she says, 'and we're okay, but I can't do this. I need to pay attention. I saw a guy from a distance. There were' – she glances down at the top of Lincoln's head – 'there had been some shooting by the entrance, and I was walking by after it happened. Then we ran and hid. That's all I know. Don't call back, though. I'll call you when we're safe.'

'I'll call 9-1-1 and tell the police you're in the porcupine exhibit,' he says, his words coming out in a rush of breath. The way he sounds when he is walking up the steep hill to his office, calling to serenade her with whatever song is stuck in his head – he is always singing – and he knows she will laugh and hang up on him. 'I love you. Tell him for me. Be safe.'

She silences the phone, turning to Lincoln. He is fidgeting uncomfortably against her, kicking out with his legs, digging at her sides with his tennis shoes. She slides her hands under his armpits and helps him spin around and get his feet under him. He stands up, and she keeps a hand around his waist.

'So that was Daddy,' she whispers.

He leans back against the rock behind them. 'I know.'

'Whisper,' she says. 'He says he loves you.'

'I know he does.'

'A little quieter,' she says.

'Okay,' he whispers.

He is bouncing his knees again, his feet steady but his

whole body sproinging. His shoulders inch up and down, and it is a strange, loose-limbed dance.

The sky is starting to pinken, long swathes of lavender stretching across the tops of the trees.

'You're being really big,' she says.

'Is the bad man chasing us now?' he asks.

'I don't know,' she says. 'But if he is, he's not going to find us here.'

Still bouncing, he turns his head left and right, taking in the new scenery. As always, he is both curious and cautious. She watches the struggle play out. His eyes darting everywhere. His feet planted.

Curiosity wins out. He takes a step toward the brick wall of the building, pointing.

'There's a water bowl,' he says. 'Like Muddles' bowl.'

'Yeah,' she agrees.

She scans the grass around them again, and, in addition to the cracked, dried-up plastic bowl that he's noticed, there are other odd bits and pieces scattered around the enclosure. An ink pen off to their right and, closer to the railing, a glittery hairband. She thinks she sees a white sock by the chain-link fence.

'Do porcupines use water bowls?' he asks.

'I guess they do.'

'They drink water?'

She can imagine clamping a hand over his mouth, holding him tight, ordering him to be perfectly still and perfectly quiet. She desperately wants that, but she cannot imagine a scenario where it is possible. If she scared him badly enough for him to stop talking, he would probably start sobbing.

'Shhh,' she says again. 'Talk a little quieter. Everything drinks water.'

'Everything?' he whispers.

'Everything,' she repeats.

'So the porcupine drank out of that bowl?' he says, stepping closer, pressing against her right side. 'And he sat by this rock, just like we're doing? Do you think it was a boy? Or was it a she?'

She cannot see any signs of terror in him. His blue eyes are big and wide, but they are always big and wide. He is slumped comfortably against her and, if anything, he seems vaguely excited to be in a porcupine's home. Of course, he has no sense of what is truly frightening – he is terrified of mascots, of Chuck E. Cheese and the Chick-fil-A cows. Last week they stumbled across one of the Batman movies on television, the one with Heath Ledger, disturbing as hell, and Lincoln insisted that the old 1960s version – he is a connoisseur of all things Batman – had a scarier Joker.

He sometimes cries at an unexpected voice over a loudspeaker, and he thinks ringmasters are horrifying, and now he is picking at the wart on his right hand, singing softly, 'Glory, glory to old Georgia! / Glory, glory—'

Still. There is no telling what is going on behind his calm, round face. She should give him some kind of explanation. Some sort of plan. He has always liked predictable schedules – likes to know that Tuesday is music day at school and Wednesday will be Spanish day and Thursday will be drawing class, and that she will pick him up every day but Wednesday, when Paul picks him up, and that Sunday night they will order Chinese food for supper and that on Saturday morning he can watch an entire hour of cartoons.

He likes to know what will happen.

'So,' she whispers, and his fingers brush her jaw, where there is a freckle that he likes to reaffirm, 'everything is going to be fine. We're safe here. It's like in a story where there's a battle and then the bad guys get taken off to jail. We just have to sit here and be quiet for a little while until the bad guy is gone.'

He nods.

'What's the bad guy's name?' he asks.

'I don't know.'

'Does he have a name?'

'Sure. Everybody has a name. I just don't know it.'

He nods again, looking back toward his wart. She presses against the rock, pulling her legs tighter, keeping one hand against his leg. She glances behind her – the rock formation completely shields them from anyone approaching them from the Primate Zone. She tilts her head up – nothing but treetops and sky. There is no way they can be seen.

Then she examines the fence around the exhibit, scanning left to right. She has not paid attention to what lies beyond their enclosure, but now she thinks that the vines along the chain-link fence are not as thick as she might like. Through them she has a partial view of the backs of other exhibits. She tries to imagine the map of the zoo and thinks she must be looking at part of the Africa exhibit, most likely the rhinos, although it could be some closed-off pen that's no longer in use. Bamboo grows dense and tall along the other exhibit's fence, and she can't see anything beyond it. Through another gap in the vines she sees a few rails of the train track and, beside it, an asphalt path that curves away so she can't see where it leads. It might be part of the regular walking path, although she doesn't remember ever seeing the porcupine exhibit from any outside path. It might be some back way that only the handlers would use. And, really, all that matters is that, if someone does walk up the path, would he be able to see them?

She does not think the gaps in the ivy are big enough.

She cannot hear anything disturbing now – no footsteps, no gunshots. No sirens. She wonders why there are no more sirens.

She realizes she never checked the link Paul sent her – she cannot afford such scattered thinking – and she grabs her phone and runs a thumb over her screen. She clicks to a local news site with two brief paragraphs slashing across the home page, racing through the phrases: 'shots fired' and 'single male' and 'multiple injuries suspected'. The final sentence of the short piece is 'Police are currently at the scene.'

The emptiness of that last sentence is infuriating. It tells her nothing. Are the police in the parking lot or a few feet away? Are they dropping down from the sky in helicopters? Is it a dozen policemen or a hundred?

Lincoln pushes free of her again, and she lets him go, assuming he needs to stretch his legs. When he takes a few steps, she grabs at his shirt and tugs him back.

'Stay close,' she says. 'We need to be still and quiet until the police come.'

'The police are coming for us?'

She has forgotten to mention that part.

'Yes,' she says. 'We're waiting until the police get here and catch the guy with the gun, and then the police will come and tell us that we can go home. But we have to be very quiet, because we don't want the bad guy to see us. It's like hide-and-seek.'

'I don't like hide-and-seek.'

'Whisper,' she says again.

'I don't like hide-and-seek,' he says, in something that might be called a whisper.

'You don't like it when you have to hide by yourself,' she reminds him. 'This time I'm hiding with you.'

He shuffles in the dirt and grass, scuffing the toes of his shoes and sending up small puffs of dust. For a while he says nothing, only watches his own feet shuffling. He runs a hand down the rock.

'Namba namba namba namba namba,' he begins to sing, and after the first five notes she recognizes the tune to the Michigan State fight song. His singing is sometimes word-less. He is packed to the brim with sound and movement, and one or the other is always spilling over the edges, and that is normally not a bad thing but now it makes her terror bubble to the surface.

She unclenches her teeth. She only realizes she has been clenching them because her jaw has begun to throb.

'Namba namba namba namba,' he is still repeating, perfectly on key.

'Too loud,' she says, and she is too loud as well.

He nods as if he has been expecting that reaction. He is

already staring at something over her shoulder. He stands on one foot, balancing.

'Let me tell you something,' he whispers, tilting his head toward the building. 'That's a biney.'

'A biney?' she repeats.

He raises an arm, pointing to a water spigot sticking out of the wall. 'Yes.'

'That thing that looks like a faucet?'

'Yes. It's not a faucet. Bineys look like faucets.'

'Tell me about them.'

'About bineys?' he says.

'Yes.'

She is not clenching her teeth. She is not breathing too hard. She thinks she sounds completely normal. She almost surely does not sound like a lawyer anymore. She is working at it every time she speaks – making sure every word is calm, relaxed, making sure she still sounds like his mother and not some crazy woman about to scream and wail and tear her hair.

He comes closer to her, but he does not sit down. Maybe he can sense the crazy woman hovering.

'Well,' he says, 'bineys have a head, a trunk and tusks. They have a long body and hairs for legs.'

'What else?' she whispers.

'They have no mouths. They eat with their noses and smell with their eyes. They can't have tongues.'

'And they live in zoos?'

'Yes,' he says. 'Only in zoos. I've never heard of a wild biney.'

'Are they dangerous?' she asks, and then wishes that she

hadn't. She is trying to distract him, and he does not need any reminders that bad things lurk.

He does not seem bothered.

'Some of them,' he says.

'Is that one of the dangerous ones?' she asks, looking toward the spigot.

'No,' he says. 'That's a climbing one. They like to climb from tree to tree, but if they can't climb, they'll crawl. Some bineys are made out of grass. Some are made out of plants or underwear. Or meat.'

She considers that. She makes herself smile, because normally that is what she would do.

She loves him like this, inventing. There was the time when he looked up at her in a hotel lobby and announced, *I have two little girls in my pocket. Tiny girls. One is named Lucy and one is named Fireman.* There was the time when he told her that all his stuffed animals went to a church where no one wore pants.

This is good, she thinks. *This is an alternative to the panic.*

'But they look like faucets?' she prompts him, so quietly. She did not know she could talk this softly.

'It's a predator,' he whispers, as if that is an answer to her question. 'Also a reptile. But they're like hippos – they can be aggressive.'

She tries to remember which of their books has the word 'aggressive' in it – the one about alligators? or about the ancient Greeks? – when her phone shakes against her thigh. She shades it with her palm as she reads her husband's text.

Can't stand it. Have to check. Talk to me.

45

She tightens her grip on the phone. Paul is imagining terrible things, of course. *If you always expect the worst to happen, you can only be pleasantly surprised*, he said to her when they started dating, and she told him, *That is the stupidest thing I've ever heard*. Sometimes it is a joke between them, his determined pessimism, but not now. Now he is justified.

We're okay, she types. We're in a really safe spot. I'll keep us safe. Are the police inside the zoo yet?

Don't know. No one will tell me anything on the phone. Driving to the zoo.

'That biney can't move, Mommy,' Lincoln whispers. 'That biney over there is not moving at all.'

'But I thought it was a climbing one,' she says, typing at the same time.

One man, she thinks. *And an entire police force. Shouldn't there be armored trucks and night-vision goggles and gas or FBI agents?* It's been at least half an hour since she heard those first gunshots.

Why is it taking so long? she types.

No idea. Going to find out. Love.

Lincoln is talking. She thinks he has repeated himself more than once.

'What, sweet?' she asks.

'It used to climb,' he says. 'That biney used to climb, Mommy. It used to—'

If you ignore him, it only makes him repeat things.

'Okay,' she says quickly. 'Right. That biney used to climb.'

He is chewing on his collar, staring at the spigot.

'I think it's dead,' he says.

She looks at him, her phone still glowing in her hand.

'I think it's probably asleep,' she says.

'Nope,' he says. 'Dead. Bineys die very easily.'

She looks down at her screen again, and she tells Paul that she will check in with him later. She reassures herself for the fifth or sixth time that the phone is definitely silenced. She forces herself to set it on the ground beside her and once again she is alone with her son, with no one to help them. No one but a dead biney.

'I think it's sleeping,' she repeats.

He is chewing on his shirt, gnawing away at the collar. Normally she tells him to stop, but this time she ignores it.

'I'm thirsty,' he whispers.

She is glad for the change of subject. She reaches into her purse, glad, too, that this was not one of the days when she insisted that he could drink from water fountains.

'Here are your sips,' she says, handing him his plastic water bottle.

'Mmm,' he says after a long swallow. He has a shiny wet mustache along his upper lip. 'Still cold.'

He drinks more, water dribbling down his jaw, and finally he lowers the bottle and wipes his mouth with his shirt.

A time or two she has used the word 'sips' instead of 'drink' when speaking to adults. It is as real and accepted a word around their house as anything in the dictionary, one of the many words that were not words before he came along. A bib is a 'neat dog', because they had a book where a sloppy dog spilled his food and a neat dog wore his bib. *Can I have a neat dog?* he'll ask if he sees his shirt getting dirty. He calls his knuckles his 'finger knees'. And he had a whole vocabulary of non-words when he was small, so small that he was not yet him. For a while he called balls 'dahs' and raisins 'zuh-zahs'. His sign for painting was a sniff of his nose, because they once tried nose painting instead of finger painting and apparently that made an impression.

He stuck one arm in the air, his wrist bent, and that was the sign for 'flamingo'.

He made a hissing sound when he was asking for more eggs. *Sssssssss*, like the sound they made when they hit the frying pan. He brought his own language into existence.

There are so many things that did not exist before him.

There is one thing that Kailynn knows for sure: it is her mother's fault. If her mother had not snatched away her phone, everything would be different. Kailynn would be standing here calling the police or her dad or anyone. People must be desperate to hear from her. She thinks of how Victoria at school posted a zillion messages after that car wreck when she got a concussion, and everyone was so worried, and that was nothing compared to being trapped in a storage closet at the zoo.

But, no, just because she overslept three mornings in a row and missed the car pool and her mother had to drive her to school, just because of that, she has no phone. There is a good chance that her mother will feel so guilty about this whole thing that Kailynn will get a brand-new phone altogether.

This is almost enough to cheer her, but not quite. The steel door is solid and cold against her hand, and she likes the smooth metal feel of it, so she spreads out her fingers, like she's making a handprint. Her hand is sticky with ketchup.

She is the only one here. When she has her phone, she is never the only one.

Also on that third day she ran late, she looked out her

bedroom window and saw the other girls in the car pool backing out of her driveway, and she ran down the stairs to catch them. It wasn't her fault they left so fast. It definitely shouldn't have counted as being late. But her mother didn't care.

Kailynn slides the bolt, cracks open the door, and peers through the thinnest sliver of space. Nothing. No one. She pushes her hair away from her face and bites into an animal cracker. A giraffe. The sugar takes away the cotton taste in her mouth, even though she would rather have onion rings or French fries.

Food always helps.

Her dad makes fun of her for never wanting to be alone, for doing her homework in whichever room has somebody else in it – in the den with him watching TV or in the kitchen with her mother cleaning the counters. He says she doesn't even like to be in her own bedroom by herself, and that must be true, because she still shares the bedroom with her sister even though they've told her that, since she's the oldest, she can move to the basement. But she likes to hear someone else breathing while she's trying to fall asleep.

She wishes her mother were here.

She is fine. She is in the safest place imaginable, and if anyone comes back, she can deadbolt this door and they will never get to her. It is dumb to be scared. Her father wouldn't be scared. When he was a kid, he took a pistol into the woods and shot animals and then cut them open to see what was inside. He set a chair on fire just to watch it burn. He never sat around, wishing. He did things.

She wishes she were someone who did things.

She eats another animal cracker. A lion.

Margaret always times her walk so that she gets to the elephants at 5:10 p.m., which is usually when the handlers are out in the feeding pen, calling out commands to make the animals go forward and backward and kneel and lift their feet. The handlers say the end-of-the-day routine is designed to check for issues with joints or hooves, but Margaret suspects they enjoy showing off.

She likes watching, regardless. It is a free circus show that no one else in the zoo seems to know is taking place, and she cannot imagine what possesses those sad old people in jogging suits to get their exercise by doing laps around a shopping mall. She comes here every Monday, Wednesday and Thursday, walking as briskly as she can manage for exactly an hour, just like the doctor recommended. She always heads back to the parking lot after the elephants are led into their metal-and-brick building.

Margaret is always prompt, but the handlers are not. Sometimes she arrives and the pen is empty of everything but a couple of puzzled elephants. The elephants are more reliable than the handlers. She suspects that the handlers are millennials who care more about yoga and inner peace than about actually doing their jobs.

So today when she sees an empty pen in front of her, it is not the lack of humans that surprises her but the lack of elephants. She can see them at a distance, lumbering through the landscaped savannah. They are off their routine. She waits for a few minutes, standing in the shade of a huge metal crate. She keeps her headphones on – she is only two chapters from the end of her Patricia Cornwell – and she stares up at the sign on the crate that asks, HAVE YOU EVER WONDERED HOW YOU TRANSPORT AN ELEPHANT?

She finally takes off her headphones, sliding her MP3 player into her pocket, and she feels the wrongness immediately. She tenses, although there is no clear reason for it. She decides it is only the silence and stillness that is bothering her. She checks her watch, struck by the thought that maybe she has lost track of time. But, no, there are still a few minutes before closing.

Normally she would see a few other visitors straggling toward the exit. Today she sees no one.

Of course, she is standing at the bottom of a steepish slope at the edge of the elephants' territory. Between the hill rising in front of her and the metal crate to her right, she doesn't have much of a view. She starts up the hill, shaking off her nerves, but before she reaches the top, she hears two quick sounds, little bursts of static or cracks of thunder. Almost at the same time she hears a voice, high-pitched, only a single note. She cannot call it a scream.

She takes another step, enough that she can see the thatched pavilion of the themed restaurant, and she hears footsteps coming toward her quickly. She can't say why, but she spins around and starts back down the hill, turning in a way that makes her bad knee buckle. She ignores the pain and hurries through the opening of the big metal crate, which is darker inside than she expected.

She presses herself against the wall, cold metal against her arms. She feels foolish, but she steps deeper into the shadows, keeping her eyes on the opening of the crate, watching the unchanging view of the sand in the elephant pen. She hears more footsteps, and then she hears hushed voices, and then the footsteps get faster. She hears someone rattle metal or glass. A door slamming. More cracking sounds.

She wonders if elephants ever feel claustrophobic. The turquoise stone in her necklace is chilly against her skin, and she touches it with her fingers. She bought it because it was the exact color of her sweatshirt. There is still a satisfaction in the perfect match.

She does not know how many minutes have passed. She has not moved, because, whatever is happening, Margaret doesn't believe in acting too quickly. She likes to consider the full context of a problem. This served her well in lightening her hair to a honey blonde that doesn't show gray, and it served her in buying a newish but uninteresting townhome instead of the pretty Art Deco cottage with roof issues, and it served her in keeping her mouth shut when her daughter decided to homeschool her grandson, who, God knows, could use some social interaction.

Margaret thinks of her daughter's face, always tired-looking because she refuses to put on lipstick when she leaves the house.

A gnat dives into the crate and gets lost in the dark. She has not heard any noise for quite a while. What felt so real for a moment now seems like some sort of panic attack, and she feels a familiar, clinical kind of concern about early-onset Alzheimer's or a brain tumor. There are all kinds of explanations for running and faraway screaming. Teenagers, likely. It is possible that she is already locked inside the zoo, bound to run into a very condescending employee, and she cannot bring herself to stand here any longer, hiding in a giant box.

So she steps outside, noticing how the sun has disappeared behind the line of trees. She slowly walks to the top of the hill, giving her knee a chance to loosen: standing still is the worst thing for it. She sees nothing but the same old exhibits – the playground off to her right and the monkeys swinging on their ropes at the primate house.

She has become a nervous old woman.

She looks down the walkway and heads toward the Sahara Snack Hut or whatever it's called. She can hear her rubber soles on the concrete, and the air smells strange and smoky. She accidentally kicks a baby's cup that has been left on the ground. She passes under the thatched roof of the restaurant pavilion, and as she steps out from under its shadow, she sees a movement through a hedge of jungle plants. The vending machines are blocking her view. It could have been the plants shifting in the wind, but it might have been a person on one of the other pathways. An employee? She might as well face him.

She starts across the concrete, angling toward the Coke

machine. There is a door leading into the restaurant, though, just before she reaches the vending machines.

She only notices the door as she is passing it.

She only notices it as it opens.

She only notices it as a hand flashes from inside, pulling her backward.

He has lost Mark. Robby does not know what to do now, standing here by himself, staring at hogs. Mark would know what to do, surely, and he cannot have just vanished. He is so quiet, though, Mark. That is the problem. He can slip away without you noticing.

No one ever says Robby is too quiet.

He and Mark were standing by the lake, right next to each other, as the first shots sprayed through the air – you couldn't see the actual bullets, but you could see brick shards and bits of leaves and branches from the parrot habitat and also feathers, bright ones, and the air was churned up and crowded like in the middle of a storm only faster and no one had ever told him guns could make it like that. There was screaming, the wordless kind, and also a lot of people's names being yelled – 'Elizabeth!' over and over. There was a moment when he was frozen by all of it, and then he and Mark started running, following the few people who could still move – a dozen or so were on the ground by then, face up and face down, and he stepped over a woman whispering nothing as he rushed up the hill and they tried the restaurant at the top of the hill but there was no luck there, and then they headed toward the jungle cats, and Mark was still right next to him. But then Robby looked over his shoulder, and Mark was gone. So Robby stopped here in this shaded gazebo by the wild hogs, only the sign calls them BOARS.

It is a pretty good place, because there are walls around him, so you can't see him from a distance, but he can look through the slits between the boards and watch the walkways. The boars are snuffling around the dirt in their pen, tusks filthy. They don't care about guns and bullets. He can tell that for sure.

Robby does not know if he should keep moving or wait here. Should he call out and hope that the wrong people don't hear him?

It is easier to wait. To watch. He is good at watching.

There are not so many things he is good at. He thinks of a birthday party from a long time ago, and he does not want to think of it – he tries to focus on the boars, on the size of their heads and how they do not have necks and, no, he will not think of the birthday, but he is somehow firing the wrong neuron, one that does not delete but instead underlines: the day when he walked into Aidan's party, the one where his mother told him that there would be s'mores, and he loved s'mores, and Aidan's mother answered the door and gave him a hug and showed him how she had set up a tent in the den.

Aidan's mother was pretty, her dark hair so long, and she was especially nice and agreed with him about how the Raiders had the scariest NFL logo. In his memory, he is having a good time talking to Aidan's mother, and it was so nice that someone was listening, and the other kids were doing something else – some sort of fishing game with clothespins and string? – and then he needed to go to the bathroom. When he was coming back down the hallway, he heard Aidan's mom talking.

'I have something to say to all of you,' she was saying, and her voice was very serious, and he'd sped up because he did not want to miss any instructions about graham crackers and chocolate.

'I want you to be nice to Robby,' she said just as he was getting to the doorway, just as he was pressing himself against the wall and making himself invisible. 'He's unique. That's all.'

Robby had known already that he was not quite the same as the others. But it changed things to hear the words announced. Aidan's mom was trying to make it sound like she was giving him a compliment, but it was not one, and he knew that and so did everyone else. And now here he is, nothing but wild pigs for company, and they are covered in mud and shit, disgusting, and today was supposed to be different, wasn't it? Finally. He was part of something. He fit. But maybe the others were only being patient, and maybe they'd planned this the whole time. No, that doesn't make sense.

He rubs his hands against his pants. Opens and closes his fingers. Sweaty hands. That was another problem with kids' parties – too many hand-holding games, and they'd say, *Oh, your hands*, and once even a grown-up called him *that sweaty kid*. But the breeze is helping, drying his palms, and he can't just stand here, pussing out. He has to think, even though he is better at feeling – well, not great exactly, but he feels plenty. He feels too much. More than other people feel, and he tells them that sometimes, but they don't understand.

He is supposed to be paying attention. He looks left and right, focusing on anything moving. He needs to be looking for people. There is a swish of the tails from the zebra exhibit farther down the walkway. The railroad track. Trees. Squirrels in the branches, running after each other. He tries to look at all of it.

Before Robby lost Mark, he heard him say that they will die if they don't get out of here. He looks at the boars again. He thinks of the whispering woman he stepped over while he was running. She had on a khaki zoo uniform, and almost exactly half of her shirt had turned purplish-red. He watches the boars and thinks how it would be to have one for a pet, and he thinks the same thing about the squirrels, about pets, but also about the two squirrels chasing each other, whether it is a game or something serious, and how do these squirrels feel about each other?

Think.

Think.

Is it so hard for everyone else to make the right thoughts stay lined up, one following the other, train cars hooked together? He is always veering off, and the feelings are pushing up again. Where is Mark? Will he be standing here alone until men with guns come in and shoot him dead, and was it the biggest mistake he's ever made to come to the zoo today? Was he stupid? He is stupid, mostly. Sometimes he is sure of it, and his mother always hates it when he says that, and his mother – he closes his eyes, tries to catch his breath. Why does he do this? Why does he always wind up, too late, wishing he could undo things, wishing he could start over, hating how he screwed up, knowing he will screw up again?

One of the boars is taking a leak on the ground. They are gross animals, ugly and stupid-looking, and why did they let themselves get caught in a cage in the first place?

He raises the gun in his hand, settling the barrel into his palm, lifting it over the fencing. He pulls the trigger. His hearing has been off, muzzy, since they came through the entrance, and he wishes they'd thought to bring earplugs with them, but now the shots don't sound as loud. He goes for speed instead of accuracy, aiming at head, belly and tail: he would like to shoot off the tail. He's only a couple of yards away instead of forty or fifty, like at the range, and this target isn't moving like the people, so he's surprised by the damage he does. The first pig is ripped open, everything spilling out of its belly into the dirt, steaming, and the second boar is dead, too, and he backs out of the gazebo before the smell gets to him.

No one ever mentioned the smells.

He keeps his fingers curved around the trigger of his Bushmaster, a classic, and he feels solid again. He's gotten the thoughts and the feelings under control. He doesn't know why Mark gave him crap about how he needed an adjustment to the handle, how the extended back strap would give him a better angle. He likes it just like it is. It feels good in his hand.

He hears footsteps. He turns, gun ready.

'Calm down, moron!' yells Mark, ducking so low he is nearly on his knees. He has his Glock in his hand and a Smith & Wesson in his holster.

Robby lowers the gun. 'Where have you been?'

'Hunting. I thought you were right behind me. You ready?'

Robby nods.

6:00 p.m.

Joan is not sure she has ever been so attentive to the shifting of the sky. The one fiery stripe she could see right after the sun vanished has spread and deepened. The entire sky is striated now, the color of a peeled peach. The colors are only intensifying.

She hears a sound from inside the Primate Zone. Something heavy slamming, either a door closing or something being dropped. The popping sound of not-balloons again – the rhythm of it like fingernails tapping fast on a desk – and then the shattering of glass. A high-pitched squeal, not human.

It is all muted, like the volume turned slightly too low, but clearly someone is moving through the building. Someone who is not afraid of being heard.

'Shhh,' she whispers to Lincoln. 'Don't say a word. Be still like a statue. He's coming.'

Lincoln does not ask her who.

'Put your arms around me,' she whispers. 'Close your eyes and disappear.'

She wants to close her eyes, too, but does not. Instead she

times her breaths to his. She feels his hands tangle in her hair and press against her neck. She can feel him against her, from his feet to his forehead.

He is not stand-offish like some little boys. He is a warm mass of affection. He knows that he has permission to come and climb in their bed at seven thirty in the morning – 'seven-three-zero', he calls it – and he respects these terms diligently. No matter how early he wakes up, he'll sing away in his bed until the precise time shows on his alarm clock, and then he will grab an armload of stuffed animals and push open their bedroom door, announcing, *It's seven-three-zero. I'm here to snuggle.*

She will lift the covers and open her arms, and sometimes he will duck his head against her shoulder or neck, squinching his eyes, and he'll say, *I've disappeared*, and she wishes it worked that way. That she could pull him against her and make him vanish.

Another squeal from inside the building, and it sounds strangely like a parrot, although there are no parrots in there.

Lincoln's breath is damp and loud. A plastic bag is blowing over the chain-link fence, swelling and collapsing in the wind like a jellyfish caught in a wave.

She inhales and exhales. Inhales and exhales.

She thinks she will hear footsteps – that is what she is listening for, because that is how it works in stories, but she never hears anything like feet stomping. She has been sure that he would be wearing boots, something with a loud tread, but there has been only silence for long, long seconds when she hears the wheeze of the glass door being pushed open – it is a much more complex sound than she has ever realized, a long whistling sound and a short groan and a sucking of air – and even then, after the door is open and done complaining, there are still no footsteps.

There is, instead, the soft sound of the door as it slides shut, and then there is nothing, and she looks across the pen at the chain-link fence, at the pine trees, and she searches for the floating plastic bag, but instead she sees a leaf levitating in midair, hooked by a spiderweb. She begins to wonder if there was anyone there at all, if it wasn't only the wind, or if, even, she has only imagined the noises.

Then the voices start, one quiet and the other not.

'Nothing,' says the loud one.

'Haven't you ever gone hunting?' says the softer voice, hoarse, like he has been coughing. 'Shut up, dumbass.'

Two of them. There are two men. They must be standing on the wooden deck overlooking the exhibit space. That means they are separated from her and Lincoln by the waist-high railing, a dozen feet, and the rock mass that is so solid against her spine.

She can't help but picture them based on those few patterns of sound. The soft-voiced one leaves her imagining a tall boy in her high-school calculus class. He was crazy smart but usually stoned, and his hair was always too long at the back, raggedly cut. He never spoke unless he was called on, and when the teacher did call on him, it was always because she had noticed he was staring at the ceiling or tying his shoes, in some way aggressively ignoring the lesson, and Mrs Vinson would yelp his name, voice sharp and annoyed, and she would ask him some specific question that he could not possibly know, only he did know it, every single time. He never missed a question, and he always spoke a little too softly, so that you had to strain to hear him, but you always did strain to hear, because there was this constant, unspoken contest between him and Mrs Vinson, of whether he would ever be caught out, and he never was.

'If there's no one—' says the voice that wants to be heard.

'No animals.'

'It's not like—'

'No more animals.'

The loud one she imagines as overweight, and she suspects his head is too large for his body. Shirt untucked, stumpy fingers. The kind of person who feels like he doesn't quite fit, so he pushes harder to make himself fit, and that only makes everything worse.

She doesn't picture them as Arabic – she has been wondering, of course. But they do not sound like that kind of terrorist. They sound like young, obnoxious white men – aren't they always young white men? – and she is not sure whether this makes them more or less dangerous than fanatics on a jihad.

She hears the second door open, the one that leads to the orangutans. There is the smallest noise from Lincoln, a shift of his head, and she can tell that he is about to say her name – 'Mommy', rather, which has become almost her name – and she shushes him, stroking his head, and he does not speak, but she wonders how long his silence will last.

His tennis shoe is digging into her thigh.

The leaf is swinging impossibly slowly on the spiderweb, and she wishes that it would stop altogether, because she does not like the movement. She wants everything to be still.

She wants the whole scene to turn into a painting, where no one can move.

'You never wanted to shoot a lion?' asks the loud one. The heavy one. 'Go on safari? I know you did.'

'That wasn't a lion.'

'No, but what the hell was it? All black and white and shaggy and those teeth on it. That thing wasn't a monkey.'

It was a colobus, she thinks. She loves their white beards and sad eyes and the way their fur makes curtains hanging from their arms. They dangle from their rope swings in a corner exhibit between the lemurs and the gibbons.

'Shut up,' says the almost-boy-from-her-calculus-class.

'There's no one left,' says the loud one. 'And, seriously, the way that boar came apart, you've got to—'

'Shut up. There's some left. Come on.'

She notices the tension in her muscles, the way her body has hardened into a shell. Her teeth are clenched again. Lincoln is drumming a pattern against the nape of her neck, his fingertips light, but other than that he is motionless.

'It's cheating, bringing that thing,' says the quiet one, annoyed. 'Where's the challenge? You fire off thirty at a time, where's the skill?'

'Jealous?' says the loud one.

Why are they still here talking? Why have they not walked through the door that they opened ages ago?

'Are you blind, honey pie?' says the loud one, suddenly much louder. So loud that she feels her head jerk. 'Are you a mole rat nosing in the muck? Are you a gunked-up, eyeless fish or some squirming, mewling larva?'

'I'm not blind,' says the quiet one, and the annoyance is gone from his voice. Although it does not sound quite like his voice. He is talking slower and deeper. Like he is playing some part. 'I'm thinking.'

'Same thing, honey pie.'

There is something strange about them, she thinks. About their voices. About 'honey pie'.

'You really think there are more?' asks the loud one.

He sounds normal again, with no trace of the drawl she heard in his voice a moment before. She waits for the quiet one to respond, but he doesn't. The silence is so much worse than the talking. Have they seen some flicker of her hair floating past the boulders? Are they right now raising their guns, lifting a leg to vault over the railing? Or did the quiet one only nod his answer? Are they standing there now tying their shoes or adjusting their ponytails? Do they have ponytails and what about knives and are they smart or stupid or insane and is there a plan is there a strategy are they suicidal are they sadistic what do they want?

How is she supposed to know anything? She cannot even see them. The enemy is right here, and this is her chance to find out something – anything – that will help her make sense of it all, but all she has is pieces – monkeys and honey pies and calculus – and none of them fit together.

She hears the creak of the wooden deck under their feet.

'Come on,' says the quiet one.

'Sir, yes, sir.'

A huff of laughter. Then the door closes, with one

air-sucking *whump* and a small echo. She realizes she is making a low, steady shushing sound next to Lincoln's ear. She sounds like a child pretending to be the wind. She does not stop, though, because he is being quiet, and she is not ready for him to speak. Her arms tighten around him. If she could, she would freeze them both for a solid hour or two, for a day, forever, long enough that he cannot remember the sound of the voices.

Lincoln jolts in her arms, the top of his head tapping against her jawbone.

'I've got the hippos,' he whispers.

She opens her mouth, but only a kind of quiet grunt comes out. She swallows and tries again.

'Shhh,' she says.

'I've got the hippos,' he repeats, even more quietly.

'Oh,' she manages.

It's one of the first puns he came up with – he means he has the hiccups. She has thought of this as his first joke, but she remembers now – as she looks down and focuses on his face and on his breath that smells of the almond butter that he had for a snack – that, before he could even talk, he would pretend to lean in and sip her coffee so she would say, *Babies don't drink coffee!* And he would shake with laughter.

He thought it was hilarious to put his feet on a book.

She scoots him away from her slightly, settling him onto her knees.

'Try holding your breath in your mouth and then swallowing it,' she whispers.

'I have the hippos,' he says again, frowning.

69

She blinks at him a handful of times before she realizes it: she always laughs when he makes the hippo joke. That is the thing: he knows she will laugh, and she has not laughed, so he is trying again.

'Silly,' she whispers, and she makes a sound that she hopes is a laugh.

Gunshots crack through the air. She no longer compares them to balloon sounds. She flinches, but even as she does, she knows they are not particularly nearby. They are close together, though, a handful of shots, barely a pause between them.

She thinks of the quiet voice telling the loud voice that he was cheating. Thirty at a time.

Lincoln hiccups again. He does not mention the gunfire, and neither does she.

She stares at their view. Only the trees are moving.

Her phone suddenly comes to life. It rattles against the hard ground, announcing its presence even when it is silenced. She watches its glowing screen, picking it up to stop its buzzing.

It will be completely dark soon, and the screen will be even more noticeable. The phone is becoming a bigger problem.

I'm outside the zoo now, her husband writes. The police have everything blocked, but there are a group of us up on Essex St., waiting. About ten of us so far, all of us asking about somebody still inside. So must be other people in there with you. Police won't say anything.

She considers the message, not sure how much she should tell him. She knows there are other people in here. She has seen them sprawled across the sidewalk. And also the police are wrong: it is not only one shooter. She must tell him that, but that means telling him the men were nearly close enough to touch.

She has to answer him.

Are they inside the zoo? Police? she types.

Still don't know. Can't even see the zoo entrance. They say to wait here. Say they're taking care of it. Not sure what else I can do.

She feels a familiar flash of annoyance – she suspects he actually expects her to tell him what to do. There are times when she feels like she is in charge of everything – what Lincoln needs to bring on his field trip and when the exterminator is due and when the milk is about to run out – and why are there a thousand small things that fall to her and why is Paul so happy to let it all fall to her? Even now he would make her more responsible? More culpable?

She looks down at his message, and the oblivious black font of it is intolerable.

And yet she longs for his handwriting. He leaves her a note on the kitchen counter every morning: *I am in love with you, especially your butt* and *You are my #1 draft pick.* He makes her coffee so that it is hot when she wakes up, even though he does not drink it.

He is the least self-conscious dancer she has ever known.

We are fine, she types. At least no mascots here.

Worst possible scenario, he answers immediately.

She can almost make herself smile.

The story online said they think there's one shooter. There are two. I heard them walk past, she types.

71

He takes longer than she expects to reply. He is surely imagining more terrible things, even knowing that they did not happen.

They walked past you? he types.

They didn't see us. But tell the police there are definitely two of them. I only heard voices, though. Saw nothing.

I'll tell them, he types.

She knows he wants to say more, but she doesn't give him the chance. She types that she needs to pay attention and that she loves him, and he tells her the same, and then the phone goes black again. There is a relief to the blackness.

'Hippos gone?' she asks her son.

'I think so,' Lincoln says.

She is trying to work herself back into the right mood to talk to him – quiet, as quiet as possible – to make everything normal and all right. A considerable part of parenting is pretending moods that you do not entirely feel. She has thought this before when she's been listening to little plastic people act out a battle scene for hours at a time, but now it seems like maybe all those eternal battles were a good thing – maybe they were practice.

She is good at pretending. She will start doing it again any moment now.

She stares at the grass. She thinks she sees a snake, but it is only a stick. Also the sirens have started up again, although these are definitely not coming from the parking lot. They are intensifying, coming from a distance and getting closer. She has a feeling that she's hearing a fire truck – or two or three – not a police car, although she is not sure how to define the difference.

72

When his words were still choppy, Lincoln was always calling the fire department from his car seat, clenching his light-up plastic phone in one hand. *Hello fireman. There a fire in big city. Bring helmet. And boots. And coat. And axe. And hoses.*

She is not sure why she cannot stay here in this moment. With this child. She seems determined to resurrect the old versions of him. They float up around her, wobbly and warm.

'I hear sirens,' he says.

'Me, too,' she answers.

He nods. 'Do you think the zoo might be on fire? From the guns?'

'I don't think so.'

'The men might have bombs.'

'I don't think so.'

'Those were the bad men?' he asks. 'The ones we heard talking? The one who was talking about animals? And larvae?'

She remembers that he learned about larvae in school. Maybe when he was studying butterflies. He listens and ponders and turns a thing round and round in his mind, like polishing a stone, and then he spits out the finished product. She thought his silence meant that he was distracted by hiccups, but really he was only shining up his other thoughts.

'Those were the bad men,' she confirms.

'They laughed.'

He struggles with this in stories. He thinks evildoers should not smile. *How can bad people be happy?* he asks.

She runs her finger across the top of his knuckles.

'Remember how sometimes bad people are happy when they hurt people?' she asks, and even as she asks it, she thinks of him saying to her, *You know, Mommy, we read about bad people but I do not know any bad people. All the people I know are good.*

'So those men were laughing because they think it's funny to hurt people?' he asks.

'Yes,' she says.

He shakes his head.

'Villains,' he says.

She looks at his face, which is calm and thoughtful. His long eyelashes swoop down as he blinks, and everything about him is plumped out and soft. Their pediatrician called him an 'objectively handsome' child.

After he was born, she said he was the George Clooney of babies. Paul told her that Muddles was the George Clooney of dachshunds, and then she told him that he was, of course, the George Clooney of husbands, and he said that she'd surrounded herself with George Clooneys. That day she had been trying to eat Thai soup with Lincoln asleep on her shoulder, and she dripped soup on his back and he smelled of lemongrass all afternoon.

The wind is picking up. She feels chill bumps rise along her arms.

'Are you cold?' she asks Lincoln.

'No,' he says.

That is probably true. He is a furnace.

'Tell me if you are,' she says.

'I will.'

If only it were that simple. If only she believed that he would always tell her what he needed. What he thought. What he wanted.

The pine trees around her have chain-link fencing wrapped around their bases. The dead porcupine must have eaten bark. There is a fine layer of pine straw over the grass – she didn't notice until after they sat down, but now she feels the sharp edges of it pricking her legs and her palms. She hears a helicopter in the distance, and she scans the sky, but she sees nothing. She hears them often, the helicopters, on their way to the hospitals downtown, and there is always something both comforting and chilling about the pulse of the rotors: the sound means someone has been badly hurt – a mother rear-ended by an 18-wheeler? a teenager who jumped from a bridge? – but it also means that there is a protocol in place. A solution in motion.

The helicopter is fading, and there is another sound. There are seconds where she follows the helicopter, straining to hear it, not willing to let it go. But she has to let it go, eventually, because the other sound is getting louder.

A baby crying.

A baby.

She does not want to believe it at first, but the wailing only gets louder, and she knows nothing else can explain the sound. It does not sound like a real infant – the cry is rusty and nasal, more like a baby doll when its stomach gets squeezed.

She knows it is not a doll.

She sees a movement outside the fence, over near the bamboo. First it is only a shifting in the darkness, not so different from a tree bending, but then a shape separates, becoming distinct from the shadows, and the shape is a woman, long hair blowing. Her arms are across her chest as she walks, hesitantly. The woman is still enough of a shadow herself that the broad curve of her arms might be empty or might be nothing more than a bulky sweater or a purse.

But the bawling makes it obvious. It is not a purse that the woman is holding pressed against her.

'I hear a baby,' says Lincoln.

'Shh,' she says. 'Be quiet.'

'Why is there a baby?'

Joan watches the woman move along the line of bamboo, and she thinks she hears a murmuring sound, but it might only be the fall air. She suspects that the woman is shushing the baby, though, because she is making all the small movements that go along with shushing – bouncing slightly, even as she walks. Rocking from the waist, running a hand along what must be a fuzzy head. But the baby is not getting any quieter, although there is a muffled quality to the sound, not quite as piercing as it was, and Joan knows that the mother – surely the mother? – must be pressing the small face into her shoulder.

'I see it,' yelps Lincoln. 'There it is.'

She claps a hand over his mouth. His lips on her fingers intensify her body's remembering – remembering what it was like to hold him against her chest, back when his legs would tuck up, so compact, wrinkles of fat condensing, soft head in the crook of her arm, such a perfect fit against her, and that feeling of trying to hush the crying.

Now he struggles, trying to shake her hand loose. She lets him go.

'Shhh,' she says.

Sometimes, back then, his mouth would land on her chin like a suckerfish. She would balance him on her forearm, close to her body, as she walked around the house, and he would wobble, rubber-spined.

'Please.'

It is one word, drifting across the air. Surely the woman is talking to her baby, not to anyone else she imagines might be listening. There is panic and a hundred other things in the word.

'What are they doing?' asks Lincoln, whispering, finally.

'Trying to hide,' she says into his ear. 'Like we are.'

The mother and baby are thirty or forty feet away from where she and Lincoln are huddled. Joan could easily call out to them. She could tell the woman that the men are likely still close by. She could warn her to stay outdoors, to not set foot in any of the exhibit halls because the men are hunting there. She could share this hiding place, which she is beginning to believe is as shielded and safe and unexpected as any place in the zoo. It has saved her once already.

The baby is so loud.

If she makes herself known, surely the woman would want to join her? To sit beside her and share comfort?

The baby is so loud.

If a woman with an infant asks for help, what kind of person would say no?

When Joan sees women with small babies, she envies them, craves the weight in her arms, wants to scoop up the stranger's baby and smell its head and run a finger across the center of its palm, because how she loved it, the feel of a small body against her, and she's wondered if she should tell Paul that she'd really like another baby, even though they've agreed that one is enough. When she sees a woman with her arms around an infant, she covets it.

That baby, the skin of its head like tissue paper. Tiny mouth wanting. Hands patting.

She does not call out. She does not say a word.

Instead she watches the dark shape of the woman shuffle past the bamboo, rocking from the waist the whole time. The baby does not quiet. And then the shape and the sound are gone, and she and Lincoln are alone again.

6:17 p.m.

'Mommy, I need to go potty.'

He has a bladder of steel, this boy. He almost never asks for the bathroom.

'Can you go like a puppy dog?' she whispers.

'I don't want to go like a puppy dog. It's too dark.'

He's right about the darkness. The sky is blue-black. She can see her hand in front of her face but only the outline of it.

'You can see plenty,' she says.

'I want to go on the potty,' he says, too loudly. 'A real potty. With something to flush.'

'Listen,' she says. 'The bad men are still out there. I need you to be very quiet so they don't find us. After the policemen come, we'll go home. But for now, you need to go like a puppy dog.'

He considers. When they were potty-training him, for months he would sit on the potty only if he was allowed to wear a bike helmet.

'They might hear me going potty,' he says. 'They might shoot me.'

She feels her nose burn – a prelude to tears, and the thought panics her as much as anything else. He cannot see her cry.

'They won't hear you,' she says. 'I'll be right here.'

And I can stop bullets, she wants to add. *I will never let you be hurt, and I am stronger and faster and smarter than anything that could ever be out there.* And the thing is that she does not even have to say it, because he believes it, and she wishes she believed it, too.

His lower lip is trembling, and she sees his shoulders begin to shake. For the first time, she sees the fear on his face.

'Mommy,' he says, stepping to her. 'I want to snuggle you.'

He has not done this outside of the morning routine in a long while – it is his old password for nervousness, for walking into a crowded room where he doesn't recognize the faces. She opens her arms, and he wraps himself around her, face in her neck. She can hear his breathing, and his mouth is damp against her skin. His hands twist in her hair. When he was a baby, he would twist his fingers in it while she fed him, and she stopped wearing ponytails altogether because of his small fingers clasping at the air, searching.

'You're my boy,' she says.

She feels her own shoulders relax as she absorbs his weight. It is possible that this says something terrible about her, that his need for her comforts her. He rubs his nose against her jawline, breathing a little too hard. He pulls back slightly, and she can feel a string of snot stretch along her chin.

He rubs his wet nose against her collarbone.

She tugs at her collar, stretching the cotton, and wipes the snot from her skin. She is still sometimes surprised that she is not repulsed by it. Not when it is his.

This is such a different kind of intimacy than with, say, a lover. With a lover you might have a perfect comfort with each other's body, a sense that his body belongs to you and yours to him, and you might have total unself-conscious freedom to put a hand on his thigh, to put your mouth on his in the way you know he likes best, for him to curl around you in bed, pelvis to pelvis – but the two of you are still, ultimately, two different bodies, and the pleasure comes from the difference.

With Lincoln, the line between their two selves is blurred. She bathes him and wipes off every bodily fluid, and he sticks his fingers in her mouth or catches his balance with a hand on the top of her head. He catalogues her freckles and moles as carefully as he keeps track of his own scrapes and bruises. He does not quite know that he is a being apart from her. Not yet. For now, her arm is as accessible as his arm – her limbs are equally his limbs.

They are interchangeable.

'You still need to go potty?' she asks, mouth against his temple.

'I think I can hold it a little.'

'No,' she says. 'I don't know when we'll be close to a bathroom. You should go ahead and go. It'll be fine.'

He shakes his head.

'I'll be right next to you,' she says. 'You can go right here.'

'Where we're sitting?' He sounds horrified.

'No. Over there. See where there's that big weed?'

She feels his head lift and turn.

'I need to take my shoes off,' he says, letting go of her, and she knows that she has convinced him.

'Shhh. A little quieter. Don't take your shoes off.' It is so much more complicated if the shoes come off. 'Otherwise you'll be barefoot in the dirt.'

There are times when she cannot affect him in the least. But there are also times when he is like a room she knows so well that she can maneuver through it in the dark.

'Dirt feels bad against my feet,' he says.

'I know.'

He walks to the exact weed she's mentioned and begins pushing down his pants, not touching his shoes. Once he starts going, the sound of urine hitting the plant is never-ending, and she has a brief moment of wondering whether she was wrong about noise not being an issue. But finally he is done, and he is concerned that he has gotten a few drops on his shoes, and she tells him not to worry and hands him a wet wipe from her purse to clean himself off with.

'Mommy?'

'Mmm-hmm?'

'I don't want to stay here anymore.'

'I know, sweet. But wipe your hands.'

Lincoln is staring down at the wet wipe, holding it between two fingers, unmoving.

She stares into the darkness, drawn to the few points of illumination – the glow from a nearby lamppost, a smaller gleam from a light on the other side of the trees, the moon. She glances down at her phone. The darkness has changed things: she knows this. She has always been concerned about the noise of the phone, but there is the light of it, too. Light is a rare, conspicuous thing now. But surely there must be some news? Surely at some point she is risking more by not looking at her phone? She cups her hands around it, shielding the screen, and when it turns on, the light is both too intense and sweetly familiar. The whole world is there in a small, neat rectangle.

She bends her body around the phone. When she checks www.wbta.com, though, the same two brief paragraphs stare back at her. She checks another local news site, and there is nothing at all. She checks CNN only as an afterthought, but there is a photo of the zoo entrance – a too-perfect PR shot. A 'Breaking News' banner is pasted in the corner of the photo, and below the caption reads, 'Presumed active shooter situation at Belleville Zoo reportedly shifts to hostage situation.'

She feels the damp impact of a wet wipe against her calf.

'I don't want to wipe my hands,' Lincoln announces.

'Shhh. Whisper. Mommy's reading something.'

'I don't want to wipe my hands!' he shouts, so loud that she flinches.

'Hush!' she hisses, dropping her phone into her purse. 'Too loud! They'll hear you.'

He stares back at her, and she releases a long breath. She takes his unwiped hand and pulls him closer. When she speaks, she is calmer.

'You know we have to be quiet,' she whispers. 'And we always clean hands after we go to the bathroom. Otherwise you'll get sick.'

Even as she says it, she is not sure why she is arguing with him about hygiene.

A hostage situation.

Hostages.

'I want to be sick,' Lincoln says. 'I like to be sick.'

She nods slowly. His volume is creeping up again. She reels in the threads of her thoughts and recasts her full focus at him. She cannot blame him for his contrariness. They are hiding from gunmen in the dirt. But also it is suppertime, and his mood is directly tied to blood sugar. There is an inevitable escalation to his hunger. If she does not feed him, there will be whining and crying and possibly screaming.

'You like to be sick?' she says.

'Yes,' he says defiantly.

Too loud too loud too loud. The terror flashes again, and she swallows it down.

'Shhhh,' she says lightly. Delicately. Like pouring an exact teaspoon of cough medicine or teasing a tangle from his hair – touch is everything. 'You know, Superman can't get sick.'

'He can if there's kryptonite,' he answers, and she feels a surge of triumph something like she imagines Edmund Hillary felt when he reached the top of Everest.

'Green kryptonite,' he clarifies. 'Like *Doom in a Tube* and *Skrag the Earth Conqueror.*'

'I like the one with Skrag,' she says.

She sees the shift in his face even before he lifts his chin and throws back his shoulders. Rebelliousness has overtaken him.

'I don't like that one,' he says.

'No? I thought it was one of your favorites.'

'It's my least favorite.'

She does not want to give him anything to push back against.

'All right,' she agrees.

'It's a terrible book.'

'All right. Keep your voice down.'

'It's the worst book I've ever read.'

He will invent arguments if he is belligerent enough. She runs a hand over her face, and the stretch and pull of her skin is satisfying. She presses at her eyelids, her eyeballs firm under her fingertips, and when she finally moves her hand away and licks her dry lips, she tastes dirt and salt and it is not unpleasant.

'Do you want to play with your guys?' she asks.

'No,' he says too quickly.

It does not count when his answer is so quick. She waits. Watches his thoughts play across his face.

'Yes, please,' he amends.

And the dark, demanding thing inside him is gone. Vanished as quickly as it appeared, which is how it always works. It will reappear just as quickly. But she will deal with that when it happens.

She opens her purse and makes a show of digging and searching, but with her other hand she reaches to sneak a look at her phone. She is nervous both of the light and of frustrating Lincoln with her split attention, but she thinks there were links to an actual story under the zoo photo and caption. It only takes a couple of brushes of her thumb to scan through the brief column of text.

- SWAT team currently at the scene.
- police department not releasing details.
- conflicting reports from witnesses.

It is still not a story at all. More gaps than substance.

'Mommy? My guys?' says Lincoln, his hand on her shoulder.

'I'm getting them,' she says, trying to make sense of it. Do the police still think they are only dealing with one man? And that the man has barricaded himself in a room? Do they believe that the danger is locked away and contained?

'Mommy?' Lincoln prompts again, more loudly. Annoyance in his tone.

She turns back to him, pulling a handful of plastic men from her purse finally. She hands them to him, not sure this is a wise choice – he is never quiet when he performs his stories; there are battles and arguments – but she cannot think of another choice.

If he makes noise, she will quieten him.

She thinks this as if it were always that easy. As if she can always quieten him whenever she likes.

'I might make up a story,' Lincoln says, trying to make the men stand up on the uneven ground. 'Do I have the Predator?'

'I think so,' she says, reaching again, one-handed.

She lays her phone inside her purse: she is more likely to miss a text with it there, but the purse will hopefully block any light from the screen. She turns her head to study every inch of their view – the trees and bamboo and railroad track and open spaces – and she sees no movement in the shadows. She does hear a far-off sound, shrill, that could be a baby crying. It is not the first time she has heard it. She is not sure that it is real.

'Mommy, did you find him?' says Lincoln.

She skims her fingers along the bottom of her purse, which is an orgy of action figures. She feels her keys and several pens and some sort of gunk wedging itself under her fingernails but also solid little legs and arms and helmets. She pulls one out – no, it is Wonder Woman. She drops it and begins digging again.

Ah. The Predator. She pulls him into the open air and brushes an old raisin from his head.

'Here,' she says, handing it to Lincoln.

She bought the Predator because it was on sale for two dollars at Barnes & Noble and Lincoln was always looking for some figure to play an alien. Then one night they were flipping through channels and she saw the old Schwarzenegger movie, and it was an edited version – no language or gore, she thought – so she let Lincoln watch, only now on regular television they can say *Don't be a pussy* and *Damn you to hell* all they want, so how are you supposed to let a four-year-old watch anything?

He did not find it frightening. He watched a man sliced wide open, hanging from a tree, and he said, *Oh, do you think those were his intestines?*

He appreciates body parts.

'Do you think he can be a zombie?' Lincoln asks, running his finger over the tiny alien's head.

'Sure,' she says.

It is possible that there are hostages. It is possible that the men she heard banging their way through the primate house have now corralled a few helpless people and all the terror has been focused in one nightmarish room. Maybe the only mistake that the police – or CNN – have made is in miscounting the number of gunmen. Or maybe the police have gotten it entirely wrong.

Those people who were lying on the concrete, bleeding, some of them were alive, weren't they? They need the paramedics, don't they? They need the police as soon as possible. And if the gunmen are still wandering around the zoo, hunting, then there is no time to wait. No time for caution.

She could tell the police that. She could have Paul tell them.

But what if there are hostages? What if she is wrong and she tells them to barge in here and then more people die? What if the shooters have locked themselves in a room and she and Lincoln are completely safe right now?

What if the shooters are on the other side of this fence and a bullet flies through her head that she never even feels and she cannot do anything to protect him?

'Zombies have green skin,' says Lincoln.

'Yes,' she says.

The night they watched *Predator*, he was hyped up. *Does the Predator go back to space?* he asked, bouncing, two-footed, on the den carpet. *What could I use for a spaceship?*

Is the Predator a boy? is it the only one? does it have friends? does it go to the dentist? does it speak English? can it live on Earth? can it breathe air? is it real? is it in actual jungles? why does it laugh at the end? does it bleed like we do?

Will you be my mommy forever? he asked, too, not long after they had watched men skinned and arms ripped off and the sky lit by explosions.

Forever, she said.

When I'm a grown-up, will you still be my mommy?

I will be.

Can I still live with you when I'm a grown-up?

Hell, no, Paul whispered as he passed behind the sofa, breath warm against her ear, but she said, *Of course.*

Because I want to be around you always, Lincoln said then, and his small hand was on her arm, in the crease where bicep met forearm.

He won't want that, of course. But it is a nice thought.

'Mommy, let me tell you something,' he says now, and the Predator – the zombie – seems to be digging in the dirt for something. 'Not all zombies are bad.'

'No?'

'No. There are some zombies called policeman-zombies, and their job is to catch bad zombies and put them in a big hole. That is what zombies use for jails.'

'Shhhh,' she says, belatedly. 'A little quieter.'

He keeps going, and she nods as she, for the thousandth – millionth – time, scans the trees and the darkness around them. Lincoln is surely maneuvering his figures more by feel than by sight, although there is a sliver of a moon and a light from the patio behind them puts out a faint glow. She can see the curves of her son's head and the silhouettes of the trees and the rooftops of the buildings. Everything around her has a shape, barely. But she would have to walk carefully if she were trying to climb out of their enclosure – she cannot make out the holes or loose rocks that might be under every footstep.

What would the pathways of the zoo be like? Are the strings of lights still glowing? Are there more light poles, beaconing the way? If there are lights, of course, she would have to avoid them. If she were going anywhere.

If they were going anywhere.

It is not supposed to be like this. She has read about enough shootings – she feels confident she knows how they work. The shooter comes in and sprays everything with bullets and people fall to the ground, dead or wounded or pretending, and it is hellish, but it is also over within minutes, and then the police come and either the shooter kills himself or the police kill him. It is a terrible pattern. But it is a pattern. There is a predictability to it, and this has always struck her as the most terrible part. The killings are common enough to have a set sequence of rolling ticker headlines and then grim snapshots of the shooters and smiling vacation snapshots of the victims and Facebook quotations and connect-the-dots for how they got the guns and released statements from the victims' families. She wants the predictability now. She wants the pattern.

This – this nothingness and silence, dead bodies still out there on the concrete, an hour later – this does not happen.

She needs to re-evaluate. Should they wait here? Hide no matter how long it takes? It is not the only option.

She knows there are boundaries around the perimeter of the zoo – 'perimeter', that's a military kind of word – but she can't bring up a picture of what the outer walls look like. Surely she has seen them in all the hours she's spent here – surely she has walked within inches of them. What are they made of – chain-link fencing? Brick? How high are they, and is there barbed wire?

She thinks that if she were sitting here alone she would be making a plan involving those outer walls.

Paul hates flying. He always wants to hold her hand as they are taking off. He tries to estimate the number of planes taking off from their particular airport, and then he multiplies that number by how many airports there are in the entire country, and he makes up the figures and puts them together and computes some imaginary odds of the plane crashing. The math comforts him.

She wonders about the square footage of the zoo. She and Lincoln are occupying about three square feet of it now. And if the zoo is one square mile and a mile is 5,200 feet, something like that – do you square that number? Over 25,000 square feet, maybe, and if she carried Lincoln out of here, they would be occupying only a couple of square feet at a time, so the chances are one in 12,000 that the gunmen would be in the same space.

She knows her math cannot be anything close to right.

'I used to have two feet,' says Lincoln, in what she thinks is a zombie voice. 'No one needs two, though. You only need one.'

Something is moving through the leaves and pine straw. She has a moment of panic – so many moments of panic, all strung together. But this time the fear fades quickly. Whatever it is, the thing is small. A bird or a lizard, maybe.

When she was small, she loved the night-time. The darkness outside was so wide open, and her mother's house was so cramped, all the dark corners full of things she did not want to think about. But outside was different. She would go out on the small square of concrete that served as a patio, feet bare, and she would sit on the splintery lawn chair – her mother had never bothered replacing the cushion when it molded – and she would try to pick out the sounds. Frogs and crickets and sometimes a dog barking, and the sound of passing cars and the chains on the swing set clinking in the wind, and she was amazed, always, by the noises, once she bothered to notice them.

It is the same here. There is that same layer upon layer of sound. Only now it does not fill her with any sense of wonder. It leaves her struggling to breathe.

She hears the baby crying again.

6:28 p.m.

The wind has picked up, and there is a new sound – something like marbles falling on a kitchen floor. An oak tree nearby, Joan guesses. Acorns bouncing off concrete. They sound, for a moment, like many small feet running.

There is something hard under her hip, and she pulls out a rock nearly as big as her fist, which she thinks might be a chunk of concrete. She tosses it a few inches away with a jerk of her wrist just as her phone flashes inside her purse.

You there? Paul is asking.

She wants her husband here next to her. Badly. She does not really want that, of course – she would never want him to be in danger – but she thinks of the hard curves of his body pressed tight against her after they turn off the lights, molded S-shaped to each other, thighs to thighs and belly to back, her belly button against his spine.

She does not want to have to answer him. She does not want to put anything into words.

She is given a reprieve: a news alert flashes on her screen. She feels a flush of anticipation, relieved that finally the phone has come up with actual answers. Something has happened – the police are coming. The shooters are dead. And even as the possibilities churn, she is pulling out the phone and reading the words, and then she is reading them again, over and over, because they do not make sense.

Dozens killed in flash flooding in Texas, the phone reads.

It is inconceivable to her that people are dying somewhere other than here. It is inconceivable that there is any place other than here. She is still staring at the words even as she swipes the news alert away. She glances at Lincoln, who is sitting, only sitting, the Predator clutched limply in his hand.

She needs to answer Paul.

Waiting, she types, wondering if I should do something different.

There is no pause for thought before his words materialize – no uncertainty at all in their straight lines.

STAY THERE.

She wonders if he thinks the capital letters will persuade her.

You know that– she starts, but then her fingers stop and she watches them, arched in the light, and she thinks their pose is like a hula dancer's, and she is sharply aware that she is admiring her own fingers.

One second. Two seconds. Three seconds.

She listens.

Something has made her stop. She knows that there is *something* for a short while before she knows that the *something* was a sound.

Then she hears it again. It is a sound that she's made herself on these winding concrete paths – the slide of a shoe on loose bits of gravel. A scrape and a scuff. Possibly a whisper. It is coming from the path behind the chain-link fence, from the vast shadowy area behind their enclosure.

She turns the phone off quickly and pulls Lincoln to her. She feels like she has always been reaching for him, grabbing him up, tightening her arms, nervous of his distance – *not too far not too loud not too fast* – except for the times, of course, when he is grabbing at her, pulling her to him, nervous of her distance.

Mama, up pease, he used to say, back when he had not mastered his 'l's.

Up pease. Up pease. Up pease.

She scans the darkness – it is total now – and she can see nothing past their pen. She knows the bamboo is out there and the train track and the concrete pathways, and she hopes maybe the woman with the baby is out there again or someone else looking for a hiding place, and this time, she tells God, this time she will call to them and help them and share her hiding place, if only that is what the noise is.

She cannot see. But she can hear.

Whispers now, unmistakable. Men's whispers, like a radio station barely coming through.

They have not barricaded themselves in a room.

'Quiet,' she says to Lincoln, even though he is not making any sound. 'Bad men.'

'Wh—?' he starts, but she shushes him, and he listens to her, and she says a quick prayer of thanks and even as she says it she wonders, again, if God is punishing her for thinking her child is more important than the other woman's child. She would do it again in a heartbeat, cannot really regret it even with the guilt weighing on her like wet wool, and she wonders, sometimes, about her ideas of God.

They are coming closer, she thinks, almost surely on the asphalt path that runs parallel to the train track. She can hear footsteps, just a slide and crackle every now and then.

The shadows are uniform, unmoving.

She does not think that she and Lincoln are visible. She pictures the light attached to the eaves overhanging the deck, and she knows the edge of the pen is illuminated, but the rocky area where they are hiding seems almost black to her. She wiggles her fingers and can only just make out the movement.

The phone, though. If they saw the light of the phone.

'Here,' says a voice, quietly, closer than she would have expected, and it is the most terrifying word she has ever heard.

'There?' says the other voice.

'No. Over there.'

She still cannot see them. But it sounds like they are within a few feet of the fence – maybe twenty feet away? Thirty? Close enough that she can make out every word they are saying, although she has to strain to hear. They are standing still, she thinks, waiting.

Have they seen her? Are they looking at her right now, aiming?

A moth skims across her cheek, wings heavy. A branch creaks overhead. Her hair blows into her mouth, and she does not spit it out.

'I don't see anything,' says one of them.

'Shhh.'

She looks down toward the phone she has stuck under her thigh, even though she cannot see it in the dark. She is certain that they saw the light from the screen, and she is equally certain that they will keep looking until they find it. It is entirely her fault. She understood the risk, and she did not weigh it heavily enough.

The price of her mistake is far too high.

'Mommy,' says Lincoln right in her ear, and she does not know whether he is as loud as she thinks he is.

Sometimes they make air kisses at each other's ears, as loud as they can. Lincoln says, *I'll make a mwah in your ear*, and he smacks his lips right at the shell of her ear, and there is the sweet, painful percussion of his kiss, and his soft breath, just like now, the damp warmth of his exhale, how it pours out of him and soaks into her skin even as it drifts into the air, gone.

'Disappear,' she whispers, so softly that she does not know if he can hear her, but he must because he drops his head to her shoulder.

She has somehow risen to her knees, she realizes, one foot already braced against the ground, ready to spring up and run. She wants to run. But she can't see, and she does not know, even if she could see, where she would go. They would hear her moving. She would have to climb over the railing, carrying him wrapped around her, and the railing is well lit.

She has to stay still.

She is not sure she can manage it. She is not sure she can make herself let them come to her.

'You sure?' says a voice.

97

She assumes they are the same two men who walked through the primate house, but she is not positive. She can no longer distinguish between their voices. They are both hushed.

'Someone is here,' says another voice.

'Hiding, huh?'

The other voice does not answer. For a while there is only wind and leaves and something far away hooting. She does not move other than to run a hand over Lincoln's head, over and over.

There is a jingling sound, a movement at the fence. Maybe a shoe or an arm propped on the chain links or maybe someone losing his footing. She thinks she can make out the shapes of heads and shoulders, as flat and featureless as paper dolls in the dark.

'You were lost but now you're found,' one says in a singsong voice, although he is not quite singing. He is chanting, off-key, voice rising and dipping. 'You were run wild / thrown out, exiled / but now you're mine.'

He keeps going. Louder. She imagines he is smiling, and she half expects him to start clapping out a rhythm.

'You led the way but you knew I'd follow / Your neck was bare / but dip your head / I've got your collar.'

Now the voice is carrying enough that she can hear it just fine. She thinks it is the quiet one from earlier. His voice is the thinner, higher-pitched one. For someone who claimed to be such an expert on hunting, he doesn't seem to be concerned about being stealthy anymore.

Or maybe he is simply that confident.

'I've got your collar,' he echoes again, and he is running his hand – or, no, something metal – along the fence, making an almost musical sound.

She tries to calm her breathing – she can hear herself almost panting. Shivers coming up from her lungs.

'I had one squab tell me that all she wanted was peace,' says one of them in that fake drawl they were doing earlier, and at least the chanting has stopped. They are talking loudly enough now for her to tell they are not overly oblivious or overly confident – or at least they are not only those things. They want whoever is out here to hear them.

The grating noise of the fence still. Steady and metallic. An acorn falls with a quiet crack.

'And what did you do?' says the other.

'What did I do, honey pie?' The drawl. 'I gave her lots of pieces. Her arms and legs and a finger or two.'

Both of them laugh, and there is something about the comfortable, agreed-upon kind of laughter – an old joke – that makes her realize: they are quoting some show.

She doesn't recognize the words, but she is sure that she's right. She had an old boyfriend who could repeat paragraphs of dialogue from *Jaws*, and back when her brother still lived with her – she can hardly remember it, a time when she was not alone with her mother – he worked *Star Wars* lines into normal conversation, and it sounded just like this. Her boyfriend and her brother would ramble on in different languages, words thrown together, all sorts of meanings in them that she was missing – she could hear the same giddy, worshipful current in their voices that she can hear from these chanting men.

So eleven hundred men went into the water, three hundred and sixteen men come out, the sharks took the rest.

These aren't the droids you're looking for.

The fence is rattling as though the men are grabbing hold and rocking it. There is no chance they can budge it, of course – the only point must be to make noise.

They have moved across the pathway, closer to the bamboo. She can make out the movement, a change of pattern in the dark. They shake that fence, too.

'I spy with my little eye,' one calls out.

But they do not see anything. She knows that now. They are playing games. Hoping to flush out their prey, like her father would use his Labrador to flush out doves back when he was still around, and the doves would fly up and he would shoot and the dog would bring one back and if it was not dead her father would pinch off its head and toss it to the ground because he said it was less painful for the dove that way but, still, there would be blood dripping from the neck hole and a little beaked head lying in the grass. He took her hunting only once that she can remember.

'What do you spy?' says one man in his normal voice.

'Something dark,' says the other.

They laugh again. She wonders if they have been drinking.

Lincoln makes a sound against her neck that sounds like Muddles when you step on his paw.

The fear in her cools and hardens as the men laugh, and she is thrilled to realize that she is furious. These stupid men are waving guns and singing nursery rhymes at her. Making her son whimper in her arms. She remembers being in a haunted house back during college, and there was a large man in front of her – way over six feet tall, with a football player's build – so close to her that she kept running into his back whenever he stopped suddenly. She had a date with her, but the large man made a better shield. And in the middle of a strobe light a masked zombie jumped out with a bladeless chainsaw not three inches from her face, eye to eye, and it made her scream embarrassingly loudly, and he must have scared the large man, too, because the guy – in a flash of white light – punched the zombie in his face, and then instead of a zombie there was a teenager on the ground, pulling his mask off, blood running out of his mouth, moaning, and she did not feel sorry for that teenager at all and in fact was very pleased with the football player.

They are teenagers, she thinks, *these men with guns. They are not men or, at most, barely men. And they are idiots.* She will not have her son killed by stupid, stupid teenagers singing songs.

If they want to play pretend, she has watched movies herself, and, really, that is what this feels like anyway. And if she is only a character, it is easier to act. She lets loose of Lincoln with one arm – her other hand still in his tangled curls – and feels in the weeds for the concrete lump she set aside earlier. Almost immediately her fingers close around it. Sharp-edged and substantial, it fits nicely in her hand, as comfortable as a baseball. She tucks it against her thigh and splays her fingers along the ground again, sweeping circles in the dirt. Another rock, bigger than the first one; her hand cannot close around it entirely.

She angles herself slightly, adjusting Lincoln forward so

she can draw her arm back. She cannot decide whether she is being very smart or very foolish, but she is already tightening her grip and tensing her shoulder, and she throws the rock over the back fence of their enclosure, hopefully through the tree branches, toward the railroad track or the undergrowth around it.

She intentionally does not take time to think too hard about her aim.

One. Two. She counts off the seconds with her arm still frozen in the air, and she hears the rock hit either branches or leaves, and it is louder than she expected and also it is not quite as far as she might have hoped, but it has definitely cleared the enclosure, and it has landed in the approximate direction of the railroad track. It has landed many yards behind the men, if they are still standing at the other fence.

She wonders if, to them, it sounds like someone has just thrown a rock to lure them away.

Apparently it does not, because they make an excited grunt and obediently crash toward the sound, smashing through the small saplings and brambles that fill in the wild spaces off the paths, and their steps are clumsy and uncertain and eager.

She supposes it is too much to hope that they might break an ankle.

With their feet still crunching through the weeds, she slides the phone from under her leg. It is cold in her hands now, a hunk of plastic, nothing more. No, it is more than that. The phone is the reason that they are sitting here, hiding from men who can barely walk in the dark.

Another sound – a gun firing. This time it sounds

surprisingly like a typewriter, with someone typing slow and firm. She does not even flinch, although she does not know why she is so unafraid. She is used to it, maybe, and she does not think they are firing in her direction, and also there is a rush to finally acting instead of only worrying.

She inhales slow and long. The tremors have stopped. She is still and solid and ready, a thing carved and polished for a purpose. She slides her thumb across the phone, lighting up the screen again, and then she hurls it as hard as she can, over the chain-link fence, toward the bamboo, where she knows she has seen pine straw in the beds. To the right of where the men had been standing before they ran toward her rock. There is a chance, of course, that the men will see a glowing thing flying through the air, and there is a chance that the phone will hit the concrete, and it will shatter, but, more than that, it will announce that it has been hurled – the impact will be obvious – and that will ruin everything. But she will not go back to cowering, helpless, so she watches as her phone spins, fast and certain, aerodynamic, like it has been built just for this time and place, and there is no clattering crash, only a soft, exhaling kind of a landing, and she wonders if they hear it.

'What?' one of them says, and the stupid feet flattening the stupid weeds stop, confused. They did hear it, and that could be good or bad, but it is something that she did – she has pulled their strings like they have been pulling hers, and she is hotter and denser all of a sudden.

There is a power inside her, watching.

She can see the phone screen shining in the distance, through the diamond shapes of the chain link, a bright dot.

Her aim was decent, although not perfect. But it is lying face up – that is what she hoped for – a few feet into the bamboo thicket. The glow from the screen lights up a small patch of smooth wooden poles and still-trembling leaves.

'There,' says one of them, and she sees the waves of shadow as they run across the concrete, into the beam of light from the eaves of the Primate Zone, and then they are past that circle of light, but they are bending over her phone, and their hands and faces and arms are ghostly for a moment.

She watches one of them raise her phone to his face. He is clean-shaven and light-haired, and he is white, just as she thought. His face is thin and unimpressive, and she wonders whether he is the thin-voiced one, whether his face somehow matches his sound.

She is not done yet.

While he is looking at the screen, she pulls her arm back, gripping her second rock, aiming past the men, farther along the path, in the opposite direction of both herself and the train track. Back toward the heart of the zoo, the exhibits, back toward everything. If she could map out the objects she has thrown, she hopes they would make a straight line, and that line would lead back to the sidewalks and bathrooms and benches and tables, back to the obvious hiding places and signs and labels. Anywhere but here.

Lincoln grunts softly, startled by the jerk of her arm, and then she's letting go again, and finally she hears the stone hit something solid and soft. Dirt, she imagines.

'They're running,' says the quiet, high-voiced one. The one holding her phone.

He must have turned off her phone or slid it into his pocket or something, because the light is gone, and she hears them jogging down the pathway, away from her and Lincoln, chasing after her rock but not chasing too fast, because they are not worried. They are enjoying themselves.

It is not rocket science, what she has done. She has probably seen something like it in her reruns of *Scarecrow and Mrs King* or maybe in *Predator* or maybe in any other action show she's ever seen. (How strange it is to think of herself in front of a television, on her couch, Lincoln pressed against her, chugging from a water bottle, his questions constant because he cannot watch any show for a full minute without asking a question.) She is sure the gunmen have seen a million of those shows as well, but she hopes they are too cocky and too stupid to consider anything very carefully.

She can still hear their footsteps, barely. Rhythmic and easy on the concrete.

Lincoln has been so quiet, it occurs to her. Other than the ache in her arm and the weight on her hip, she has almost forgotten that he is here.

'Sweet?' she asks.

He only pushes closer to her, not even lifting his head.

He and Mark are running nearly elbow to elbow, and their breathing is one rushing sound. Even though they have seen no sign of whoever dropped the phone, speed makes everything feel smooth and perfect. Robby has never felt as fast as he feels tonight. He has never felt so much like his body is a powerful tool, ready to do anything. There is a backless iron bench ahead of them, and it would be easy to go around it, but he leaps over it, one foot landing loud on the metal. When he is running, he is not Robby anymore, and sometimes the gun in his hand makes him feel that way, too, but not always. The darkness around them and the flashes of light overhead and the big leaves waving in the wind – it all feels right. It is what he has wanted for forever: rightness.

When it felt wrong before – back with the hogs – that was because he forgot that he was not Robby anymore. It is only Robby who can feel so lost, so legless and armless and brainless, only a stump.

'This way,' whispers Mark, turning left toward the giraffes. He doesn't bother to wait and see whether Robby will follow. Robby always follows.

Mark has slowed to a jog. His Adam's apple is sticking out of his skinny neck, his head is sort of nodding up and down, and the guy has never looked more like a bobblehead. He can't have gained ten pounds since middle school – *hell on Earth*, Robby's mother called it, half laughing, but Robby knew that if she could laugh, then she didn't understand – and it was back then that Robby had first invited Mark over, and Mark had seen the DVD sitting on the shelf and grabbed it and yelled out, '*The Hidden Ones*?!' in a voice that other guys might use if they'd found porn, and Mark had reached for the remote control without even asking. Then they were watching that first scene, the one Robby had watched by himself a dozen times already, where blackness filled the screen and then, so slowly, tiny spots of light appeared in the blackness.

It is like you are looking into space, but then the camera pulls back and you are actually looking into a gap in a tree trunk. The spots of light are some kind of insects, like maggots or termites, only they are fluorescent, and then you are looking at the whole tree, giant, and then you see the other trees and you realize this is a jungle, but it is not like any jungle you have ever heard about. You never see the sky. The trees are so thick that everything is shadows, and the leaves are as big as a grown man. Those giant leaves flap against helmets and curl around rifles, and Robby has always thought that it would be hard to breathe if the trees were crowding you like that, even though trees are supposed to make oxygen, at least Earth trees. And that is, actually, the coolest thing about the movie: you never know if this is Earth or some other planet. Because the men are humans,

108

but at night the leaves glow like Extra gum, and the things that the men hunt are always covered by their headdresses, all feathers and dreadlocks.

'You know we've lost her, right?' says Mark, a beat between every couple of words while he sucks in a breath. He has never been much of an athlete. 'There's no telling where she is.'

Robby is still half in the movie, and it takes a second to reconnect himself to his body.

' "She"?' he says.

'The woman who dropped her phone.'

'How do you know it's a she?'

Mark holds out the phone, turning it so that the cover catches the light. Robby can make out some vague image.

'Picture of her kid,' says Mark. 'Gotta be a woman.'

Robby is not convinced of it, but there's no point in arguing.

'Then why are we still running?' he asks.

Mark raises his arm, and then there is the sound of the phone bursting on the pavement, and it is a beautiful sound. In another second, they are leaping over cracked pieces of screen and casing and innards.

'The hunt goes on,' Mark says. 'We are order. We are hope.'

Robby knows, then, that Mark feels it, too. How they have left the rest of it outside the gate, back in the parking lot. In here there is no history.

Starbucks – eight months. Applebee's – four months. Bud's Burgers – five months, and, God, he'd been ready to leave that one because that place had been full of, like, seriously obese freaks, like, only fat people were allowed through the door, and the bellies would just hang off them like batter over a cake pan, and it made you want to take a knife and slice it all off and see what the poor guy would look like without the blubber.

And there was Dog-Eared Pages bookstore and Chick-fil-A and Sears – two months – and now CVS, not even one month.

His stupid boss, full of himself because he is a manager at a drugstore, and, hey, you're forty years old and manage a drugstore, so, yeah, wow, you're really setting the world on fire. Louisa Brunson, who he was sure had a good time when they went bowling, but then he called the next night and she couldn't even be bothered to stop watching television while she talked to him. She said her mother thought she should be focusing on college instead of dating, but he knows that really her mother just didn't want Louisa dating him. Because that is what parents think, especially Louisa's mother, who has bulging frog eyes and has never worked a day in her life, one of those women who is a terrible person and probably was since she was born and her parents should have just drowned her like a cat. And before Louisa there was Angela Willard, who was nice at first, sweet, shy, but she turned out to be a dumb whore and he should have known it from the beginning.

Whore and *sweet* and *shy* are the sounds that his feet pound into the pavement.

His eight-year-old cousin asked whether Robby paid his mother rent. He wonders what conversations she overheard from her parents to make her ask that. That side of the family says they're Christians, but they love to rip people apart. They're nasty, petty people. So many nasty people – a world of them – but no one sees the grossness of each other, no, no, everyone is too busy thinking Robby is the screw-up, the lazy one, and they are so blind and they are miserable and don't even know it.

All of them are wiped away. All of it is wiped away.

We are order / We are hope.

We are order / We are hope.

That is the chant that gets louder and louder as the camera pulls back, and the rhythm is like something army men would yell while they march, voices rising on the final *hope*, but for several seconds there are only trees on the screen until a figure comes running, silently. It's being chased by a dark-haired soldier in a sleek, smooth uniform, and you almost feel sorry for the shadowy shape, which is thin and mostly naked except for the huge headdress. Then just as the soldier grabs the thing's hand – is it a hand or something stranger? – its other hand touches the soldier's face, and the soldier freezes and then arches back, spine curving, and collapses.

There are more soldiers coming – a neat line of them, synchronized – and the creature dives under a bush. You see Lieutenant Harding for the first time, and he raises a hand without saying a word. Then he steps to the bush, and he reaches into the branches. He pulls out the squab by one ankle, kicking and gibbering. He grabs the squab's wrists in one gloved hand, keeping her poisonous hands away from his skin. He sings to her, smiling, *You were lost, but now you're found*, and from that moment when you see Harding's face as he wraps his fingers around her neck – you can tell it is a her because there are breasts, even though they are covered by some sort of purplish metal – you know that the squabs are evil and that the soldiers are good. And when the lieutenant snaps her neck, you are glad.

'Back toward the lake,' says Mark, tugging his jeans up. 'Let's finish the loop.'

'All right,' says Robby.

'Shhh,' says Mark.

You are glad when Harding realizes that the original mission of containing the squabs is flawed. Containment is not enough. Because the squabs have begun to venture past the borders of the jungle and into the town, which has no name, and Lieutenant Harding realizes the creatures could easily wipe out an entire population. They must be wiped out instead.

The squabs say they mean no harm. They send a babbling contingent, three of them, to the soldiers' camp, and one of them comes forward – feathers and dreadlocks blowing in the wind – and they say the only word they seem to know, *peace, peace, peace*, and they hold their hands up, but their hands are weapons, aren't they? They can kill with a touch.

Harding carries a long needle with him, and at night around the fire he pulls out the needle and begins popping the blisters his boots have rubbed on his feet. He slides the needle into his bubbled-up skin, and the sores burst and pus runs into the dirt, and he never changes his expression as he shoves his boots back on. Later he stabs the needle into a skinny squab's neck over and over again, and tears come down the squab's face as it screams. The tears look just like pus as they hit the ground – no difference.

The squabs look fragile. That is the thing Robby hates most about them. Harding is smarter and stronger and there is no weakness in him. You have to admire that, don't you? A guy who doesn't make mistakes? And if he does make them, no one notices, and that's the real talent, isn't it?

When they fired him from CVS, he told them that he was late because he slept through his alarm again. What was he supposed to do? His boss – with his goatee and his ego and his skinny jeans and his fake-British way of saying *Carry on* – said that Robby's alarm is not his problem. Maybe he was right. Maybe being late is Robby's own problem. But what can he do? How can he undo something that's already happened? Is he supposed to invent a time machine and go back and make himself wake up? Throughout his whole life he has never understood why he has to be blamed for things that are out of his control. Why he is constantly being punished for those things. He can't control that he's a deep sleeper. He can't control that he forgot to look at his speedometer and accidentally went fifty miles per hour in a school zone. He can't control that he mistyped an order and a table got Bacon Burgers instead of Black Bean Burgers. It wasn't intentional. Even if people are right and he is lazy or rude or selfish – well, it is what it is, right? It's genetics. It's not a choice. But that doesn't matter, does it? No one cares that he's trying, do they?

But, no, Robby is the one who is trying. *He* is not Robby. He is not that same constant fuck-up of a boy who left home today.

Are you blind, honey pie?

The squabs are the cleverest villains ever created, he sometimes thinks. When they bleed, their blood is bright pink, and it is impossible to know if it is the weird lighting or if it is meant to be inhuman. The blood splatters and drips on moss, and it is like some painting project he did once in Vacation Bible School.

It's the color of that antibiotic stuff, Mark said back then, on that first afternoon. *You know, amoxicillin? Did you ever have that?*

And Robby thought that, yes, actually, the blood was the exact color of amoxicillin. He remembered the taste, sweet and chalky and delicious. He told Mark that he loved that stuff.

You liked it? Mark said, and he said that he'd never met anyone else who didn't think it was disgusting. Mark said how, when he was a kid, he snuck downstairs in the middle of the night and drank a whole bottle of it.

It had been so long since Robby had felt like he was the same as someone.

Sometime after that his mother brought them a bowl of Doritos, not speaking, not making eye contact, and Robby felt bad, because he was sure that she knew he didn't want her to do anything to remind Mark that she existed. He wondered whether that hurt her feelings. He wondered whether she was trying to make him feel guilty. And then he caught her looking back over her shoulder, and he can still see the way she was smiling. She was so happy that he had found a friend. She was so relieved.

There are times when he almost hates her. But he hates himself for it, so that's something.

'Check-in time,' Mark says, slowing to a walk, huffing and puffing.

Robby glances at his watch, which still feels weird on his wrist, but they all needed a watch. 'Yeah.'

'Unless we don't,' says Mark.

They are nearly back to the lake now. He can see the lights flashing, all the pretty Halloween decorations twinkling away.

'No,' Robby says.

'All we have to do,' says Mark, for the thousandth time, 'is go over the wall. We follow the track around and we find some dark spot and pop out on Cherry Street or over on Havers. We walk back to my car, and we're out of here. No one knows.'

This is Mark in a nutshell – he wants everything easy. He never wants to pay the toll. If there's a paper due in a class, he's the one who never writes a page of it and gives the professor some excuse about a migraine and still bitches about getting a zero and Robby is the one who works his ass off in the computer lab until 4:00 a.m. but still only gets a couple of pages done and gets a fifty or sixty on it, and they both fail out, so who is smarter, really?

'And then we'll do what?' Robby says. 'Go to Peru and live on the beach forever?'

'Peru doesn't have a beach, dumbass,' says Mark. 'We do whatever. We go home and eat pizza. It doesn't make any sense, Robby. It ends the same for him. He gets what he wants. We've done what we said we would.'

They step off the concrete path, the grass and pine straw crunching under their feet. Robby sees a movement in the bushes, but it is only a duck on the other side of the chain-link fence.

'No,' Robby says. 'I already told you no.'

Since Robby never argues, Mark hasn't had any practice trying to convince him, and it shows. He'd be a crappy salesman – he just keeps repeating himself.

'We can walk away,' Mark says, stepping closer. 'We can wake up tomorrow morning.'

When he was little, Robby watched some cartoon about a robot or a mouse or maybe a dog. All those things could look pretty much the same in a cartoon. But when the robot-mouse-dog popped onto the screen, some deep voice yelled out, 'And now the star of the show!'

Robby sometimes hears that voice in his head when he sees Destin, the one who made all this happen. The one who saw something special in them. The star of the show. Robby is going to finish this like he promised Destin.

The ending is, really, the most important part.

Robby looks over at the lights shining on the lake. He smiles.

6:40 p.m.

'I'm hungry,' Lincoln says.

Joan has to strain to make out the words. It is the first time he has said anything in a while. They have been sitting silently, Lincoln reclining against her chest. It is entirely too dark for his guys now.

It is too dark for anything.

She is absurdly glad to hear his voice, regardless of how much she wishes he had said something – anything – else.

'Let me look,' she says, even though she is sure that she has nothing. She grabs blindly inside her purse, feeling in the pockets first.

'So,' she says, 'what sort of training do you think Batman does? To make himself faster and stronger?'

He says nothing.

'I think he lifts weights,' she says.

She can feel crayons. She wonders why she hasn't thrown away all these receipts.

'I think he Hula-Hoops,' she says, desperate. 'I think he does ballet.'

117

She pulls out a squashed Snickers Miniature and unwraps it, handing it over.

'Here's a candy bar, sweet. A Snickers.'

His fingers touch hers as he takes it. 'Do you have more?'

'I'll check,' she says. She does not have more. Still, she keeps her hands in her purse, and she hears the wet sound of his mouth closing around his fingers – he always seems to put the food farther into his mouth than necessary – and then she hears his chewing.

After a few seconds, she hears him licking his fingers.

'Did you find more?' he asks, so quiet and sedate.

She can see, just about, when his head moves toward her. She cannot make out anything of his features, not even his eyes or his teeth, which she would think might flash white in the dark. She leans back against the rock wall, and it is cold and hard, the edges of it snagging at her hair.

'I don't have any more, sweet,' she says.

'I'm still really hungry. Do you have any crackers?'

'No. Hey, do you still have your guys?'

'No.'

'Where are they?'

Nothing.

'You don't want to lose them, sweet. We should find them.'

He doesn't answer. She reaches out, her hand landing on his thigh, and she feels until she has his fingers in hers. She takes his hand and he does not pull away, but he does not curl his fingers around hers as he usually does.

'Let's just feel around on the ground,' she says, 'and see if we can find them. Like an Easter-egg hunt in the dark. Only for guys.'

He likes Easter.

He takes his hand from hers.

'I'll start feeling around for them,' she whispers, and she knows she sounds too cheerful. 'Now, who-all do we have out?'

She cannot help filling the silence when he does not respond.

'I know I gave you Batman,' she says, running her hands through the dirt, and the grass is so dry that it pricks her skin. Almost immediately she feels smooth plastic, and she knows which figure it is by the horned helmet. 'And I've got Loki. Who else am I looking for?'

'Thor,' he says. Flatly. 'Predator. The blond boy.'

She has found three of them already. It seems crucial to her that he does not leave anything here in the dirt, and her hands speed up, circling. She feels a sharper prick – glass? a shard of rock? – but she does not mind it.

'Are they gone?' he asks, so softly that she can barely hear him.

She rubs her hands on her skirt. She closes her purse, carefully snapping it shut so that no guys will fall out accidentally.

'The bad men?' she whispers.

'Yes.'

'I don't know. Until we know, I want to stay here and be quiet.'

'Are the police here?'

'I don't know.'

'Will they kill us?'

'Who were you using the blond boy for in your story?'

119

'Will they kill us?'

She can hear him breathing. His breathing is possibly louder than his words. She wishes she could see his face.

'They might,' she answers. 'If they found us. But they won't find us.'

She can feel his warmth pressed against her from hip to shoulder. He says something else, too softly – too softly! – and she leans closer so she can make out his words.

'What?' she whispers.

'If they killed us,' he says, 'would our bodies go to heaven?'

'It's souls that go to heaven.'

'Oh yeah,' he exhales. 'And our bodies stay here?'

'Yes. But we don't miss them. The souls are the important part.'

'But we can't see our souls. Or touch them.'

'Not now,' she says.

The wind has picked up again. She is cold but not miserably so. She does not want to ask him if he is cold, because it might plant the idea in his head.

He shifts against her, but he does not ask any more questions. He does not hum or blather meaningless words. She listens to the leaves and the crickets and thinks of Paul – no way to reach him now – and wonders if the men might circle back around, and it is harder to sit here, actually, in this silence that pulses and expands.

'It won't be long,' she whispers to Lincoln.

'I'm still hungry,' he says.

She wonders, for the thousandth time, where the police could be. She might be able to pacify him for a while, but his blood sugar will keep dropping, and he will become a little more like a wild animal with every passing minute, and there will be a breaking point.

She could leave him here while she makes her way back through the Primate Zone, past the playground and the elephant habitat, around the side of the Savannah Snack Bar to the vending machines. If all goes well, she could grab a pack of crackers and be back in only two or three minutes. He could wait here, and she would be back in the amount of time it would take her at home to run to the bathroom or to run upstairs and grab a book.

This is a pure dream, and she knows it. He will never sit here quietly, of course, calmly waiting. Not even for two minutes. He would not let her climb over the railing before he'd lift his arms, insisting she take him with her. And if she ignored him, he would scream as she walked away.

And what if it is not such an easy trip for her to get him a snack? What if they are out there, waiting? What good will she do him if they kill her, and then he is here, crying her name, and they find him?

No, even if he would wait here, it is hard to imagine the benefit. It is somehow a much more terrible thing to think of them finding him alone, to think of him small and scared as they raise their guns. It gives her an ugly kind of comfort to think that if it came to that, she would be holding him and—

She shuts down the thought. She thinks of how sometimes she can see so clearly some terrible accident – him stepping backward into the street, a car crumpling him. She finds herself practicing what she would tell Paul if she had to call him with the news. She has fought off an attack of near-terror watching Paul's sister strap Lincoln into a car seat and drive off with him, because she can so clearly see the accident they will have on the interstate, and then she will be the one getting the news, hearing her sister-in-law's voice on the phone, sobbing.

She goes into his room way after midnight, sometimes, to make sure he is still breathing.

She drops him off at school and, more days than she likes to admit, squelches thoughts of school shootings and men pushing their way into classrooms, teachers screaming, and how many children might get out the window before the gunmen break through the door and whether his teacher might choose him as one of the first to escape, and this is not rational, she has always told herself, but here they are, so apparently her imaginings were not so unhinged.

The morbid fantasies have actually lessened as Lincoln has gotten older. When he was an infant, she went through a phase where she could hardly look at windows. Any windows. She was always imagining him falling from them.

Now, sitting in the dirt, the whole world shadowed and filled with noises that she can barely decipher, she cannot imagine him being shot. The image does not come. She will not let it.

'Do you want to lie down?' she asks. 'You can use my lap as a pillow. Or I'll hold you like when you were a baby.'

Sometimes he is fascinated by what she did when he was a baby. By the parts of his life that he cannot remember. He is intrigued by the idea that milk came out of her breasts.

'No,' he says. 'I want to eat supper.'

'You might feel better with a little rest,' she says, although she knows that trying to steer him will not help her cause. Still, she is not willing to let go of the slender hope that maybe he will go to sleep. That maybe she could hold him and stroke his face until he drifts off and then they could stay here endlessly, and she wishes, for once, that he still had a pacifier, because it was Pavlovian the way his eyes would drift closed as soon as he started sucking – *A paci is a friend that you keep in your mouth*, he told her once – but he gave that up willingly on the night that he turned four, and it is sitting on the shelf in his room in its little paci house made of popsicle sticks with its doll's bed and blanket.

'I'm hungry,' he says again. 'I'm starving.'

The way he pronounces it, it comes out 'staw-ving'.

'Just lie down for a minute and see,' she says.

'I don't want to lie down. I want to eat supper.'

'We'll eat supper a little later.'

'But I'm starving.'

'Lie down for five minutes,' she says. 'Just five minutes and then we'll see.'

'Okay,' he says, but his face is scrunching up, his lip sticking out and his eyebrows jutting down, his breath already starting to stutter. 'O-kay. O-kay.'

'Lincoln—' she starts.

His crying always starts with words. He tries to talk through the weeping, and the words stretch into wails, and then the words evaporate and the tears come, and once they are falling down his cheeks he has passed into something monotone and rhythmic like the ocean, only more grating.

'Shhhh,' she says. 'You have to be quiet.'

123

'O-kay-y,' he says, in many syllables, more moan than word.

She scans the darkness. He is too loud too loud too loud. She is running her hand over his head, pulling him closer to her, shushing and stroking, and none of it is working.

She does not know how to buy more time. He cannot make noise. Whatever other factors are at work, that is the most important piece of the puzzle. Soon the tears will turn into stomping and sirenish screaming, and he can make you cover your ears from sounds that are not quite human but more mechanical. Like the gears inside him are stripped or a muffler has come off somewhere.

'All right,' she says. 'Do you want to get supper?'

The sobs stop almost immediately. His breaths skip and catch, and he sniffs wetly, but the sobs are gone.

He wipes his nose on his shirtsleeve. 'Is there a restaurant?'

'What about a treat?' she says. 'What about cheese and crackers for supper? Or peanuts? And a candy bar for dessert?'

Even though she cannot make out his face, she knows the look he gives her is disapproving.

'That's not big strong food,' he says.

'No,' she agrees. 'We can get something out of the machine. Whatever you like.'

'Food out of a machine for supper?'

He sounds hopeful now.

'Yes,' she says.

This would be different if she were alone. If she had been strolling through the zoo by herself when the gunfire started, she would have run, surely? She would have hidden. But then what? She is reasonably strong and reasonably fast, and she is smart, and if she were alone, she would by now have decided that she should not be waiting around for anyone to save her. There must be some point in the perimeter of the zoo where she could climb over, even if it meant getting a little bloody on some barbed wire. She can envision herself creeping from this pen, peeking around corners, and then escaping, escaping into the open air and the trees and the endless winding pathways, and she would be silent and quick, and they would not see her.

She does not think that these men are particularly competent, and if she were paying attention she could avoid them, and she could find a way out. She would look for others, too – she would be selfless if she were alone, she would not only rescue herself. She would find the woman and her baby, and she would reach out a hand to anyone else she found hiding, and she would lead them all to safety. She would stick to the shadows, and she would lead the way. She would take her time and never make a sound, and – in the surely thousands of feet of fencing – she would eventually find a weak spot. Or a policeman, watching.

She sees herself, a shadow.

And if the men found her, she would run. She would dash around a corner, and she could run for much longer than they could – she tries to do six miles four times a week – and there is a thing she loves about running, how, when the humidity is low and your muscles are loose, after a while you go weightless, sloughing off gravity, and the ache in your thighs and lungs gives way to helium, and you feel nothing.

Sometimes she can no longer feel her feet. Sometimes her entire body has turned to air. When she runs.

'Mommy?' he asks.

'Are you ready?' she whispers. 'You have to pay attention and do exactly what I tell you. And not make any noise.'

'Or they'll kill us,' he finishes.

She considers it.

'Or they might kill us,' she agrees.

She thinks she can see him nod.

She stands up, taking his hand. She lifts him, and his legs lock around her waist, and she absorbs the weight, settling more firmly onto the ground, and everything is utter dark around them, so she cannot see the first step that she takes. She keeps one arm under his butt and presses her other hand against the rock wall, balancing herself just in case.

He keeps his head against her jaw, and she feels his hands moving in her hair. She takes her first step so slowly that she can feel each muscle in her foot move. Her heel pressing down and the tendons in her ankle stretching, the arch of her foot curving as the ball and then the toes roll onto the ground, the smallest crunch of dry grass.

She feels like she is managing about two steps per minute, her hand dragging around the rock, measuring her progress as she moves inch by inch along the back side of it around to the angled end – she steps on a branch and it feels like a bone under her sandal, and it snaps, too loud, but maybe not much louder than a branch falling from a tree? – and then she is in front of the rock, facing the wooden boards of the deck, looking straight at the spotlights lighting up the two doorways: one that will lead her back to the main paths and one that will take her into the recesses of the orangutan exhibit.

The doors are lit up like choices on a game show. She blinks at the brightness.

The spotlights spread to the edge of the railing and slightly beyond – she can see spiderwebs strung from the wooden planks all the way to the ground, and they make her think of firemen's nets that would catch you if you fell.

Moths are circling the spotlights, ecstatic. Falling leaves zig and zag from trees that she can no longer see except for where the highest branches catch the moonlight. There are smaller winged things that are not moths hurling themselves into the glass doors with soft taps. All around her, nothing but blackness, but in this lit-up bubble of space, everything is frantic.

She stays in the dark for a few more moments, then she runs to the railing and lifts Lincoln to the outside ledge.

'Hold on,' she says, still keeping a hand on his back.

She has to let go of him entirely to boost herself over the railing, but his fingers clamp tight around the wood and he is silent, and then she has swung both feet over the side and landed on the deck and the moths are still swooping, oblivious and exalted, and she reaches over the rail, sharp edges biting into her hip bone, and she lifts Lincoln over, his tennis shoes thudding – *fwunk fwunk* – on the railing, and then he is tucked against her again and she steps under the eaves, into a far corner away from the door, back in the shadows, and she catches her breath.

6:58 p.m.

It feels good to stand, spine straight against the brick – she wonders how long she had been sitting. She moves her hand to her purse, patting the side pocket, her body remembering her phone independently of her mind.

Her phone.

When she felt it leave her hand, there was nothing but relief, and she has not, really, reconciled herself to the fact that the foreign thing she flung away, the thing that was leading the men to them, is the same thing that let her talk to her husband and have some connection to the world outside.

Now, whatever might be happening outside the walls, she is no part of it.

This does not bother her as much as it probably should. The outside world is irrelevant. It is, somehow, clarifying to feel her shirt snagging against the bricks behind her and to feel the pain in her left shoulder where Lincoln's weight pulls and to know that it is only the two of them, and it has been from the beginning. The phone only gave her the illusion that they were not alone.

It was surely no different for those poor people in Texas,

the ones floating face down, dead now, and maybe they were gulping lungfuls of water in the same seconds she was listening to gunmen rattle a fence.

There is no one coming. There is no such thing as the police.

Everything is sharper now that she knows this.

There is Paul, of course. He must be terrified. But there is nothing she can do about that. Paul is beyond her control, like almost everything, except which door she will open and which way she will point her feet and how fast or slow she will move. She considers what must come next: the building strikes her as the most dangerous part of their route – if the men are hiding or watching, she and Lincoln will have nowhere to go. There's no exit other than the main door to the Primate Zone, the same one they ran through on their way to their hiding place, and it was a perfect hiding place, safe, and she is moronic to leave it, negligent, and she should turn around now, but he is nearly shaking from hunger, or possibly from something besides hunger, but she does not have a fix for that – how long has she been standing here, wasting time? – but, yes, to get to the main exit, they'll have to wander down the narrow hallway with solid walls and glassed-in exhibits all around them, no doors or turn-offs. They'll be trapped.

But there is no choice, or, at least, there is none that seems better.

'Mommy?' he says, more high-pitched than usual.

Will he only speak in one or two words from now on? Have all the unending questions and inventions and stories dried up for good?

'It's all right,' she says as she gathers him to her and steps into the light, moths flashing silver above her head. She takes four long, fast steps and then pushes open the glass door, slipping inside quickly, despising the groaning door as it closes behind her, even though she has kept a hand on it, gently guiding it.

The door, finally, is closed. Inside, the silence presses down like humidity. The air is heavy with quiet. From this angle, flattened against the craggy wall – she is finding that she likes having her back against something – she can see only the faux-stone walls and fluorescent lighting along the baseboards and the smooth, shining surface of the floors. The exhibits begin past the first curve of the walkway, and for now it is like standing in the middle of some futuristic cave or an underground bunker. It is both entirely natural and entirely man-made. She sighs at the warmth. It usually seems cold in the building – she is always rubbing her arms while walking through – but now it's several degrees above the outside temperature.

She listens, and there is nothing. No sound of a heating system, no animals chattering. No wind shaking the sky-lights. She could make a long list of all the sounds that she might hear and does not.

Her boy is so quiet.

She considers letting him walk – he might like to stretch his legs. She would not mind giving her arms a rest. But there is something about holding him that seems much safer. He may weigh her down, but wrapped around her, he cannot be separated from her.

She listens, and there is still nothing.

'Here we go,' she whispers.

He doesn't answer, and she steps forward slowly, measuring the almost-sounds her feet make against the red-brown tiles. In two – three – steps she is far enough from the wall that she can no longer touch it, and she feels off-balance, as if she is walking on the deck of a boat. There is too much space around her. But another few steps and her hand lands on the porous surface of another wall as she comes to the first curve in the hallway – there are portraits of extinct animals, dodos and passenger pigeons and Pyrenean ibexes and great auks, and none of them are primates, and the logic of this place escapes her. Keeping her shoulder against the wall and her hands locked under Lincoln, she tilts her head around the bend. She has already ducked back by the time she processes what she has seen.

There is a monkey sitting on the floor.

She steps from behind the slab of rock, turning the corner, and there is glass on either side of her: the tiny squirrel monkeys on her right and what should have been the colobus exhibit on her left. But now that exhibit is only a square hole in the wall, exposing ropes and concrete. There is barely any glass at all, except for what is smashed all over the tile floor. No lights are on inside the enclosure, but the hallway fluorescents throw a glare over the rocky ground and the fake creek. She only glances at the landscape, though, because she is focused on the monkey in front of her.

It is a colobus, of course, black and white, head hanging forward, with its hands – paws – dragging on the glass-covered tiles, and because of the angle, it takes her a moment to realize that there is a second colobus lying unmoving on the ground. She can only see its black feet and rump. The rest of it is hidden.

She watches its feet carefully, and she cannot see the slightest twitch or tremor – the doves her father killed would jerk for long seconds even after their heads were gone – and she is fairly sure it is dead. The other colobus, the living one, is standing so close that its long white fur mixes with the fur of the dead one, and Joan cannot tell where one stops and the other starts.

She tightens her arms around Lincoln, wishing she knew more about primates.

The living colobus has not looked in her direction. Its back is hunched over, and its fur is smooth and silky and touchable, and she wonders if people have ever made coats from it.

Only its fingers move, curling and straightening a few millimeters from the floor. It does not seem to have thumbs.

She thinks of the time in Mississippi when a possum meandered onto the sidewalk in front of her and she decided to cross the street because she did not like the look of its teeth. And in Honduras, during that unending contract with the coffee cooperative, when she woke to find a cow in her bedroom, its wide head dipping toward her mattress, thick tongue swiping into the air. Her uncle caught her baby squirrels when she was small – this was after her father had gone, and, of course, her father would probably have shot the squirrels – but they were really her uncle's pets, not hers. He wouldn't let her hold them because they would bite, and his thumbs were bloody and scabbed even though they loved him and rode on his shoulder and jingled his earlobes with their tiny claws.

The colobus is swaying its head slightly from side to side, rolling its neck, and she thinks of Stevie Wonder and frightens herself by almost laughing. Her mouth begins the smile before she can stop it, and then she has to work to make the muscles in her cheeks do what she tells them to do.

She wonders if the live colobus dragged the dead one out here. Do they have burial rituals? Do they mourn? Did the dead colobus live for a while after it was shot and try to escape out here, and the unhurt one follow it and, really, why wouldn't all the monkeys run like hell and get as far away as possible when the first shots sprayed around them – why is this one still here? Did it get trapped by the closed doors and come back eventually, or has it been here the whole time, standing watch over the body?

She and the monkey are both frozen, refusing to acknowledge each other's presence. It strokes its white beard with one finger, contemplatively, but it never raises its head.

The glass barrier makes all the difference. A dog or a cat – a domesticated thing – is totally different. A wild animal in front of you, not a pet but a *real* animal, is every impulse all at once. You believe it is sweet and affectionate, and this can be true, but it will also make you bleed without remorse. Scabbed thumbs and dear, dangling earlobes. You cannot know a wild thing.

She cannot stay here frozen indefinitely. She could turn around and go the other way, but it would take much longer to wind through the orangutans and the baboons and several other animals she cannot recall. She would have to go back across the lighted deck, and she would much rather go forward.

'Mommy?' Lincoln says, his head still pressed against her.

'Mmm-hmm?'

'What is that monkey doing?'

'Just thinking, I guess.'

'Do monkeys think?' he asks, and she thinks that, yes, it has been good for them to get moving, because at least the change in scenery – wild animals lurking in hallways – has made him less catatonic.

'Yes,' she says.

'Do they bite?'

It is, she acknowledges, the more relevant question.

'I don't think so.' That is not true. 'Not unless you scare them.'

'Like bumblebees?'

'Sort of like that.'

As she speaks, the colobus lifts its arm over its head, and the sudden movement sends her scuttling backward. It opens its mouth, yawning, and its canines are long and vampire sharp. But it only picks at its fur.

She decides to move slowly and steadily, non-threateningly. First, though, she glances down at the shards of glass on the floor by her feet, and she squats down and slides her fingers carefully around the biggest piece, almost a perfect triangle. There is a sting in her palm, and she knows she's cut herself, but she stands back up, thighs screaming, and shifts her grip on the glass. She likes that it's too sharp.

She stares at the monkey, at its closed mouth filled with teeth. Once, when they were watching some horrible news story, her uncle said it worried him that if he walked in on a burglar pointing a gun at someone he loved – and if he had a gun in his own hand – he wasn't sure he could make himself pull the trigger. He wondered if that made him a bad man, that he might let someone hurt her just because he couldn't bear the thought of killing another human being.

If someone were trying to hurt Lincoln, she could splatter brains on concrete.

If this monkey comes toward them, she will aim for its eyes. She will slit its throat.

She moves to the right, pressing herself against the squirrel monkey exhibit. She watches the colobus the whole time, and at one point it almost glances toward her, a turn of its head that makes her sure that it is aware of her movements, but it never actually lays eyes on her. She inches along sideways – her palm damp with blood – and eventually she is past both colobuses, and she looks back and the live monkey is still sitting there, mixing its fur with that of the dead one.

The path turns. She passes the gibbons and the tamarins, and there is a wet patch on the floor, dark like spilled soda, and then the lemurs are straight ahead. All the other glass windows are intact. The habitats beyond are dark, although each has a dim round light at the ceiling, moonlike.

She reaches the entrance door more quickly than she expects, and she keeps to the side of it and does her best to study the view outside. The spider monkeys' outdoor playpen fills up the space to either side of the door, so she can see only a narrow tunnel of sidewalk and sky and then – barely visible – the edge of the playground and two empty green benches.

She bends down, setting her jagged piece of glass on the floor. She does not want to slice herself more than she already has, and glass will not be any help against men with guns.

'Are we at the food machine yet?' asks Lincoln from her shoulder.

'Almost,' she says, and she pushes open the door. The air outside is somehow colder than she remembers from only a few minutes before. But she likes the feel of it on her skin. She prefers the outdoors, the openness, the lack of walls, even though she is aware that she was thinking just the opposite not long ago. But looking up at the sky – clouds have rolled in, thin and spread like pulled cotton – the height and breadth of it makes her chest loosen.

The door closes, nearly catching on her hip, and she is slow to move, because when she steps forward, they will be in a spotlight – another damn spotlight – but she boosts Lincoln higher on her hip and then sprints to get free of the light. Once they are past the spider monkey cages, she slows down, safely in the shadows again. Although there are light poles dotting the pathways and more strings of lights looping, for now they are in a pocket of darkness at the edge of the playground.

The moon is blurred behind a cloud. *The moon was a ghostly galleon tossed upon cloudy seas,* she remembers from a poem her uncle used to read to her, and *Goodnight room, goodnight moon, goodnight nobody,* and once, when they were first married, she and Paul stood on the porch and saw an orange moon hanging so low and huge it was like something nuclear, something painted by Dalí, and they walked out, not even locking the door behind them, and followed the moon through the neighborhood for miles, getting closer and closer, holding hands, running sometimes, and they would round the corner and it would be almost reachable, and then all at once it was back in the sky, its normal size and color, and they walked back home like they'd shared a dream.

Not far away, the light streams down from the light poles, cones of brightness spreading across the concrete. It is a patchwork of light and dark. The shadows are tropical around her at the edge of the playground: tufts of pampas grass. Fences made of wooden poles and ropes. Banana leaves, waving.

She takes stock of the play structures, all fiberglass and metal. There is a fake mountain that Lincoln likes to climb, and its outline is like a giant cactus. The African drums are in a line, empty and silent. The wooden masks rest on poles, black and gold and open-mouthed, slightly demonic, and one of them has a tongue that looks like a penis, although she cannot see it from this distance. There is nothing here she has not seen countless times before, although rarely at night and rarely without crowds. There are no broken bodies and no pools of blood. If it were not for the grieving monkey and the shattered glass she can still feel crunching slightly under her sandals, embedded, she could tell herself that she has imagined the past few hours.

She stays still, listening, always listening. Waiting for any shadows to separate themselves and turn into men. There are wind chimes nearby, and they are playing a tune as if a fairy might appear at any moment. The wind picks up the echoes, twisting them around, and the sweet song comes at her from all directions.

She finds herself almost swaying to the chimes, and it strikes her that she is still tense but that the fear has been pushed back ever since she heard the men singing at her. She wonders at her calmness – no, that is not quite right, she is not calm, but she is focused and without the fast breaths she remembers from those early moments, when it felt as if she might break into pieces, and she thinks maybe it is not possible to maintain that level of fright indefinitely.

There is a rock near her feet, covered in green moss, nearly luminous. Her hand is barely bleeding anymore.

She freezes at a movement to her left, something bigger than a swaying branch or a flapping bug. But when she turns, it is only a lone African painted dog moving through the shadows of its sad exhibit. The dog is too scrawny, all legs and ribs – it is prowling, pacing back and forth along the fencing of its cage. Usually there are two of them in there, but she can only see the one. It looks hungry and desperate, like it is planning an escape.

She imagines it finding some latch on its fence.

The moon has come from behind the cloud. The landscape around her is whitewashed, eerie, and she moves past the playground, keeping to the edges of the path, anywhere there are shadows. There are enough trees that she can stay under the branches, close to the trunks, stopping often. They pass the tall fence that hides the rhinoceros, and the prowling dog is out of sight. The elephant exhibit is up ahead; the thatched roof of the Savannah Snack Bar is coming into sight, and past the far wall of the building there will be the snack machines. They are close.

She scans the path ahead of them. A sippy cup. It is there on the concrete, spilling a wet puddle. She steps around it, speeding up to cross a patch of lit ground, landing safely against the bamboo fencing of the elephant habitat, back in the dark.

She does not let herself look back at the abandoned cup.

She does not let herself think again of the woman or the baby, and she does not let herself think about the woman who scanned their membership card today and told Lincoln she liked his curls or of the grandmother and the little girls who had been only a minute or so ahead of them on the way out – had she seen a shape wearing the woman's navy-blue dress? had the little legs she'd seen been wearing pink tights? – or of the older boy in glasses who had picked up Thor when Lincoln dropped him on the sidewalk.

She does not let herself wonder.

She feels the small cup behind her, dripping.

7:06 p.m.

Looking over the elephants' domain, Joan can see no animals. She sees only grass and dirt blanched in the moonlight. Her eye is drawn beyond it all – a fifth of a mile across the entire exhibit, maybe? When she has watched the elephants lumbering along before, their habitat has appeared endless, but now, as she scans the shape of it, the space does not seem so large. The illusion of Africa persists only up to a thick barrier of pine trees, and past their Christmas-tree edges she sees the iron lines of the zoo's train track in the moonlight. Beyond the track, in brief flashes through the trees, she can see streetlights, the lit-up letters of a Walgreens, a stream of cars easing around a curve.

They shock her, the cars. Driving past steadily, lights on, unhurried. Shouldn't someone have put a stop to people headed out to buy toilet paper or grab a martini? Shouldn't there be only orange cones and police tape and sirens and possibly tanks and black armored trucks?

The cars driving by, unconcerned, are unbearable.

Her eyes go back to the hard curves of the train track. Its rails blink silver, only a gleam here and there, catching the moonlight. She focuses on the gleaming. Her uncle used to take her on picnics and fishing trips in the country, and it was a good thing, because if it had been up to her mother, Joan would never have gone anywhere but home, school and the mall. In the countryside there was nothing but cows and farmland, and the dirt there was dotted with mica, which she could pull apart in thick silver sheets. She thought it must be worth something, but her uncle said no, only shiny, and she pretended that the pieces of mica were meteor fragments. So beautiful, that mica, a revelation. One time she filled a Ziploc bag with it, like a scientist with valuable specimens, and she brought it home to show her mother, who never went to the country – she and Joan's uncle defied any kind of argument for genes or heredity; they were different creatures entirely. But on that day her mother was plucking her eyebrows, black little apostrophes all over the bathroom counter, and when Joan held out the mica, her mother said, *Don't bring rocks inside the house.* Joan was still young enough that she did not give up. She tried to explain, *You have to peel off the top layer, and it gets shinier, like treasure, just look under the dusty part*, and her mother said something like *It's not actually worth anything, Joan*, and of course Joan knew that. But she didn't have the words to make her mother understand the wonder of it, the loveliness, and her mother wasn't really listening anyway, and she wouldn't even look inside the bag. Not a single glance. Her mother stood there, one hand pulling at her forehead, staring into the mirror as bits of her eyebrows floated down.

Joan looks away from the railroad track, rubbing her

cheek against Lincoln's head. He has never seen mica. She would like to show him how to peel it with a fingernail.

Then she hears a snap and a crackling sort of impact, and she is halfway to the ground – down on one knee – curling her body around Lincoln, before she realizes it was probably a twig or a nut falling. She turns in every direction, seeing nothing but light patches and dark patches and shadows and plants.

She stays low and quiet and watching.

Finally she stands. She cannot bear to consider everything that might happen, here on this spot of concrete. On the concrete ten feet in front of them. Or twenty feet ahead, under the shadows of the massive thatched roof.

She puts one foot in front of the other.

She looks again at the track, which is one smooth circle. Countless times the train has taken her and Lincoln so close to the outer fences that they could have hopped off – the train is so slow – and they could have pressed their hands against the iron or brick of the walls, and they could have been that close to outside.

She has been moving even as she considers the train track. She and Lincoln are still paralleling the elephant exhibit, drawing closer to the thatched pavilion of the snack bar. The speakers are playing 'I Put a Spell on You', and the sound of the singer is startling. She looks ahead, trying to spot the speakers, but she is not close enough yet.

'Can I walk?' whispers Lincoln, and the sound of his voice somehow surprises her as much as the music.

'You want to get down?'

She can count on one hand the number of times she remembers him actually asking to walk when she is holding him.

'Yes,' he says.

So she lowers him to the ground, keeping hold of his hand with her undamaged one. The relief she feels at being freed of his weight – the sudden lightness – is balanced by an emptiness. She tightens her fingers around his. He is stepping closer to the bamboo fencing, pulling her with him.

'What is that?' he asks.

She tries to follow the line of his pointing finger. The elephant exhibit looks astonishing at night – there is no denying it. The low-growing trees and the scrub grass seem to levitate over the swells of the hills, and there is a golden glow to the sand, and it strikes her as some alien landscape, like the moon or Mars.

'That plant?' she asks, noticing a shrub with the look of tentacles.

'No,' he says. 'That thing on the ground.'

She looks again, and it takes her several seconds to make out the ink-stain shape on the ground, and she is even slower to recognize what it must be.

The men have killed an elephant.

Its body is wide and dark and solid, but the trunk is curving along the ground, snaking up, and there is a part of her that feels like it is separate from the rest of the body, still alive, struggling to break free and inch its way across the dirt. But it is not moving.

'What is it, Mommy?' Lincoln prods.

'The elephant,' she whispers. As the clouds shift overhead,

she thinks she can see the fine hairs on its rough hide moving in the wind.

'Lying down?' says Lincoln.

'Yes.'

'Why is it lying down?'

She could tell him that the elephant is asleep. It is probably the kinder answer, but she does not want to say it. It is somehow insulting to him to lie straight to his face when he has made it through these hours with her, jawbone to jawbone, hand to hand, and also she wants to say the words to someone and he is the one who is here.

'It's dead,' she says.

'Oh. Did the men kill it?' he asks.

'Yes.'

She cannot stop looking at it. Its tail is worm-like and pitiful.

'What's its name?'

'I don't know,' she answers. 'What do you think its name was?'

He makes a hum, a considering kind of noise.

She lurches away, pulling him with her, speeding up, annoyed that she has wasted energy and time on the elephant instead of keeping her attention on all the angles and walls and hiding places around them, and he comes with her but his head is still turned toward the elephant. He likes to name things: he has a family of tiny toy rabbits in clothes. One is named Softball and another is named Baseball and there is a brother named Little Bunny No Ears – Muddles ate his ears off – and a sister named Suzie Cat. There once was a baby named Suzie Witch, but Muddles ate her entirely.

He has a million plastic football players and a foldable cloth field, and he names and renames the players. One lineman is named Chewed Humpy. There is a receiver named Susan.

'Was?' Lincoln asks.

She has lost the thread of the conversation. 'What?'

'Doesn't it still have a name? Do you not have names when you're dead?'

'I meant "is,"' she affirms. 'What do you think its name is?'

'Marshmallow,' he says.

She tightens her grip on his hand.

When he plays with his football guys, he makes his quarterbacks yell out pep talks: *Everybody play strong! Play fast! Do we make mean tackles? No! Do we make nice tackles? Yes!*

He is an exceptionally sweet child. It would be easy to hurt him.

He has stopped again. He's twisted around toward the elephant. Or maybe a moth or a stray leaf has caught his interest.

'Lincoln,' she whispers, bending to his ear. 'We have to keep walking. We can't be looking at things that don't matter.'

There is so much space out here. So many potential hiding places that she would never notice until someone took a step out and raised a weapon. She looks and looks everywhere, but she knows she cannot see it all.

If she thinks about it – about how much she cannot see – it gets hard to breathe.

Walk faster. Pay attention, but walk faster.

The elephant is yards behind them. They are nearly at

the restaurant, with its pavilion and speakers – and another speaker is set into the fencing, she realizes as the music swells, obliterating everything else. Still, she stays pressed to the bamboo fence and the dark strip of grass that the lamp-light does not reach. She tugs at Lincoln's hand. She cannot stand being out here much longer. Not only can she not see everything, but with the music blaring – 'Werewolves of London' – she cannot hear anything.

The restaurant is immediately to her right, and the thatched pavilion stretches toward her. But between her and the building is a swathe of illuminated concrete where, nor-mally, children are running and falling and drinking from juice boxes. The pathways to all the various exhibits come together here, and it is a terrifying wide-open space. If she sets foot on that empty concrete, they will be exposed and she will be deaf to anything but wolf howls and the pound-ing of the keyboard.

The music is making her head throb.

She decides that they will walk up slightly farther to the turtle exhibit, where a huge tree spreads across the entire concrete walkway and they can cross the concrete under the shadow of the tree. Once she has made the decision, she is set on it, focused. They stay crouched, close to the fence, inching along, and she would not have been distracted except that the music pauses for a few seconds as the howl-ing fades out and the next song begins.

In that moment of quiet, she hears the baby scream. She thinks it is a monkey at first, but then there is a hitch in the scream, a breath being gulped down, and she knows it is no animal. It is a gurgling, furious cry, and it is close. Close enough that she remembers being in bed, the house silent in the wee hours of the morning, Lincoln's crib in the next room, ten feet away, back when she would wake a split second after he made the slightest sound of discontent, feet on the floor before her eyes were even open.

She jerks her head toward a bench that is a few feet ahead of them – a little viewing area for the elephants – expecting to see the long-haired mother huddled, still shushing the child, but the bench is empty.

Then the music has kicked back up, a disco beat obliterating everything else, and she can almost tell herself that she has imagined it – that her mind is playing tricks on her. But she knows. And she does not have to reach any new decisions: she is only keeping to her planned course as she approaches the bench, set in a zigzagged corner of the fencing, and there is nothing to it but iron framework and the solid shape of a metal trash can on one side.

She pauses, back hunched, still in shadows. There is no one here. There is obviously no one here, no baby, no mother. Lincoln is twisting his fingers in hers, not because he is trying to break free but because he is impatient. She feels him leaning forward, testing whether or not he can hurry her.

There is obviously no one here.

But she pulls Lincoln closer, lining up his back against her legs, and she moves them forward until she has her hands on the cool metal of the trash can, slightly sticky, and she flattens her palms and lifts the lid in one heave. She knows what she will find – even though she tells herself that it will not happen, she knows that it will – and, yes, when the lid is gone, she sees a baby screaming up at her.

She can hardly hear it over the music, even as she watches its mouth move. The moonlight is dim but sufficient. Nestled a foot deep inside the can, the baby is on top of a blanket, which is covering most of the actual trash. It is small and soft and wriggling. It is Moses in a basket.

She sets the trash-can cover on the concrete, and then she leans in, making shushing sounds that she cannot even hear herself. She looks at the small fingers, reaching. Hands patting. A head fuzzy with dark hair, not a newborn but only a few months old, loosely swaddled in a second blanket, some sort of pastel – green or yellow or white? – but kicked free enough that she can see its onesie, also pastel, and its fat thighs, but mostly she is mesmerized by its rage, its closed scrunched eyes and wrinkled forehead and stretched, open mouth that for all its efforts cannot compete with the speaker system.

That woman – or some woman – has left her child in the trash. In the trash.

It is unthinkable.

Lincoln is pulling at her hand, saying something. She has no idea what. She leans down closer.

'Say it in my ear,' she tells him.

'What is it, Mommy?' he screams, but still she can barely hear him.

He cannot see, she realizes. He is too short to see over the edge of the trash can, and he can hear nothing but the music, and she is standing here, frozen.

'Nothing,' she says, and she is not sure why she is lying to him.

'Then what are you looking at?'

She straightens again, looking at the baby. Then she notices that her hands are inside the trash can, reaching. She steps back.

'I thought I heard something,' she says.

The child's mother must have panicked. Maybe she could see the gunmen coming or maybe she was simply weak or selfish, but she couldn't quiet the child, and she gave up. She saved herself. She is likely tucked away safe and secure, leaving her child rolling around with empty soda cans and hamburger wrappers, and Joan hates her intensely. Her hands are, again, hovering over the trash can, and why is she not touching the baby?

Lincoln is tugging at her skirt again.

She cannot take her eyes from the child. It is not such an awful hiding place, once she gets past her immediate reaction to the trash can. If you can get over the fact that the woman has literally thrown her child away, it is a fairly brilliant spot. Right by the speakers, the child can scream as loud as it – is it a girl or a boy? surely she should not think of it as 'it' – regardless, it can scream as loud as it wants and no one will hear. And the child will scream, of course, because it is alone and scared and probably hungry and there's no soft warmth where its mother's body should be, and babies judge so much by smell and it will smell the strangeness and filth and rot of the trash can. But the sound of the crying is blocked out and also the trash can is a crude kind of bassinet, walled in, a place the baby cannot crawl free of.

There could be rats or roaches in there, crawling into eyes and mouth. Roaches. It is not safe. It is a trash can. Lincoln is capable of walking, and this baby would weigh nothing. She could carry them both, even, briefly.

This disco music is ringing in her brain.

She reaches inside and runs her hand over the baby's face, which is purplish-red even in the moonlight. Its skin is as soft as she expected. Its crying does not ease. It does turn its mouth to her and latch onto her thumb, and she lets it suck for a moment. There is a candy wrapper near its face, and she tosses it aside. The baby kicks a leg, and she sees a flash of something under a pale, soft thigh. Sliding a hand under, she finds a pacifier.

She wipes the pacifier on the inside of her arm and then offers it to the child, and there is another thing she remembers – the perfect O of a small mouth and the satisfying pull and slurp as a pacifier is accepted.

The baby sucks twice and then spits it out. It screams. She can already feel its weight settling into the crook of her arm.

Lincoln has not quit pulling at her. She looks down and he tugs her closer.

'I thought you said,' he yells into her ear, 'that we couldn't look at things that don't matter.'

She straightens quickly, reorienting herself. She realizes she is illuminated – the same patch of light that shines on the baby is spreading across her arms. She has let go of Lincoln's hand, too. It is the first time she has completely let go of him since the moment they climbed from the porcupine pen. And she was not watching him. If he had wandered off, she would not have seen. If the men were right here, guns aimed, she would not have seen.

She was not looking.

The baby is screaming, still.

She squats down, back in the shadows, her arm looping around her son.

'Yes,' she says to him. 'You're right.'

She has to be fast. She cannot do it otherwise. She half stands, keeping as low as possible, and she runs her hand over the baby's head again. She slides her thumb over its mouth and lets it latch onto her – no teeth yet – and then she puts the pacifier into its mouth once more. She turns away quickly, wanting to believe the baby keeps hold of it this time. She reaches to the ground, picking up the trash-can lid.

She eases the lid back into place. It is not as quick as she would like – she has to line up the edges exactly – and the whole time she stares off at a point in the darkness. For a moment the baby is a vague, pale flutter beneath her, and then the flutter is gone and there is only the dark dome of the trash can.

'Come on,' she says to Lincoln.

She squats down low to the ground again, taking a few steps, and already the music is slightly quieter, not pounding in her head. Another step and another step, and she just has to keep taking them and that is all, and she does not have to feel anything.

She only has to keep him safe.

'What was in there?' Lincoln asks, pressing his face to her hair.

'Nothing,' she says.

She knows he is still talking, not willing to let it go, but she speeds them up, leaving the trash can behind. The music intensifies. An electric guitar spirals into something ecstatic, and a flurry of leaves, yellow even in the dimness, scatters across the grass in front of their feet. When they reach the wide mass of the tree by the turtle exhibit, they run across the shadowed concrete, holding hands, and then she kneels by a low fence. A pause and a reassessment. They are only a few steps away from the snack machines, which are mostly hidden by a bamboo partition, but she can see the electric lights glowing in red-and-white stripes through the poles of the wood.

A few more steps. She slides a hand into her purse, feeling in the side pocket. She tucks her credit card against her palm and closes her fingers around it.

'What kind of crackers will they have?' Lincoln asks.

'Cheese, surely,' she says. She is unreasonably angry that he has brought up crackers again. 'Whisper.'

'I want cheese.'

She can feel him slow down, and his drag increases like a fishing line caught below the surface. Her hip brushes against the bamboo fence cordoning off the snacks.

Another ten or twelve steps and she can feed him.

'I don't want peanut butter,' he says, voice rising. 'I want cheese ones. Unless they have the cookie kind with peanut butter in them that Daddy likes.'

'Hush,' she snaps. It is unfathomable that he might bring down gunfire over peanut butter at this stage, and does he not realize what she has done for him? He does not, of course, thank God. But she cannot argue with him over crackers.

She calms her voice. 'There'll probably be cheese,' she says.

'Promise me,' he says.

Tears come to her eyes – she was wrong: it is not exactly anger she's been pushing down. Her hand is sticking slightly to his as she yanks him closer to her: she will not think of the syrupy gunk on the trash-can lid. As he stumbles toward her, Lincoln makes a whining, growling sound, like she has tried to wake him too early in the morning, but now they are past the fence.

She freezes.

Then she staggers backward, stepping behind the fence, pulling Lincoln against her legs. She feels panic again, and that is good, because it burns off every other emotion. She is scalded clean.

Between the bamboo fence where they are standing and the bricked side of the Savannah Snack Bar there is near-daylight. Glowing machines are lined up against the wall: Coke and Pepsi and Dasani water and, at the far end, a metal box full of small packages. She has never seen them at night. The cheerful lights feel aggressively mechanical. The machines are completely unaware of her predicament, and she hates them for their brightness.

She has to shield her eyes from the light.

To the left of the machines, the bamboo fence bends around, eventually abutting the wall of the restaurant. Banana plants are growing thick and high at the curve of the fence, and so on that side, at least, there is some kind of barrier.

But from where she is standing to the credit-card slot of the vending machines – please, God, let the credit-card reader work, because occasionally it doesn't and she never has coins – from here to the machines there is no hiding. Nothing but concrete. Not only are the machines themselves lit from within, but the recessed lights along the eaves spotlight the entire area.

She studies the thicket of banana plants past the machines. Their leaves spread out in parasols, and underneath them are thick trunks sloping into the mulch of the bed. Three trash cans are jammed into one corner of the fence, but the corner next to the building is dark and empty. The banana plants offer cover, and she thinks she and Lincoln could push themselves deep into the plants, against the fence itself.

There is no advantage to standing here endlessly. They are not safe here, either.

She studies all the things she can see and considers all the things she cannot. She lifts Lincoln again, waiting until his arms and legs are around her.

'This way,' she tells him, darting across the light – her shadow massive and shapeless on the cement – past the drink machines and past the food machine and right to the edge of the banana plants. Up close she can see decorative stones set into the dirt, square mosaics of black and white. She lowers him into the leaves, pressing herself against the brick wall of the restaurant. The snack machine is close enough that she can touch it. It is blocking them from some angles. She gently pries his hand from hers and pushes him backward, steadying him, step by stumbling step, into the bed.

'Stand on that stone,' she whispers. 'Stay there and I'll get food.'

She is satisfied with his position. She can barely see him, even this close.

From this side of the machine, she can stand in the shadows and expose only her arm as she reaches around with her card. Fumbling slightly – her fingertips are so dry – she slides in the card, and the machine accepts it, and she chooses the cheese-and-wheat crackers, shoving her wrist through the slot at the bottom of the machine and grabbing the crackers before they hit the bottom. She pulls them out and listens. Then she buys a second pack because, really, how much more dangerous are the extra five seconds – only she hits the wrong button, A6 instead of B6, and a Zero candy bar falls out, but she snatches it up.

She steps back into the shadows, and the leaves are damp against the back of her neck.

7:12 p.m.

His shirt rides up as he eases down into her lap, and she thinks of the boniness of his spine and the narrowness of his hips. He was a huge baby – over ten pounds – and he had multiple chins for a while, although it was a handsome fatness that made unknown women stop her on the street to squeeze his thighs. He stayed round for so long, but somehow he has turned long and lean.

She unwraps his crackers and hands him one – the wrapper is louder than she would like, but she tears it down the middle, the crackers falling loose on top of the plastic – and she adjusts herself so that she is solidly on stone instead of mulch. The wide, flat leaves, cold, fall against her head and shoulders. The speakers are now playing the whirling instrumental number that always signaled the Wicked Witch in *The Wizard of Oz*. The woodwinds are loud and frantic. The sound is grating, but she does not want it to stop. She does not want to hear anything else.

Lincoln has eaten two crackers before she realizes it. She fishes his sips from her purse, shakes the cup, and thankfully it is at least half full. She pops the stopper and sets the bottle between his knees, which are tucked between her knees.

'Thank you,' he says. He is bouncing slightly, his rump nearly levitating off the ground. The crackers have had an effect that seems barely short of magical.

'You got a candy bar?' he asks. 'What kind is it? Can I have some?'

She breaks off a piece and holds it out to him. She is slow making the words come. 'It's called a Zero Bar,' she says. 'It's white chocolate and caramel.'

'You don't like white chocolate. It makes you throw up.'

This is normally true. It is a remnant from her time in Thailand. She had been working with nuns in Ireland before she went to Bangkok, and it had been Lent, so she had given up chocolate because when you are around nuns you pick up ideas of self-denial, and then it was Easter Day in Thailand, and she bought a solid white-chocolate bunny – why did they even have Easter candy in Thailand? – but she ate it all, and then she threw up, and that was it for her and white chocolate.

'I used to like white chocolate a long time ago,' she says. The edge of the rock is sharp under her thighs, and when she shifts to adjust herself, she scrapes her hand against the stone. She feels a sting and then a rush of liquid – she has reopened the cut in her palm.

'Before I was born?' Lincoln asks.

'Yes,' she says, clenching and opening her fist, feeling the stickiness of the blood. 'Way before you were born.'

'Back when you went to different countries?'

'Back then.'

He tries the candy bar tentatively, and he hums a pleased sound, and the whole piece disappears in his mouth.

'You ate this all the time before I was born,' he says. 'When you liked white chocolate. But there was no white chocolate before I was born, so that can't be right.'

'No?' she says.

There is a malfunction in the Coke machine – some kind of short. The Sprite button is flashing softly, on and off.

'Before I was born,' he says, 'there was no chocolate at all. There were no houses. Only castles. There was no furniture. No plates, no hats, no dirt. There were no dinosaurs. There was no world. There wasn't anything. But there was one hospital, where I was born.'

She looks at him.

He once started crying at a voice over the loudspeaker in the grocery store. He thinks the monsters on *Scooby-Doo* are terrifying. And he seems, at the moment, to have no recollection of the past hour. He has sprung back into his normal shape.

'I didn't know that,' she whispers.

'I know you didn't.'

They should leave here soon. They are right next to the building, just off a main walkway. She shrinks against the brick wall, making sure they are both tucked into the shadows, and, thanks to a trickle of light through the leaves, watches him eat.

'Good, sweet?' she whispers.

'Yummy,' he says, mouth full of wet crumbs. He is back to the crackers. 'Yummy. So good I said yummy twice.'

'Shhh,' she says. 'Quieter. Remember not to wolf them up. Enjoy them.'

Another of his word inventions – 'wolf them up'. Instead of 'wolf them down'. And he has asked her, *Why do you say good grief? Shouldn't it be bad grief?*

'I am enjoying them,' he whispers, proving it by taking a bite so small it barely grazes the cracker.

She often tells him to savor his food, but she particularly wants him to go slowly now. She likes watching him caught up in the pleasure of processed cheese. He chews loudly, not quite open-mouthed but with his jaws and lips moving more than necessary. He licks his wrist, and she assumes there were crumbs.

She wants him to think only of crackers.

He wriggles closer to her, his hip hitting hers, and she thinks of her uncle in his old recliner – penny-colored – sliding over to make room for her own small self, saying, *One of us must be getting bigger.* Her uncle always smelled of cut grass and a nice sweat, and after she'd squashed herself into the recliner, hip to hip with him, he would lay his cheek on her head and she would feel his heart beating against her temple, and she was so content to feel him solid and safe next to her.

From what she can tell – from movies and books and lunches with friends – people are not content. They want different jobs and different spouses, and, at her age, she is supposed to be hitting some great existential crisis where she should start questioning all her choices and wishing she could start over, and it should be even worse because she is a woman and she has a child and she works, and she is supposed to want it all but be thwarted at every turn, drawn and quartered by her desire to carve a place for herself in the world and by her maternal longings.

She does not feel that.

She read a story when she was small, back when she was obsessed with anything involving spontaneous human combustion or voodoo, and she assumes this story was from one of her thick books filled with ghosts. It was about a man who was given a watch by the devil, and the watch could stop time. All the man had to do was push a button on the watch, and his life would freeze forever, unchanging. He would never die. He would never grow older. He would live each day exactly like the one he was currently living. All he had to do was choose his time and push the button. But he was never quite ready to push it – he kept thinking he would like to meet the right woman, and then, once he thought that he had met her, he decided that he would like to be a father, and then, once his child came, he was not so sure the woman was the right one, and then he wanted to make more money, and, finally, he had become an old man, and the devil came to claim his soul. The devil told him, well, he had been using that trick for an eternity, and the kicker was that no one ever pushed the button. No one was ever willing to say that this moment – *this* moment – was the one that was perfect.

She would stop the clock. Any day. Any moment.

It is possible that contentment is her one great gift. She appreciates what she has. Her son is warm and pressed against her, and that is nearly enough to cancel out everything else.

160

Only her hand is wet again, blood dripping down her fingers.

She lifts it, ready to put pressure on her slashed palm, but it is the side of her arm that is bleeding now, a raw spot just above her wrist, and as she stares at it, she realizes she has been rubbing her skin against the jagged piece of stone under her, back and forth, and it has been hurting, it occurs to her, but also – a red drop has splashed onto her thigh, too close to Lincoln, and she jerks her hand back – she would like to rub it against the rock some more.

She presses the scraped skin against her skirt.

She would like to stop the clock. Lately she'll catch the reflection of herself in a lacy nightgown, maybe the one with the see-through bodice and the slits up to the hip, the one that Paul asks her to wear when he comes home at lunchtime on a Thursday afternoon, and she'll think, *One day I won't wear these anymore. One day my skin will be loose and there will be bulges and I will be an old woman who does not wear sexy lingerie, and one day Paul will be dead and I won't have anyone to wear it for anyway.* Or she will do cartwheels for Lincoln, counting them – eighteen, nineteen, twenty – and part of her is proud and part of her is laughing, and another part is thinking, *Someday I won't be able to manage cartwheels and I hope that he can at least remember the days when I could, and what if I died in a car crash tomorrow, would he remember me this way and would he remember how we say magic words to make the stoplights turn green and how we turn the dining-room table into a fort?*

She does not know when she started imagining the end of things. It's possible that turning forty triggered it or that

Lincoln triggered it the moment he began changing from a baby into a boy and she realized how he was going to vanish, over and over again, until finally he was grown and gone, and it's possible that she has such dark thoughts precisely because there is nothing she wants more than for life to stay exactly as it is, never changing, and maybe she loves it all the more because she knows it can't last. She wonders if everyone has these thoughts of car accidents and dead husbands or if she is unusually morbid.

'Whatever happened to my Transylvania Twist?' asks the bass voice on the speakers.

Lincoln has one cracker left in the wrapper. She should get up. They should find somewhere more remote.

No. She should decide what comes next. She does not need to step back into the light until she is sure of where they will go. And he is being so quiet. So still. When he is this silent, they are almost invisible. Also, when they move, she has to pick a direction, and that involves deciding whether to go back past the trash can or to avoid it.

The torn skin on her arm is throbbing, and she thinks it is possible that a few more bloody swipes against the edge of the stone would make the ache go away, like scratching an itch.

The impulse scares her. She is not someone who has these kinds of thoughts.

'Do you want the rest of the chocolate bar?' she asks Lincoln.

He pulls out his final cracker with one hand and holds out his other palm for the chocolate bar.

'Yes, please,' he whispers.

She hands it to him. Something crawls across her foot, feathery and quick, and she makes sure not to look down to see what it was. She learned that in her mother's house: if you can avoid seeing it, you can pretend it's not there.

Still, she imagines. She thinks of glossy black shells and twitching antennae.

There is a scene in *Scarecrow and Mrs King* where Lee and Amanda are hiding in a swamp, huddled in plants and dirt just as she is now, and Amanda shivers and Lee slides his arms around her. This is Joan's secret: she has been rewatching more episodes of *Scarecrow and Mrs King* than she has admitted to anyone. She thinks that she feels about these episodes she spends hours watching as some people must feel about alcohol or porn. Sometimes she abandons her home office and sneaks in a show at lunchtime. Sometimes she climbs out of bed at night, kissing Paul's shoulder, and stays up until 3:00 a.m. binge-watching.

She should not be thinking of television now. Or maybe she should. There are worse things.

She used to think that Bruce Boxleitner was handsome, and she still thinks that he is – the 1980s version of him – and that version is right in front of her, anytime she wants, because these people – no, they are not people, they are characters – they have not changed at all. Lee and Amanda were grown-ups, she used to think, and now she is older than they are. They are splendidly frozen.

When she was a little girl, she would sit on the too-shiny hardwood of the den floor, next to the coffee table that was sickeningly liquid because her mother always used too much polish, and the slickness of the floor was worse because of the roaches, which would skitter across it noiselessly, like on ice, always roaches, because her mother thought an exterminator might accidentally kill the dog. Joan would turn on the television as soon as she got home from school – was she the only one who never wanted to leave school? Who walked as slowly as possible out the double doors when the last bell rang? Who looked in the classrooms to see if there were any teachers she could finagle into conversations and maybe get to perch on their desk so she could breathe in their attention? Teachers liked her. In sixth grade there had been the Maypole Dance, and only twelve girls were chosen by the teachers, and she was one of them, and it had meant long hours of practice after school – heaven, not home until after dark.

But they would not let you stay at school forever. So she would turn on the TV and watch her shows until her mother got home, and then her mother would take over the television – she had her own shows to watch. Joan would wait until late at night, after her mother had gone to bed, and then she would come back to the television, sitting close, neck craning up, because they had lost the remote control – no, not only that, but she liked to be close enough that she was more in the television than in her den. And she would be content. But sometimes she would be sitting there after dark, cross-legged and barefoot, slick, slick floor, and a roach would crawl right over her ankle or thigh or fingertip, and she would run to the sofa, choking back a scream, but she would go back to the television always, even if she did not know which direction the roach had gone and she was forced to keep checking under the chairs. The worst terror was always that first moment when she saw, from the corner of her eye, a dark shape creeping. She could never get close enough to them to kill them. The best she could do was throw shoes at them and hope she got lucky, and sometimes she would spray them with hairspray until they were drowning. She liked to watch them die like that – but even when the roaches were threatening, she would go back to the television. She could not stay away.

The Sprite light on the machine is pulsing like Morse code. Lincoln is still chewing. The speakers are singing out. *'It was a graveyard smash / It caught on in a flash—'*

She would watch a *Scarecrow and Mrs King* episode and then rewind it – she always taped it – and watch the good parts over again. Rewind, pause, play. Rewind, pause, play. She remembers an episode where Lee and Amanda walk into a hotel and he's holding her hand as they step into an elevator and then he lets go of her to push a button and Amanda reaches for his hand, groping in the air, and the look on his face is wonderful when he realizes Amanda is reaching for him. Joan watched that scene a hundred times. This was back when they were in love but hadn't admitted it, so every single look was so important, and Joan wondered if anyone would ever look at her like that.

That patch of floor in front of the television stand is the only piece of her childhood house that she can see so clearly. The wall of bookshelves, painted beige, lace overhanging every shelf, the coffee table to her right, shining, with silk flowers in a brass bowl and magazines scattered. The television and VCR, the silver knobs and black buttons, the satisfying hum of a tape rewinding.

She did not like the other rooms. The kitchen drew the roaches the most. Once she reached into a bag of potato chips and felt a hard, slick shell move under her fingers. The hallway was long and carpeted, and she would run down it at full speed – so much empty space to cover, the soles of her feet hot against the nubs of pale-green carpet – and her bedroom was at the end, and she would vault from the hallway onto her blue bedspread, hoping nothing would be moving in her sheets.

She never went a single night without seeing five or six or ten roaches. Sometimes she lay awake, listening for the sound of their little legs scuttling. Sometimes she could not sleep at all.

Her mother never saw them. Joan could make a monument to the things her mother never noticed – a grandson, for instance, whom she has visited twice since he was born – but there is still a shudder of fury in her that her mother never saw the roaches.

Joan asked, again and again, for poison. *You're overreacting*, her mother would say. *You know the dog could get ahold of it. And there aren't that many of them.*

She remembers when she liked to use the den carpet as a stage for her little plays, and she would ask her mother to watch her perform. *Do it for me while I rest my eyes*, her mother would say, lying on the couch, and she would have her eyes closed already.

She remembers her mother insisting on taking her for a manicure: *It'll be fun*, her mother said. *No*, Joan answered, older by then, with a temper closer to the surface. *It won't. I hate getting my nails done. I hate the smell, and it hurts when they use the tools. I always hate it. You're the one who likes it.*

Her mother slammed her hairbrush onto the counter, her make-up mirror rattling, but the next day they went to Lovely Nails, and surely her mother believes to this day that Joan loves manicures.

Her mother never saw.

Her mother never even bothered to look.

You are supposed to be more forgiving of your parents, aren't you, after you have children yourself? After you understand what parenting really means? But it has worked the opposite way with her. In her twenties Joan reached some vague peace with her parents, but once Lincoln came, the fury returned. The best she can manage is to keep her head turned away from it so that it stays a dark shape, creeping.

Lee Stetson said things like *This Bordeaux is to die for*, and he drove a silver sports car, and he kissed Amanda's hand, and that is what Joan thought adulthood would be like. Everyone beautiful and witty, cocktails and exotic locales and montages. She had a mother who slept with a Lhasa apso, who didn't mind smears of dog poop on her sheets but who sneered at touching treasure-bright rocks, and she had a father who could spend entire days hunting tiny animals but could never find his way back to a full-sized daughter.

The Sprite light is speeding up its rhythm, frantic.

She realizes that Lincoln is motionless, maybe asleep. White chocolate covers his fingers, which are relaxed and pointed skyward. His head has fallen onto her bicep. She looks at the soft curves of his cheeks and his eyelashes sweeping down and his nose that has a ball on the end of it, a perfectly round ending point. He used the word 'arsenal' in a sentence yesterday. He has entire worlds inside his head.

She sees him.

With her unbloodied hand, she closes her fingers around his wrist, softly, a bracelet. She feels the bones under his skin.

She sees him.

Only him.

The trick is to keep her focus.

'I wish I had Sarge,' he murmurs, and she is surprised both because he is not asleep and because Sarge is usually a second choice next to his best-loved stuffed animal, a floppy giraffe. Sarge was her own stuffed dog, more than thirty years old now; his left ear has a hole big enough to slip your finger inside, and his nose has partially rubbed off. Her uncle would make Sarge creep onto the breakfast table and beg to have a taste of her eggs, and she suddenly misses Sarge, too, his stuffed-German-shepherd body, worn nubby. He has known everyone she has ever loved.

'Why do you want Sarge?' she asks.

'Because he's a police dog.' Lincoln's head lifts slightly. 'He protects things.'

She is about to reassure him that she will protect him, but then there is a sound and a movement, out in the middle of the bright light.

In the second it takes her to realize that a door is opening – the door on the other side of the Coke machine – there is already a voice, and then there is a face lit pink by the red-and-white swirls of the vending machine.

A face. Long hair swinging. Dark eyes staring at them.

It takes her a second or two – time is gluey and slow, like a roach's legs in hairspray – before Joan realizes that the voice belongs to a girl, and she barely manages to swallow down her scream.

The girl reaches out an arm, fingers curling and her whole body visible, just for a moment, then it slips back behind the machine. The body belongs to a young black woman, a teenager, with hair falling in braids, streaked with bright red like a crayon. Her face is small under all the hair.

'Come in,' says the girl. 'Fast.'

7:23 p.m.

Joan stays perfectly still, studying the girl's face to decide whether she might be a girlfriend of the shooters, someone sent to play games with the prey. But the girl looks very young and very nervous, and it is hard to suspect her of anything.

'If you want,' the girl says, only the back of her head showing as she turns and looks out into the darkness, sounding both uncertain and annoyed.

It is the annoyance that convinces Joan. She wraps one arm around Lincoln and lifts him up, waiting until his feet are under him, and then she pushes herself to her knees, swiping the banana leaves from her face. She pushes her son in front of her, past the Coke machine, shoving, scuttling, his hand twisting in her shirt, everything awkward, her thighs aching, and then they are stepping inside the restaurant and the glass door is closing behind them, too loudly.

Squatting on the balls of her feet, Joan keeps an arm around Lincoln's waist. There is a long crack in the door, she notices, a silvery line that spreads across the glass in the shape of a chicken's foot.

The girl is in front of her, motionless, also bent low to the ground. They are next to the lunch counter, with the cash register to their left. There is an entire wall of windows to their right. The ceiling lights are off, but the display cases of the restaurant are lit from within, so there is a fluorescent glow to the room, and the white plastic tables and chairs – she thinks they are white – are now the pale green of deep-sea creatures.

The girl has turned toward them, reaching over their heads, her armpit coming close. She smells pleasantly of powder and bread.

'The door,' the girl says, flipping the deadbolt.

Then the girl is bent down again, moving forward, past the food counter, and they follow her. A few tables have the chairs neatly turned over on top of them, legs in the air, but other chairs and even tables are scattered sideways across the floor. There is a red rope strung between two poles, the kind used to tell people where to stand in line, and the poles themselves are turned over so that their round bases are standing up.

'Back this way,' the girl is saying, waving them forward, as if they are not already so close that they might step on her feet.

'Who is that?' asks Lincoln, his voice warm and damp against Joan's cheek.

His hand is still wrapped in the hem of her shirt, pulling.

'I don't know,' she says, and she realizes she does not know many things, like why she has decided to close herself in this building with a stranger. The door opened and there was another human being, which seemed like a godsend – although if God were sending anyone, why a teenager? – and maybe this is a terrible mistake. Still, she cannot think of turning around. She feels compelled to move forward, and why is that?

Her brain is spinning off, pell-mell, but her feet are plodding along. Hunchbacked, they pass the empty metal-and-glass cases where food used to be – muffins, she thinks, and apple Danishes. They are keeping below the level of the windows that line the wall. Glancing through those windows, she can see the underside of the thatched roof and the darkness beyond the spotlights. The dark looks total in a way that it did not when she was outside – she sees nothing of the elephants' domain, nothing of the faraway pine trees or the lighted streets. The straw roof stretches forever, and the world beyond might as well be actual Africa.

She wonders about the reverse view – from outside the restaurant looking in. Just how clearly are they outlined and highlighted? Is there someone outside thinking that her skin looks pale green like a sea animal's?

She faces forward again. The girl's hair is dyed a dark red in this light. Streaks of black and rust.

The music outside is a monotone hum.

There is a dead ladybug on the floor. Lincoln does not see it, and the shell crunches under his shoe.

The girl is picking up speed. Joan stays close, with Lincoln wrapped around her but moving by his own power. Her thighs are screaming from this squatted-over walking.

They round the counter and turn into the kitchen area, passing stainless-steel counters and a massive stove with many knobs of all sizes. The tile floor is slightly slick, and she takes care to place her feet carefully and to keep a tight grip on Lincoln's hand.

'Nearly there,' whispers the girl.

The kitchen comes to an end – no more appliances – and the tile floor curves into a short hallway that ends with a stainless-steel door. The girl pushes open the door, and they step into a room with steel counters on both sides and cardboard boxes stacked under the counters. The lights are off, of course, but one square window high on the wall lets in some combination of moonlight and the glare of the outdoor spotlights.

There is a woman sitting on the floor. An older woman, white-haired and pale-skinned, leaning back against a stack of boxes. She is wearing jeans and a sweatshirt, and she nods once, her face shadowed.

'Come on in,' says the woman.

'This way, Lincoln,' Joan says, steering her son into the room as she nods back at the woman.

The cardboard boxes fill every inch of floor space other than a narrow path down the center of the room. Joan can make out plastic forks and spoons in one box and coffee filters in another, but most of them are taped shut. Above the counters at least a dozen ladles hang along a magnetic strip. There is a block of knives. Farther down, a pool of shining red makes her flinch, but then she sees the ketchup bottles, seven – eight – glass bottles of ketchup in a neat line. The lids have been removed, and in one spot the ketchup has overflowed onto the counter and pooled onto the floor.

'I was marrying them,' the girl says, sliding the lock on the steel door.

Joan looks back, and the door is so polished that even in the dim light there is a reflection of the girl, a wraith, mimicking the lift and fall of the girl's arms. The reflection in the door collapses smoothly to the floor just as the real girl does, limbs folding until she is sitting, cross-legged.

The real girl is wearing a maroon beret, the same color as her braids, and her jeans are loose around her hips. She is bird-boned.

'I mean the ketchup,' the girl says. She props an elbow on a cardboard box labeled NON-DAIRY CREAMER. 'I was marrying the bottles when I heard them come in, and I spilled some, and it seemed dumb to clean it up after, you know?'

'Ketchup?' repeats Lincoln, crowding close, his feet tangling up in Joan's feet as she shoves at a box, trying to make a space.

As Joan sits, she studies the room. Only one door. And the one window is too high, surely, for anyone to see inside. She finds it easier to focus on the space around them – the strengths and weaknesses of it – than to make sense of whatever the girl is saying about condiments.

Other than the girl's voice, it is quiet in the room. Joan can no longer hear the Halloween music. She is not sure that she likes the silence.

Her feet, she realizes, are almost touching the older woman, who is silent and watching. Joan draws her legs closer to her body, and she situates Lincoln on her thigh. His legs land in the space between her knees.

'So you were here when the shooters came into the restaurant?' she whispers to the woman.

'Not me,' the woman answers, voice low. 'I was by the elephants. I had headphones on, so I didn't even hear the shots at first. But she found me. Like she found you.'

'They didn't know,' the girl says, not whispering. Like she is sitting on a couch somewhere, gossiping over pizza and *Dancing with the Stars*. 'The men. They didn't know that I was here. They didn't even look hard. That's the weird thing. Wouldn't you think they would have checked harder? Like, that they would have been really serious about it? Aren't you supposed to have a plan for things like this?'

The girl's questions use up so many words.

'Should we talk more quietly?' Joan whispers.

'Why?' The girl gives a slight roll of her shoulders. 'You can't hear anything in here from outside the door. Trust me, I've tried, because when the manager wants to tear a strip off someone she'll come back here and close the door and there was this one girl who was always eating coffee cake, like a crazy addiction to coffee cake, and all of us wondered, I mean – anyway – I was saying how I was back here when the men came inside. No customers were here, which is a good thing, I mean, because – but after the men walked out again, I opened the door and watched them leave, and from the window I could see a man and a woman going down the path and I heard shots, and then they fell. But maybe they got up later.'

Joan is having to focus very closely on every word the girl is saying. It is like arriving in a country where she thinks she speaks the language, but then some taxi driver or concierge starts speaking at full speed, and she realizes all her practice and CD-listening have not prepared her for it: even though she has the vocabulary, she's only getting one out of every three or four words.

'Maybe,' she says to the girl, and she catches the white-haired woman's eye.

They study each other for a moment, and she notices that even though the woman is wearing a sweatshirt, she is also wearing silver earrings and a necklace, and her hair is carefully styled – it looks like it would bounce back into place if you touched it. Her nails are manicured. Nothing flashy – some sort of pastel color. Tasteful. Cautious.

Joan suspects this is a woman who never leaves the house without fixing her face.

She regrets following the girl. She does not want to be here.

The girl tilts her hair-heavy head backward, staring up. She is swaying slightly, making her hair swing over her shoulders.

'Have you ever heard about how if anyone pulls a gun on you and tries to force you into a car,' the girl says, 'you're better off running away from them, because the chance of killing you with a shot from even, like, six feet away is only something like 60 per cent? And if you get ten feet away, it's like 30 per cent? So they might shoot you, but they probably won't kill you. And if they were thirty or forty or fifty feet away, it's not likely at all.'

Joan looks down at Lincoln, who has shifted on her thigh. He seems to be absorbed with what looks like a potato masher – she does not know how it wound up in his hand – but he is often listening more closely than she realizes. She does not want to discuss the ins and outs of gunshot wounds.

'How old are you?' she asks the girl.

'Sixteen.'

The girl sounds proud. Joan has nearly forgotten that feeling – to feel delighted with your age.

'So what happened?' she asks again, because the more she knows about the gunmen, the better. 'When the men came in here?'

The girl leans back farther against her cardboard box. Her jaw works slightly, like she is sucking on a cough drop or chewing gum.

'At first?' the girl says. 'At first I heard a scream outside. But there's screaming sometimes, you know? Like kids running around – you know that elephant statue that sprays water? And they let them feed the giraffes and sometimes kids freak out at their tongues. Also the music is up loud anyway, and I'm busy with the closer's list. Then the screaming went away, and then everything was pretty quiet for a while. Did you hear the guns?'

The girl's voice is still so loud. Joan fights the urge to shake her. *We are going to die if you keep talking like this*, she wants to say. She understands, logically, a soundproof door, but logic is not asserting itself.

'We heard them from a distance,' Joan says calmly. Logically. 'He and I were in the woods in the children's area. I didn't know the sound was gunfire.'

Lincoln drops his potato masher, and he stands up to

retrieve it. The older woman hands it to him. He takes it from her cautiously.

The girl is nodding enthusiastically. 'Me neither. They were far away at first. We were already closed – door locked and everything – and I was back here when I heard somebody at the door.'

'Shhh,' Joan says, unable to help herself. 'A little quieter.'

'They can't hear us,' the girl repeats.

The white-haired woman reaches out a hand, touching the girl's arm. Not a light touch but a firm one, her manicured hand closing on the arm.

'Shush,' says the woman, and there is a surprising authority in her voice. 'She's right. Keep your voice down.'

The girl looks surprised, but she nods. The woman pats her arm before she lets it go.

'Very good,' says the older woman.

Joan considers her again, reassessing.

'Anyway,' says the girl, finally whispering, 'I was marrying the ketchups – it always gets on my hands, and no matter how hard you try there's splotches on your arms and wrists, and you don't notice it until it's dried – and I heard a knocking, and at first I thought someone maybe needed to use the bathroom.'

The girl stretches her thin legs out straight, then she folds them on top of each other like origami. She is always moving.

Lincoln is watching the girl now, eyes big and attentive. The potato masher is forgotten.

'No,' the girl says, chewing again, 'do you know what I actually thought? Did I say how I used to work at Hawaiian

178

Ice? The lady who runs it goes to my church. Anyway, there was this old woman who came in every Saturday . . .'

The girl pauses, but she never seems to be looking for a response. The pauses are only part of her rhythm.

'She always wanted to touch my hair,' she continues. 'Ladies do that sometimes, white ladies, no offense, but she just wouldn't leave until she'd felt my hair, and sometimes she'd run late, and I'd have closed the windows because it was closing time, and she'd bang until I opened.'

This pause seems like an opportunity. Joan is no longer sure the girl can stop herself.

'But you were telling me about the gunmen?' she prompts.

'Yeah. So I cracked open this door' – the girl nods at the solid door over her shoulder – 'and I could see the men kick the side door open, and I could see the gun. Like a rifle or something? They came inside and started tossing things, and that was stupid, don't you think? I mean, I wouldn't have known they were here if they'd been quiet about it. But when the two of them came in and started wrecking everything, I just locked this door behind me. The lock's on the inside. Somebody got stuck in here one time, I think. You can unlock it from outside, too, but you need the key, and I have the only one. So it's safe in here.'

The girl swallows whatever she was chewing.

'She's wearing a hat,' announces Lincoln.

'You like hats?' asks the girl, touching her beret.

He nods. It has been years since he would watch the sidewalks, scanning crowds of pedestrians and bikers, and he would point his finger as he named headgear. *Hat. Helmet. Hat. Hat. Helmet*, he would call out.

'I still haven't seen the men myself,' says the older woman, flexing her leg with a grimace. 'I would have walked straight into them if Kailynn hadn't grabbed me. What about you?'

'We were nearly at the exit when I saw them,' Joan says. 'Then I ran up to the old porcupine exhibit.'

The older woman smiles down at Lincoln. It is a nice smile, completely detached from everything going on around them. 'Did you pretend you were a porcupine? With sharp quills?' The woman taps one finger against Lincoln's head and jerks her hand back. 'Ouch!'

Lincoln laughs. It is a shocking, bubbling sound. The light from the window catches the woman's face, and her expression is cheerful and focused, and Joan has a suspicion.

'Are you a teacher?' she asks.

The woman dips her head, lips curving slightly. 'Third grade. Thirty-six years. I retired last year.'

'Which school?'

'Hamilton Elementary.'

At a cocktail party or a luncheon, Joan would say, 'Oh, I have a friend who sent both her kids to Hamilton,' and the two of them would keep going in the universal way of small talk, but the back-and-forth of it feels wrong now. She will not act like everything is normal. And she does not want to know more about these people. There is no need for chatter.

Kailynn, the woman said. The girl's name is Kailynn.

'When you saw the men,' Joan says to Kailynn, 'did you see any sign of hostages?'

'Hostages?' the girl says. 'Why would they be shooting people if they wanted hostages?'

Joan shakes her head. It doesn't make sense. Maybe it is a waste of time and energy to even try to fit the pieces of the puzzle together.

'You want to try on my hat?' Kailynn says to Lincoln.

'No, thank you,' he says.

The girl twists around, lifting the flap of a box on her left. With a rustle of cellophane, she pulls out a small bag.

'You know what I have?' Kailynn says. 'Some animal crackers.'

Even in the dim light, Joan can see Lincoln's teeth flash.

7:32 p.m.

Lincoln has nearly finished his animal crackers. Joan supposes it is a good sign that he has an appetite – the thought of eating anything makes her throat close up.

She may not be the only one. The teacher finally gave in to Kailynn's repeated offers, but she has made no attempt to eat the single cookie she pulled from the bag. She is holding it between her thumb and finger, tapping one lacquered nail against it.

Kailynn does not seem to have any problem with her appetite either. She has just torn into another bag. She is also rocking from left to right, swinging her hair from side to side.

The girl is slowly driving Joan crazy.

'You know what I really want?' the girl says, chewing as she talks. 'Onion rings. Maybe mashed sweet potatoes and corn on the cob, but not the frozen kind. Do you have a deep fryer?'

Joan shakes her head. So does the teacher.

'I've been begging my parents,' Kailynn says, 'begging them to get one, because usually I'm the one who makes dinner, and a skillet isn't the same. With a fryer I could do onion rings or mozzarella sticks. Fried fish. You know, Mom might feel so terrible after this whole mass-murder thing that she might buy me one.'

No one answers her.

Kailynn wipes her hands on her jeans and looks down at Lincoln. 'So what's your name?'

'Lincoln,' he answers, still chewing.

'Like Abraham Lincoln?'

'Yes,' he says.

Joan is not surprised that the girl does not ask her name. No one ever cares about her name anymore.

'You know who Abraham Lincoln is?' the girl is asking.

'Yes,' says Lincoln. 'The president. He got assassinated.'

Joan cannot help but smile down at him, knowing it is odd that the word 'assassinated' charms her, but, still, how many four-year-olds know it? It is a leftover from when he loved presidents – yet another bygone phase – when he loved that Reagan liked jelly beans and that Nixon liked bowling and that Obama likes basketball. He liked George Washington's wig. He liked Franklin Roosevelt's wheelchair. When they played doctor, she would examine him and tell him he had an ear infection or a bellyache. He would tell her that she had polio.

A soccer game on the front porch: he wanted to be Gerald Ford, and she would be Ronald Reagan. *Gerald Ford is showing control!* he yelled, one foot on the ball. *Gerald Ford is kicking and . . . Gerald Ford scores! Ronald Reagan is trying to take the ball from Gerald Ford! Ronald Reagan kicks the ball out of bounds!*

'He kept papers in his hat,' Lincoln is saying.

'How did you know we were outside, Kailynn?' Joan asks.

She is wondering how obvious they were as they crept through the dark, as she tried to scan every inch around them and not step on a single dry leaf. She also remembers the darkened Koala Café they passed on their way out of the Woodlands and the Kid Zone, with the chairs on the tables and no sign of life, but, of course, there might have been zoo workers in there, too. They might have been tucked away in the kitchen or crouched down behind the cash registers, a few steps away from where she put her palm against the door. Maybe she has passed a dozen people holed up in safe places, watching through darkened windows, and maybe all of them let her pass by without a word.

Small fingers reaching, hands patting.

She could tell the others. The thought keeps rising. She could tell them about the baby, and she could even go get the baby and bring it here, absolve herself of her sins, and she tells herself that she does not do it because if she got herself shot, then where would Lincoln be? And also what if the room is not so soundproof and the wailing baby brings death down on them all? But these reasons are not what keep her quiet.

She cannot imagine telling them. She cannot imagine telling anyone.

Kailynn is answering her.

'And then I heard the snack machine,' she is saying. 'You can hear the vibration through the wall. I go out there and get PayDays on my break sometimes, and I heard the sound. So I looked out and saw you just as you were going into the plants. And I waited a while, and I planned to get you when you came back past the door, but you didn't come out. So I opened the door and came and got you. It's not safe out there.'

Joan still cannot make sense of the girl. With her animal crackers and her endless, mindless chatter, she does not seem like the heroic type. But she has risked herself to lead them to safety – there is no denying it.

Kailynn brushes the crumbs from her jeans. 'I promise they can't get inside. There's no reason to worry.'

Maybe the girl is neither heroic nor mindless. Maybe she is only confident in the way that sixteen-year-olds can be. She is swinging her hair again, flipping it from one shoulder to the other. Back and forth, back and forth.

Joan looks away. She feels better when she cannot see the girl. The teacher has the right idea: she is sitting there, eyes closed. Silent and apart. She is still holding her untouched cookie in her hand, and she's shifting it between her fingers like a talisman.

Then, as if feeling Joan watching her, the teacher opens her eyes.

'Everything's going to be fine,' she says, in a tone that is calm and slightly condescending, and Joan wonders why she is speaking now and why these are the words she has chosen.

'Will it?' Joan answers, probably more sharply than she should.

'God wouldn't bring us this far just to let us die,' says the teacher.

Joan forces a smile. She does not bother to tell the woman that she does not believe God brought them here at all. What does that even mean? Did he bring the gunmen here, too?

Those dead bodies on the concrete – was he guiding them along?

'We've been lucky so far,' says the teacher, rubbing at her knee. 'Someone is taking care of us.'

'That's a nice thought,' Joan says, and now she is the one who sounds condescending. And the truth is that she feels condescending and she dislikes this woman's too-perfect hairstyle and her naive answers, but it is not the woman's fault that she believes stupid things.

Joan tries again.

'It's nice of you to say,' she says, and her voice is better this time. She appreciates that, to her credit, the woman only nods and closes her eyes again.

Lincoln drops his empty bag to the ground and pushes himself to his feet. He must be feeling at ease, because he is moving away, knees bending and straightening, feet not quite leaving the floor. He bounces toward the far wall, where he will likely trip on the lid of an opened box of paper plates. But it is good to see him letting go of her.

'You're going to trip on that box,' Joan tells him.

'No, I'm not,' he says.

She watches him, and, next to her, the girl is swinging her hair.

'Do you know what my dad used to always do?' Kailynn says. 'We'd play hide-and-seek—'

'Can you shut up?' interrupts Joan. 'For God's sake! Just for a little while can you please shut up?'

She regrets the words as soon as they leave her mouth, and then she catches the look on Lincoln's face, and everything is worse.

'Mommy,' he says, and his eyes are huge.

Joan takes a breath. She is not sure she has ever seen him disappointed in her. The teacher is staring at her, too, disapproving. And the look on Kailynn's face is worse. Wounded.

'I know I talk a lot,' the girl says. 'I'm sorry.'

'No, I'm sorry,' says Joan. 'I shouldn't have said that. Go on and tell me about your dad.'

She does not really expect the girl to keep talking. And there is a part of her actually hoping that Kailynn is the kind of overly sensitive, sullen teenager who will sulk and withdraw. But, no, the girl is apparently resilient.

'Well,' Kailynn says, cautiously, hopefully, as if Joan might change her mind, 'so we would play hide-and-seek. With my dad. And me and my sister would always be the ones to hide, and my dad would seek, but he would always do it with big scary steps and heavy breathing, where you'd be shaking when you heard him coming. And then everything would go silent, and you'd know he was close, and then there he'd be – his hand grabbing at you under the bed or yanking the sheets of the laundry, and you'd just scream and scream. He loved to scare us. He'd always laugh.'

Joan thinks the girl's father must be a dick, not that it matters.

'One time,' the girl continues, 'I was hiding in the closet, and he jerked open the door, and I was so surprised I fell backward into a shelf and I cut my arm and it was bleeding and it was, like, more blood than I'd ever seen come out of me. I couldn't stop crying.'

'Did he laugh?' asks Joan, without meaning to say anything.

'No. He picked me up, and I could see how bad he felt – he kept saying he was sorry, over and over – and he wrapped a paper towel over my cut and set me in his lap, and I was still crying and he told me to be brave and I told him I couldn't because I was bleeding. Then he picked up a knife off the counter and he cut himself across his arm, just sliced his arm right there in front of me. And then he was bleeding, too, and he held out his arm and he said, "Breathe with me, baby girl, in and out. You and me together." And I did. And then we put on Band-Aids.'

Joan can see this. She sees it more clearly than she wants to. She can see the tears coming down Kailynn's face, and she would have had pigtails, surely, when she was little, maybe with barrettes, and she can see a little bloody arm and a father making himself bleed.

She smiles at the girl. A girl who saw men waving guns and people falling down dead. A girl who left her safe hiding place to come help people she had never even met.

'Breathing helps sometimes,' Joan says.

Kailynn tilts her head forward, hair rocking from side to side, and for the moment the motion does not grate on Joan. It is a child's habit, she thinks. It is a comfort, maybe, the feel of hair swishing.

'I want him to be here,' Kailynn says softly.

Joan leans in closer. It is the first sign since they've been shut in this room together that the girl truly understands that she is here, in the middle of this reality, feeling anything like the actual weight of it.

'Yeah,' says Joan.

'You wish your dad was here?'

Joan sorts through possible answers to that question.

'Well,' she says, 'my dad had a lot of big guns.'

Kailynn laughs, only a quiet giggle. Joan feels something loosen inside her, and she is not sure whether the looseness is good or bad.

'Why are you the one who cooks dinner?' Joan asks.

'Mom and Dad both work late,' the girl says. 'And I like cooking.'

'My daughter made cakes,' says the teacher, eyes closed. 'Five or six layers. Back when she was still a little thing. Like you see in a bakery.'

Joan studies the woman, who seems relaxed enough that she might fall asleep at any moment. Her hair is smooth and unruffled, and the pendant of her elegant necklace is perfectly centered at her throat. She is so calm. Maybe she is praying. And Joan can admit that it is appealing to believe that they are being watched over. That God is with them. She would like to believe it. She is turning the idea around in her head when Lincoln, hopping up and down, side to side – an uncoordinated dervish – falls backward as he collides with the box she has already warned him about.

The room is flooded with light. Joan is confused and blinded for a moment, but then she looks to her son and sees the light switch right above his matted curls. She lunges for him, pulling him away from the wall as she slams her hand against the switch and turns the overhead light off.

They are quiet in the darkness.

She hears herself breathing. She closes her mouth, but the sound is worse when she breathes through her nose. She

189

finds Lincoln's hand with her own, and his fingers latch on to her.

He does not move from her lap. They all sit, waiting.

'It was just for a second,' Kailynn says, and it is possibly the longest she has gone without speaking since they stepped into this room. Joan is glad to hear her voice.

'It doesn't matter,' says the teacher. 'We're fine.'

Joan appreciates the effort they are making.

'Mommy?' says Lincoln, and his voice is unsteady. She has been careful not to say a word of blame to him. Still, he has picked up on something, either from her or from the others. She has heard before that children are like dogs: they can smell fear.

'It's okay,' she says. 'It's okay. We're all okay.'

A roomful of light, off and on and off. Like a damn beacon, calling all comers.

'It's okay,' she repeats, squeezing his hand.

His fingers are small.

He is so small.

The feel of his soft knuckles – no part of him is roughened or calloused yet, not even his heels or elbows, and sometimes she runs the tip of her finger over them after a bath, just to see if he is toughening, hoping he is not and feeling guilty for the hoping, because of course he has to. The feel of those knuckles and his hard, smooth nails, like seashells against her palm, breaks open something in her, something that shattered hours ago, only she has been doing such a good job of holding it together.

She has refused to think it: he could die.

She cannot think of such things and still function, and

she has needed to function, and she has never wanted to be one of those women who won't let their children eat raw cookie dough or wander a block down the street without a chaperone, and you have to manage the terror or you can never watch your child walk out the front door. And here they are, where death is shoving its bloody snout in their faces, and she has not considered it, not really, because she has some vague idea of what she will unleash if she does, the great, gaping chasm that will open up. That is what you do when you have a child, isn't it, open yourself up to unimaginable pain and then try to pretend away the possibilities.

She focuses on his hand – on thoughts of his evil-villain laugh, *mwah-ha-ha-ha*, and the way he smiles when he wakes up from his nap and sees her leaning over him – and the terror recedes.

As they are all, probably, trying to think of something to say to fill the silence, gunfire crackles and pops outside, distant enough that it has the feel of firecrackers.

There is a chorus of different blasts and small explosions. There is a mumbling voice so loud that Joan thinks a bullhorn must be involved. And just as she is sorting through it all, she hears some kind of banging that she can't identify. It reminds her of stacks of baking sheets falling to the floor. The cacophony is multi-toned and expanding. She knows what it must mean, all this gunfire and racket and yelling.

Finally, something is happening. Someone is coming for them. She should surely feel relief or excitement, but she cannot summon much of anything.

'See?' says Kailynn, jerking her head toward the window. 'The police.'

'Yeah,' Joan says.

'They'll be here soon,' the girl says.

'Yeah,' Joan says, crossing her legs. She wants to stand. To move.

Her hand lands in something sticky on the floor. She lifts it, sure that she has seen a paper towel somewhere close by, and Kailynn catches hold of her elbow.

'You hurt your arm,' the girl says, and from her angle she can see the raw skin near Joan's wrist, not the cut on her palm.

'It's not bad,' says Joan.

'You don't want it to get infected,' Kailynn says. 'We don't have stuff here. But you could at least wrap it up.'

Before Joan can argue, the girl has lunged toward the countertop and pulled open a drawer. She collapses back onto the floor with a thin white dishcloth in her hand, and she begins twisting it around Joan's wrist.

'It's clean,' she says.

There is a surprising efficiency to her movements, and it keeps Joan from objecting. She only watches as the girl wraps the towel tight and ties it off with two quick pulls.

'See?' says Kailynn, leaning back on her elbows, hair skimming the tiles. 'Better?'

'Yes,' says Joan. And the truth is that the wound does feel better with the cloth pressing against it.

She is still studying her wrist when gunfire explodes through the room, so loud that it is a new thing entirely. Joan jolts backward and slams her head against the edge of the counter, and her arms clamp around Lincoln tightly enough that he struggles against her. The sound of the bullets is all around her – she hears it echo in her head like cymbals.

She hears Kailynn screaming, and Lincoln is yelling something into her ear, but she can't make it out.

The noise is physically painful, and it takes a moment to fight through the urge to clamp her hands over her ears. To clamp her hands over Lincoln's ears. She has turned so that her back is to the door, and Lincoln is tucked under the curve of her body.

One thought is coherent: *someone is inside the restaurant. Someone is outside the steel door to their room, trying to get inside.* She feels the noise in her teeth. With every single shot, she is sure that a bullet will come through the door.

The shots pause. There have been a dozen of them, maybe. They start again almost immediately.

Kailynn has scrambled to her feet and backed into the far corner of the room, boxes tumbling around her, coffee filters and paper cups spilling onto the ground. The teacher is almost upright, her hands bracing against the counter.

The bullets stop again, and the quiet is more frightening than the noise.

'They can't get inside,' says Kailynn. She is crying, although only her wet face gives that away. Her voice is strong. 'They can't.'

Joan does not feel so sure. The door is only steel. It is not magic. There must be a limit to what it can withstand. She touches her face, wondering if she might be crying, too, but she is not. It is a waste, crying. She has learned, over the course of this evening, to unclench her teeth. To make herself breathe in and out.

Breathing does help.

193

There is still an echo of the gunfire in her ears.

'The window,' she whispers, and she is standing, lifting Lincoln to the countertop. She climbs up behind him and shoves at the window and it opens, thank God, with hardly any effort. Only a twist of her wrist and the handle turns: the glass pushes outward, but it judders to a stop after a few inches. The gap between the window and the frame is plenty big for Lincoln but tight for her. The gunfire has not resumed – maybe the men are working on a strategy? and why have they not said anything? shouldn't they be performing rhymed couplets? are they positioned by the door, or is one of them waiting outside this window? – and then there is a new sound, a heavier thudding against the door, and by now she has directed Lincoln to stay still on the counter while she clambers up.

The light is bright by the window. Definitely more street-lamp than moonlight. She looks up and sees ladybugs, tiny black buttons, speckling the ceiling.

'Come on,' she says to the others, mouthing the words more than speaking them. She is not going to try shouting over the racket.

Kailynn moves toward her, lifting a foot to the counter, climbing up in a split second, all knees and elbows.

The pounding sound – is it a battering ram? – is vibrating through her skull as the teacher shakes her head.

Joan keeps one hand on Lincoln and beckons frantically with the other, her hand blurring, and still the teacher is shaking her head.

'I can't make—' the teacher starts, and any other words are buried.

Then there is a shift in the noise – another thud, but this one with a new tone in it. A different kind of impact against the door. There is a clinking and a crash.

For a moment everything is quiet – blissful – and then the door moves. It barely drifts open, only an inch. Such a small movement that at first Joan can tell herself that she did not see it. But the door continues to swing farther, slowly, and she knows it is opening, and she looks down at her son and sees a crumb on his cheek. Kailynn is pressed against her back, warm and with a tremor of movement, and the teacher is standing closest to the door, backing away, and the light is catching her hair so that it shines. The moment stretches out, slowing and slowing and slowing, and then the door slams open entirely, banging against the shelves behind it.

A man is there.

Joan cannot help thinking that she was right all along: he is hardly a man. He may not even shave yet. He is not wearing boots, as she had imagined. He is wearing tennis shoes.

One second.

Two seconds.

She slides in front of Lincoln, her legs dangling from the counter. She thinks she is blocking him entirely, and maybe there is some chance the shooter will not notice her boy – could she push him through the window, even? Without his being seen? There is a set of knives behind her, a foot or two away, although she doesn't want to look toward it.

She looks at the man instead. It takes effort to look past the long gun that he's lifting toward them all – toward the teacher – but she does look past it.

He is holding an axe in his other hand, but as she watches, he tosses the axe behind him. His jacket is too big, and his jeans are too tight, and his belly overflows them slightly. He is thickset, but there is a softness to him. She is feeling on the counter behind her, trying to think of how – even if she manages to grab a knife without his seeing it – how she might get to him before he shoots her, and if he shoots her, can she still manage to stab him, even if she is dying? – she thinks there are a few seconds before the body knows it is dying – and how much force would she need to drive the knife into his heart? Or maybe the neck would be easier, softer, no ribs would be in the way. As she thinks all this, fingers scrabbling behind her, she is trying to see his face.

Three seconds.

Four seconds.

She cannot see enough. His head is tilted down, and all she can see are wide, dark eyebrows. The shadows frustrate her, keeping her from making out the details. She wants him to look at her. His gun is chest level with the teacher, but he is still looking toward the floor.

Joan wants to see his face.

Her fingers close around the block of knives, and she runs her fingertips up to a handle. Should she pull out the knife or should she be trying to lower Lincoln through the window? But if she does that, if she moves that fast, she will surely draw the gun in their direction – and it is maybe too late now, because the shooter is looking up, finally.

He is staring at the schoolteacher. Without turning, he reaches behind him, his hand slapping against the wall, and he flips the light switch when he finds it. The room is bright again, and she squints as her eyes adjust.

He has not looked away from the teacher. The teacher is staring back, blinking in the light, chest rising and falling.

Five seconds.

Six seconds.

His gun dips down.

'Mrs Powell?' he says.

The teacher only watches him, not moving or speaking. The elastic in her pants leg has snagged around her knee, exposing a pale calf. She is arched backward against the counter so that an inch of belly is exposed under her sweatshirt.

Lincoln shifts, and his foot jabs into Joan's side.

Say something, she thinks at the teacher. *Do something. Whoever you are, tell him you're Mrs Powell.*

The teacher straightens. 'Yes,' she says finally, as calmly as if someone is calling roll. She tugs her sweatshirt down.

The teacher is the only one of them who has moved. Joan has her hand on the knife handle, but she has not moved to pull it from the block. She cuts her eyes toward Kailynn, and she can see the wet shine of the girl's cheeks. She can see that the girl's legs are trembling, either from fear or from the strain of perching on the balls of her feet for so long.

A ladybug falls from the ceiling to the floor.

'Yes,' the teacher repeats, just as calmly as before. 'I'm Margaret Powell.'

The gunman takes his left hand from his gun, opening and closing his fingers. Over and over. Grabbing at nothing.

197

'I'm Rob,' he says, and his voice is loud enough that Joan recognizes it. He is the colobus killer. 'Robby—'

He stops, frowning, maybe frustrated with himself for announcing his own name. Joan thinks that maybe he will make up for his mistake by shooting them all, but he only glances at his feet, lowers his gun farther, and starts again.

'I had you in third grade,' he says. 'Robby Montgomery.'

Again the teacher is silent. Too silent. She could be charming him, but she clearly has no sense of strategy. Maybe she is frozen in terror, or maybe she does not want to admit that she cannot remember him. She only looks at him, at his hair curling long past his collar and his loose jacket and his guns: the rifle in his hand, some kind of pistol under his jacket, and something else big strapped across his back.

The teacher's hands are still clasped around her sweatshirt.

'Robby,' says Mrs Powell.

He nods.

'Robby Montgomery,' she says.

He looks at them all then, but only briefly. He glances at Kailynn, still crouched on the counter. He glances at Joan, and when he tilts his head, she knows he can see Lincoln over her shoulder.

Then he steps backward, pressing himself against the doorframe.

'This way,' he says, his voice filling up the room. 'Come on out.'

He is back to looking at the teacher – Mrs Powell – and it is not clear whether he is including the rest of them in his order, whatever kind of order it may be. It is possible that he will spare the teacher and then come back for them. Or maybe he is leading her out to be shot first, and then he will come back for them.

But when Mrs Powell steps toward the door, Robby Montgomery waves his hand toward the rest of them. Joan slides to the floor and lifts Lincoln into her arms, moving slowly as she considers whether she should try to take one of the knives with her. Then she is turning around – still unsure – and she has lost the chance. She hears Kailynn's feet hit the floor, and she settles Lincoln on her hip.

Joan steps over paper cups. She focuses on the floor. When she looks up again, she sees that Robby Montgomery is touching the teacher. He has put a hand on her arm as she passes through the doorway.

'You don't remember me, do you?' he is saying.

Mrs Powell looks down at his hand, and he lets go of her arm. The teacher, as usual, is slow to speak. But once he has removed his hand, she reaches out and lays two fingers on his wrist.

'You sat next to that little boy who put glue in his ear,' she says. 'Harrison . . . Harrison something. And you liked to help me staple the bulletin boards. Any kind of stapling. You liked the staple remover – you said it looked like—'

'Vampire teeth,' he says, and he smiles.

'Mommy?' Lincoln says softly, his breath warm and cheese-smelling. She knows that he is interested in the mention of vampires. But she is watching the gunman smile, and it is a strange sight, and she thinks maybe she is not so different from Lincoln – she does not think villains should be happy.

Then Robby Montgomery is jerking his head at them, and they are moving. Joan follows Mrs Powell through the doorway, trying not to brush against Robby Montgomery or his gun as she passes him. Kailynn is behind her, and she feels the girl's hand close around her arm, just above her bandage, keeping close.

They are back in the hallway then, the dark stainless-steel gleam of the kitchen in front of them.

'Look,' Robby Montgomery says, 'you need to go somewhere else. Not up here. The police are coming through the entrance – but don't go that way. They're still shooting.'

'Who is "they"?' asks Mrs Powell.

'The police,' he says, easily enough. 'And Destin. Unless he's dead, but he's done up for it, and the police wouldn't still be shooting if he was dead.'

'Who is Destin?' asks Mrs Powell. There is a primness to her voice – as if she is considering whether to approve the boy's choice of a prom date – that is almost funny.

'Destin is the star of the show,' says Robby Montgomery in a voice that is not his own. It is a TV newscaster's voice, overly dramatic.

Joan takes a step away from him. She does not like his pretend voices.

Mrs Powell frowns, and it seems that Robby Montgomery notices. When he speaks again, he is talking normally.

'You see a tank on legs, that'll be Destin,' he says. 'He's got himself the good stuff – Level IV plates that'll take rifle hits and a Blackhawk helmet and the whole deal. You don't want any part of him. And then there's Mark up here with me, but he ditched me again. Lucky for you. Come on. You need to get moving.'

'Mommy?' whispers Lincoln again.

'Not yet,' Joan whispers back, so softly that she can barely hear herself.

He is letting them go.

He is letting them go.

That thought is so overwhelming that she cannot push past it at first. Even when she does, it is hard to make sense of what he's saying. There are three men involved in this, including this boy, and he is throwing names out as if they do not matter. Surely he should not be sharing such details: she wonders if he fully understands what is happening. What has happened and what will happen. Or maybe he does know what will happen, and that is why it doesn't matter if he tells them names.

That last thought is sharp enough that it makes her look behind her. She glances back toward the spilled paper cups turned up like sandcastle turrets. Back toward the knives that are too far away now. The third man, Destin, does not sound quite human. She imagines some monster from an Arnold Schwarzenegger movie. Monsters are not swayed by old teachers.

'The police—' she starts, but apparently Robby Montgomery does not want to make conversation with anyone but Mrs Powell, because he cuts her off, hardly glancing at her.

'That way,' he says, pointing with his rifle toward the side door of the restaurant. 'Out that way and head back down toward the sea lions. You know the sea lions?'

So they all shuffle toward the side door – Kailynn in front, Lincoln and her in the middle, Mrs Powell in the back with Robby Montgomery. The door is only barely attached to the hinges now – he must have forced it open, and she is surprised they didn't hear him break it, even beyond their soundproof door.

Outside, the Coke-machine lights are psychedelic after the dimness of the restaurant. Beyond the trees, there is still the sound of guns and shouting. The banana leaves are flapping, and she heads down the walkway.

'Faster,' calls out Robby Montgomery, and Joan picks up her pace.

Margaret Powell is well aware that she may die in the next few minutes, shot in the back by one of her students. She is not completely surprised.

Kailynn and the other woman are moving much faster than she is, getting farther and farther away, but Robby is only a few feet behind her. She glances back at him, trying not to be too obvious. He seems to be doing an impression of a soldier in Vietnam, peering left and right up into the trees, and it would be ridiculous in a different situation. She is still not quite sure if he is protecting her or leading her to slaughter, and she is not sure that he knows, either. He is clearly a psychopath. Or close enough that it doesn't make a difference. But even Hitler was kind to puppies, wasn't he?

Her knee is throbbing. Sometimes sitting is worse than standing.

They are long past the shadow of the thatched roof. There is still gunfire, off and on, from the front of the zoo. And Robby is still back there, following. She did not expect him to stay close like this. She slows, looking back again, and this time she does not try to disguise the fact that she has noticed him.

'Are you coming with us?' she asks.

He shakes his head, but he is coming toward her. He is tall, even though he still has some baby fat. His gun is loose in his hand, bobbing along like a metal detector or something else that doesn't kill people.

She has begun to think that the more she talks to him, the better. The more he hears her voice, the more he has to accept that she is a real person. A person who held his hand in line and who helped him tie his shoes. (She does not remember doing those things, but she imagines she did them for all her students at one time or another.)

'You're moving too slow,' he says. 'You've got to go faster.'

She stops entirely and turns to face him.

'I am sixty-eight years old,' she says. 'I have a bad knee. This is as fast as I go.'

The mother has paused ahead of them, her little boy on her hip. She is looking over her shoulder. Margaret wishes the mother would not wait.

'Walk with me, Robby,' she says, using her teacher voice, which has worked on every child she has ever taught. She is sure she is conveying that she would like his company: that usually works best with the troubled kids, the bad kids, the ones the other teachers might scream at or send to the principal's office. Those kids are the ones who most want attention, and that is the secret to winning them over.

She does not want his company, of course. The truth is that she does not like him back there behind her. She wants him where she can see him. Another secret: you always assign the troublemakers the seats closest to your desk.

She is not surprised that she taught him. She has envisaged some version of this – imagined, countless times, having some thug pull a gun on her and demand her purse, only to say, 'Hey, is that you, Mrs Powell?' She has taught so many students – thousands over the years – and she has taught them all in this same city, so she runs into her former students constantly, in malls and restaurants and parking lots. All those eight-year-olds transformed into men in suits and women in high-heeled boots.

'Mrs Powell!' they always say, always smiling, and she never has any idea who they are, because, of course, they have grown up, but she knows they were her students by the way they say her name.

Sometimes she remembers them. Sometimes she can even remember where they sat or what they gave her for Christmas. They hug her and they tell her that they are lawyers or doctors or car salesmen or that they have three daughters or a son in college. They want her to know how they have turned out.

There are others. Ones who have never introduced themselves, but she knows how they have turned out. Demetrius Johnson was the first one to wind up on death row. He killed a boy in a fight over a television, and when he was in her classroom, he kicked a little girl hard enough that he made her leg bleed. But he also was very good at jigsaw puzzles, and it was a real talent, the kind that could have meant something. Then there was Jake Harriman, who was the sweetest boy, never gave her a bit of trouble, but his family was bad and he had bruises on him. She told the principal about it, and DHR visited, but nothing ever happened, and then a couple of decades later she saw his face on the news after he'd killed a woman in the Kmart parking lot and stolen her car. Death row. Horace Lee Block was loud and could never sit still, and he had a mean streak even then, and she had to pry his arms off when he gave her a hug. Death row.

She sees their names in the newspaper and stares at their unrecognizable photos on the news. By her count she has taught four murderers, six rapists and nine armed robbers. She does not mean to keep track of the numbers, but they add themselves up anyway. Three of her boys and girls have been murdered, including one young woman whose husband set her on fire. She remembers one long braid, tied with those little hair twists that have plastic balls on the end of them. It is all horrible, and plenty of times seeing the mugshot of some dead-eyed monster and remembering a skinny little boy with ashy elbows made her want to quit teaching altogether, because the worst part is that it is hardly ever shocking. They are set on their paths before she ever meets them. When they come to her angry and sullen, full of swear words, violent, their parents are usually angry and sullen and full of swear words, violent. When they come to her desperate, empty, their parents are desperate and empty. She sees which direction they are headed, usually, and there is nothing she can do about it. Sometimes she has tried, and it is like huffing and puffing at a brick house.

They walk out of her classroom, and they never even look back. They are gone.

But Robby? It does not make sense to her, although she is still struggling to remember him clearly. He could not stop talking. She knows that. Poor thing, his voice was so loud, like there was no volume knob on it, so when other kids whispered away, she caught him every time. He was awkward socially, but he wasn't a discipline problem. She thinks of a thickset boy who laughed too loud at other kids' jokes and said 'Yes, ma'am' every time she told him to be quiet, and he was a rule-follower, she thinks. No, not a rule-follower – he was a pleaser. The effect was the same, but the reason was different.

She feels the moment he catches up to her: he is warm. He smells slightly of onions.

'Why do we have to hurry?' she asks him softly, and she remembers how he would ask to help with the bulletin boards, but she cannot think of a single conversation she ever had with him.

'Mark,' he says. 'Partly. He'll be coming.'

'Is he your friend?'

'Yes.'

'If he's your friend,' she says tentatively, 'can't you tell him not to shoot us?'

She is facing forward, not looking at him, and he takes a while to answer. They pass under the spreading oak tree, and there is a signpost full of arrows that are unreadable in the dark, but she knows they are following the ZOO EXIT sign.

'He's got ideas of his own,' he says finally, and then he is lifting his gun. She is about to scream a warning to the others, but he keeps lifting it, firing several shots at the tops of the trees, and it feels as if her ears might have cracked open. She touches them, checking for blood.

She can barely hear his voice as he yells.

'Stay where I can see you!' he calls out, and she realizes that Kailynn and the woman and boy were disappearing around a bend in the path. They are no longer disappearing – they are statues.

'Don't stop!' Robby yells at them, more frustrated than before. 'You can't stop. But stay close.'

His gun is pointed at the ground again. The others start moving, looking back frequently. She can feel her pulse in her bad knee.

'You'd told them to go fast,' she says.

He doesn't answer. She freezes when she sees him reaching for her, but then his hand is on her elbow steering her forward, gently enough. He is not hurting her.

'We all go fast,' he says.

It is clear that he wants her to shut up, but she is discovering that it does not really matter what he wants. She is no longer quite so afraid of what he might do to her: death is not as terrifying as she once thought. That would make more sense if she were standing here imagining heaven with golden streets, or if she were daydreaming about a tearful reunion with her parents, who she would love to see again, in any form, bodies or souls or angels. But she is not thinking about any of that.

She has been told all her life that there is a God. It surely is true. She has been trying to remind herself of it. She has been talking to him. But she wasn't thinking of God in the moment when the edge of that counter was cutting into her back and she was looking into the black hole of the rifle: she was thinking that her daughter is grown and has made it very clear that she does not need much of anything from Margaret anymore, and her own parents are dead, and her ex-husband has remarried some woman who is both younger and fatter than she is, and there is nothing left that she has to do. She is not eager to die, but the thought doesn't panic her.

So she limps along and says, 'Did you kill people today?'

He shrugs. It is the most juvenile answer she can imagine.

'You're saying you're not sure?'

He shrugs again. The longer she is with him, the more she can see the third-grader underneath.

'Are you sorry for it?' she asks.

He ducks under a tree branch.

'No, ma'am.'

Then why, she wants to ask, *didn't you kill me? If it comes so easy to you?*

They are nearly at the bottom of the hill as they pass under the carved wooden arch that announces AFRICAN TRAILS, and now they are out of Africa entirely. His hand is still loose on her elbow. For someone she remembers as a chatterbox, he does not use so many words. Maybe the evil has changed him. Maybe the third-grader is no longer in there after all.

Kailynn and the woman disappear around a bend in the path again, and this time he does not yell at them. So it is only her and Robby, and just when she has given up on him talking, he starts again.

'You know when you pop a blister?' he says. He squeezes her elbow lightly. 'That's what it's like. Don't you feel like, you know, there's this satisfaction to it, popping things? Like zits, too, and blisters and things that are puffed up and shouldn't even be there. There's something in you that wants to burst them. Maybe that should tell you something. Because you may think you're solid, but the least prick and we're all just skin and pus and infection, and I think we know that. We make things up, you know? All the things we think are so important – none of it matters. None of it's real. And maybe it's better, maybe, to pop the bubble. Did you ever think that? That maybe you'd be better off to let yourself drain out? Because otherwise we're just swelled-up blisters dripping pus and blood, but we pretend like we're goddamn unicorns – excuse me – unicorns or fairies or something, like we're beautiful and magical, but we're sacks of nothing.'

He inhales loudly. Margaret is not sure if it is embarrassment at his monologue or only a lack of oxygen. She hits a patch of uneven concrete, nearly turning her ankle.

She thinks and thinks, but she cannot come up with a response that feels helpful. She does not want to encourage the talk of people as pus-filled sacks. She spins her bracelet around her wrist – a Kate Spade that she paid twenty dollars for on sale.

'You think none of this is real?' she says.

'I think we live our lives doing stupid things and believing stupid things,' he says more quietly.

He is trying to convince her, she realizes. He is laying out his argument.

'So you killed people because you think they're better off dead?' she says.

'I don't know if that's why I killed them. It's not that they're better off. It's not like I'm Jesus saving souls or something. But they're not worse off. We can't be worse off.'

She swallows, tasting acid. She was right in the beginning: he is a psychopath, and he is making her go fast enough that she is almost stumbling. She can no longer hear the music, but the sounds coming from the front of the zoo are getting louder – voices, men's voices, lots of them, and the bang of something metal.

'Do you still have oranges for lunch?' he asks.

She is surprised enough that she does not consider her answer.

'Sometimes,' she says.

'You cut the peel off instead of eating around it,' he says.

She does not know how he remembers that.

'Yes,' she says.

He stops and scrapes something from the bottom of his shoe. She does not want to think about what kinds of things might be stuck to the bottom of his shoe.

'Did you ever learn how to use an axe?' he asks.

She thinks back. So he'd been around the year she had two trees fall in her yard within six months of each other, and it was absurd the money that landscapers wanted to charge to chop up the things. After the second tree, she'd bought an axe and had been determined to learn how to chop wood herself. All the little boys in her class had been very taken with her idea.

'No,' she says. 'I ripped open my hands on the handle. I wound up paying someone.'

'I used to imagine you out in your yard in overalls,' he

says. 'With your axe. And then you'd go rock on your front porch and drink lemonade. Do you have a front porch?'

'No. I used to have a deck in the back.'

'Do you live in the country?' he asks.

'No.'

'I always wanted to.'

'Live in the country?'

'Yeah. Where you could walk in the woods.'

A flash of light makes her look up from the concrete unspooling in front of her. She can see the pond through the branches, all lit up. A few steps in front of her, the train track cuts across the concrete, and Kailynn and the woman and boy are standing there.

Robby lets go of her and waves toward the pond.

'I'm going back up,' he says. 'Go somewhere around the sea lions and the birds. Find a place and hide. Wait until it's done.'

He is turning around before she realizes that he is leaving. And for some reason she remembers a moment from who-knows-how-many years ago, and Robby was surely not in her class then, but she was doing a science lesson about roots, and she was talking about moss. She'd found big hunks of green moss in the park, and she'd passed them around to talk about how they lacked true roots, but the children did not want to talk about roots. They wanted to put the moss on their heads to pretend it was hair, and they mashed their faces against it to see what it would be like to sleep in the forest with a moss pillow, and she'd given up on the science and just watched them hold the plants.

'Come with us,' she says to him.

He stops, mouth slightly open as he turns back to her.

'Why?' he asks.

If she were honest, she could tell him it is because he has a gun. If they run into his friends, that gun would be worth something. But also, if she were honest, she would tell him that she is sure she can save him. She feels the rush of it jolt through her, sharp like the scrape of worn-out cartilage against bone. She can see it all play out: bringing him, hands up, to the police and visiting him in prison and bringing him pie, if that's allowed, and she would write him letters asking him if he'd rather have chocolate or coconut. She could save him and also save them all, and it is impossible not to imagine the headlines announcing how she had convinced him to put down his weapons, how she had reached him when everyone else had failed.

He is still watching her, waiting. She has to put together all these thoughts of second chances and pies and moss.

'We can tell them – the police – how you helped us,' she says. 'We can tell them—'

He smiles at her; she can see his teeth in the dark.

'It's okay, Mrs Powell,' he interrupts.

'What's okay?'

He has turned around again.

'You don't have to tell them anything,' he says, voice as loud as it ever was, and she hears every word clearly.

He walks up the hill, and he never even looks back. He is gone.

7:49 p.m.

The clouds are thick again, blocking the moonlight. The large pond spreads out in front of her, and Joan can see the decorations hung on the fencing and even floating, some-how, in the water itself. A multicolored sea monster blinks in the middle of the pond, and she can see other lit figures along the edges. Beyond the water, of course, is the noise coming from the zoo entrance.

If she turns her head, she can see the teacher and Robby Montgomery back there, cozy together, and she is almost panting with the effort to stay still. There is no time to stay still. She needs to move – she needs to get Lincoln away from the gun and from Robby Montgomery, and also when she is moving she does not have to think as much, and everything is simpler when she is simply pushing herself so hard that her muscles scream.

She needs to keep moving, too, because of what she thinks is on the concrete a few yards ahead of her, past the railroad track. She is being careful not to look.

Still, despite her itch to cover ground, she has paused at the track, undecided. Robby Montgomery has told them not to

214

leave his sight. He has threatened them. Yet if she turns right, a copse of trees shades the way to the flamingos and sea lions. The shadows are tempting. She considers running, taking her chances, but she does not consider it for long, because she is slumping slightly from Lincoln's weight and she knows that Robby Montgomery or his bullets would catch them in a heartbeat.

And there is still the thought of Mark, and Destin, whoever he is, covered in armor and wandering around with plans of his own.

'What is she doing back there?' whispers Kailynn, standing so close that her hair blows against Joan's shoulder. Her hand has found its way to Joan's elbow.

'Wasting time,' Joan answers, and she feels a twinge of guilt, because she has been thinking that the teacher should charm and wheedle and guilt the killer into helping them, but now the sight of the two of them huddled together leaves her revolted.

She takes a step to her left, twisting away from the water, with Kailynn still holding on to her, and instead of pulling free from the girl, she wraps an arm around her shoulders and steers her, partly because she knows the girl needs comfort and partly because she needs to keep the girl and Lincoln from noticing what's spread across the ground past the train track.

Finally Mrs Powell is coming the rest of the way down the hill. Something is clearly wrong with her leg – she is hobbling. Even the sound of her footsteps is awkward and off-balance.

'He's gone,' says the teacher when she reaches them. 'He says to go hide.'

Joan glances behind her. 'Is he really gone?' she asks.

215

'He wouldn't come with us,' says the teacher.

Joan chooses not to comment on that. She cannot afford to spend any more time or thought or words on unnecessary distractions. 'You sure he's not hiding?' Joan asks. 'You saw him go back up the hill?'

'I did,' says the teacher.

'Come on, then,' Joan says, and she puts a foot on the train track. She is determined to keep facing the track. The wooden boards are so evenly spaced. So beautifully repetitive. Nothing unexpected. She can follow them forever.

Mrs Powell puts a hand on her shoulder. Her grip is solid.

'He said to go toward the sea lions,' the teacher says, pulling Joan back slightly.

All her thwarted movement, all her disgust and fury, all her frustration, even, with the teacher's weak leg comes pouring out of her.

'I'm not going to go where he said!' Joan snaps, and she struggles to tamp down her voice. 'Don't be foolish. We get going in the opposite direction, and we get as far away from him and all the others as possible.'

'But why not go to the sea lions?' says Mrs Powell. 'Maybe he knows something. He would have killed us already if that was what he wanted. I know this boy – I think he—'

'You don't know him,' she tells the teacher.

'I remember—'

'You didn't hear him with his friend,' interrupts Joan. 'You didn't hear how he is. He's *bored*. It's just a game. Maybe he wanted to turn us loose and find us all over again, just to make things more interesting. I promise you, he's not worried about us being safe.'

216

She holds Lincoln closer and focuses on the track again, on the smooth iron rails that make her think of blacksmiths and tools and everything that is strong and unbending. The silvery chunks of rock – too big to be called gravel – shift under her feet. They look like the pebbles Hansel dropped in the woods.

And then Kailynn is talking, and that is one problem with being around other people: someone is always talking. Someone is always complicating things. Joan has to pause again. She has moved three rungs down the track, only a couple of steps.

'Why not go find the police?' says Kailynn, but she has followed Joan. She is holding on to her shirt.

The sound of gunfire explains why they will not go toward the police, but nonetheless Joan turns back toward the front of the zoo, even though she has sworn to herself that she will not look this way again. She glances across the pond, and the chasing lights on the sea monster make the creature shimmer, a wave of orange and red racing.

Her eyes dip down – it was inevitable – and she cannot help but look at the shapes on the concrete. They become more than shapes, and then she cannot look away. She keeps one hand on Lincoln's head, his forehead firmly against her cheek. She cannot let him see. But she sees all of it, every line and curve of the two bodies sprawled on the ground. There is something righteous about memorizing them. She owes it to them or maybe to God.

She sees the soles of the girl's high-heeled sandals. The girl is on her stomach, with her too-short skirt tight against her thighs, bright orange with black lace. The boy is on top of her, covering most of her body, and surely he thought he might save her, surely that was his last thought. There is more blood than Joan would have expected, sprayed and splattered and pooling on the concrete all around them. She knows it is blood, because it is shining dark wet like the pond.

Her brother told her once, when he was going through medic training, that the instructors would cut the legs off goats, and his job would be to transport a legless goat from the pretend battlefield to the pretend medic station without the real goat bleeding to death. His job was not to keep the goats from dying, because the goats would definitely die, but he just had to make them bleed slowly instead of fast, and he said the blood would pool around your feet while you were working on the tourniquets.

The boy's hand is on the girl's head, on her hair. His mouth is open.

Finally Joan makes herself look away, even though she will never be able to not see them – and that is fair – and she stares across the pond that spreads out in front of them, gleaming, and beyond it is the long, wood-paneled entrance building and the drab, outdated ticket counters, but none of it is recognizable.

Although the various spotlights throw the zoo entrance into relief, everything is blurred, both because of the distance and because of the smoke. The reds and blues of what are probably police lights are reflecting off the haze. She can see the branches of the parrots' perches poking up above the smoke, but they are only an abstract design. Everything is abstract. Around the double iron gates – swung open? – she can see a cluster of dark figures, and she is sure they are police, because there are so many of them. They must be whatever kind of police you send to deal with this sort of thing.

She sees a movement around the building, maybe a door opening. There is a shifting from the police, and some of them move forward, a dark mass.

It is all smoke and noise and silhouettes. She listens to the guns sound, and she looks down at the bodies again.

'Go where you want,' she says to Kailynn and the teacher.

She starts running, making sure her feet land on the wooden planks, one after the other, picking up speed, trying to avoid any loose gravel. She is used to this – she has been doing it forever – as she hefts Lincoln higher on her hips, tugging at his ankle so he will wrap his legs around her more tightly, and he must be used to it as well, because he obeys her signals without a word. Her shoulder is malfunctioning – a sharp pain shoots through it if she moves her arm backward instead of forward – but her body is otherwise holding up.

She moved fast enough, apparently, to dislodge Kailynn's grip. But she can hear one or both of the others behind her, the rocks crunching. She grips her sandals with her toes. The *whap-whap* of her soles has started to sound louder to her, and she hopes her shoes are not coming apart.

Here is what she has not explained to the others, because she is through wasting time and it does not matter what they think: the track will take them to the outer edges of the zoo grounds, and even if Robby Montgomery is only toying with them and getting ready to hunt them all over again, even if Destin in all his armored plates comes after them, once they get close to the outer fence, it seems possible that

219

they can find a way to get over it. Maybe more police are waiting. Police who are not in the middle of a gun battle. Or, worst-case scenario, there are acres and acres of woods out here, and if she can find a hidden place in the dark, she and Lincoln will be all right until the police take care of all the shooters.

A string of white lights loops from pole to pole alongside the track. There are patches of darkness and slashes of unavoidable brightness. A few steps of safety and then exposure. For now, she cannot avoid the light: the track is hemmed in by the pond on the right side – a rough split-rail fence along its edge, because everything is so fakely natural – and a creek on the left side, a rushing, tinkling sound coming from it.

'We're on the train track,' announces Lincoln, and he is throwing her off-balance, trying to lean over her arm and look down at the ground. 'We'll get run over.'

The sound of his voice makes her tense. It is one more noise – one more trace of them for someone to follow, and there are two questions, now, repeating in her head, always: *Can they see us? Can they hear us?*

She will not let anyone find them again.

'Put your arms back around my neck,' she whispers, taking a breath between every couple of words. 'Trains don't run here at night.'

He accepts this, and his arms are where they belong and his head is bumping along against her shoulder.

She hears her footsteps and the footsteps behind her, and it takes her a while to realize that she does not hear anything else. The gunfire has stopped. The night is quiet, but the silence does not comfort her.

The quiet is nice. Robby has been waiting for it.

He imagines Destin, and even in his head Destin is huge, not fitting into the frame. His arms are like Popeye's, no wrists at all. He imagines Destin on his horse – his horse! – and he thinks of the one time Destin took him riding through the hills, but Robby only pretended to like it. The idea of it was better than the real thing. And he thinks of the Gila monster tattoo on Destin's bicep, cool as hell, and how once Destin called Robby a team player. Destin never called Mark anything at all.

There are crickets or something chirping in the hedges, and when Robby walks past, they get quiet, too. Good.

There is a game show that has a cardboard character climbing a mountain like Robby is climbing this hill, and if the stupid contestant misses a question, the cardboard guy falls and disappears. He's just plodding higher and higher, never knowing when he might get knocked off the board.

Left, right, left, right, left.

He can hear Mark pounding across the pavement some-where up ahead, somewhere past the AFRICA sign. He is almost positive it is Mark – the police should be coming from the front of the zoo. He looks over his shoulder – he thinks he can see them moving toward the pond, coming through the smoke.

Robby faces forward again. He tries to hurry, but he can't, because he is only cardboard.

And then Mark is in front of him, sprinting, his arms flying around, his form completely inefficient. He barely slows down when he sees Robby. They bump together, shoulder to shoulder, Mark bouncing off like a pinball.

'I think they killed Destin,' Mark says, still moving downhill. 'I think. They must have.'

'Yeah,' Robby says, watching Mark get farther away. A roach runs across the concrete by his foot, and the roach, yeah, that guy is freakin' efficient.

'You know they're coming!' says Mark.

He has paused now, realizing Robby is not following him.

'I know they're coming,' Robby says, and he is proud that for once in his life Mark is louder than he is. Mark is the one who needs shushing.

'What are you doing?' asks Mark.

Robby is not sure. He is not sure of anything, and it's not the worst feeling. Everything is fuzzier than it was before. He has been rolled up in tissue paper, like the bags of pralines his mother shipped him when he tried one semester at State, or he is like the dead squabs that Harding wraps in brownish-red moss before he buries them. Mrs Powell turned him back into himself, partly, and he is stuck now, in between. He saw her in that storage closet, and he recognized her right away, because she has not changed at all, not

222

in fourteen years, except maybe her hair is lighter, and he could not believe that she didn't yell out his name the way she used to when he drifted out of the line to the lunchroom, and then he figured out that she didn't know who he was, but he couldn't stop himself from saying her name.

'Robby!' yells Mark. 'Come on!'

He is going to make himself move in a second. He knows Mark is freaking out. But first he has to push Mrs Powell someplace where she'll leave him alone. It was too much to hope that she might understand, that she might see that he is accomplishing something here, that he is, actually, someone who has thought about things. She did not see it. But maybe she did. Maybe that is why she asked him to stay with her. Maybe, by the end, he had gotten through to her, and maybe she will think of him after. She will remember him.

She gave him some orange. Back then. She gave him some orange.

Was that him back then?

He has not thought about it in years, but he could almost taste the orange when he saw her. He sat close to her desk, and they were doing some kind of worksheet when he smelled the fruit in the air. He was always hungry back then, no matter how much his mom fed him, and he stood and tried to figure out a reason to go to her desk. His feet started moving and he was there, in front of Mrs Powell, before he had thought of a good question to ask her. He watched her slice an orange into half-circles, and she looked up and told him that she hadn't had a chance to eat breakfast that morning. *I like oranges*, he'd said. *I like how they smell.*

Instead of sending him back to his desk, she sort of laughed and held out an orange slice, and he ate it in one bite, ripped it off the rind. No one else got an orange piece, only him.

He couldn't kill her, and that was maybe all right, but he couldn't kill the others in front of her, either. Not even after that awesome bit with the axe, which was hanging there on the wall like it was made to chop through a doorframe. That part was just like the movies. But he couldn't kill them, and so he fell off the rails, just like he always does. How could he have been so sure of what he wanted and so clear on the plan and then have gone and done the exact wrong thing without even realizing he was doing it?

Only he does not care that much, he realizes. He is all wrapped up.

'I'm leaving,' Mark says, and he is running with that stupid uncoordinated stride that he has. 'I'm not just standing here waiting for them to find me.'

'Destin is dead,' says Robby, although it comes out as partly a question.

'You know he is!' yells Mark.

Robby gets himself moving. The truth is that he does not really want to be alone when it happens. And it won't matter where they are. The police will find them.

He feels like he has been running up and down this hill forever. A shell of another roach – not quite fast enough – crackles under his boot.

Destin would stomp roaches with his bare feet.

Destin said that the best cure for poison ivy was to slice off the top layer of skin with a razor and then pour bleach on it, and Robby watched him do it once, and Destin smiled when he poured the bleach.

Maybe there is something after this life, because it seems impossible that a man like that can disappear into nothing.

He could have learned so many more things from Destin if he had more time. They only met him about ten months ago, if meeting online counted. Robby was arguing with Mark about what would be the best jungle weapon. He thought an M14 if your men were good marksmen or maybe a Stoner, either semi- or full automatic, and Mark thought AK-103s, and they googled to settle the question. They clicked around a few message boards, and they started to realize that people were out there talking about everything from homemade hand grenades to how to can deer meat. A while later they were following a thread about a family rescued by a sheriff's deputy after three days in the Wyoming wilderness, and a guy commented that you should never drive anywhere without a log chain and a come-along, and they didn't know what the hell that meant.

So they asked the guy, and the guy was Destin, and he explained it when they asked. Destin knew everything about everything, like how bandannas could be used as filters and as handcuffs and as tourniquets, and how you should keep a spare sidearm between your shoulders in case someone made you put your hands behind your head. Everything. Robby has always been impressed by people who know everything. And it turned out that Destin lived outside the city – thirty miles or so. After a whole load of e-mailing, they met him for beers one day.

They talked about a lot of stuff, and they met for beers

again, and they were lucky, so lucky, that a guy like that wanted to hang with them. Then one day Destin said, *Do you want to live forever?*

Mark said, *Yeah.*

And Destin said, *I know how we can do it.*

He told them about how Columbine had changed everything with the police. Before those two guys shot up the school, if the police got a call about someone with a gun in a public place, they figured it was a hostage situation, and they'd wait for the SWAT team to show up and negotiate. But then Columbine rewrote the rules: the cops realized you might have a shooter firing at anyone and everyone, killing them as fast as they could. So the cops didn't wait anymore to go inside: they had a new template. Whether one policeman showed up or twenty showed up, they'd rush inside right away, and they'd head straight to the shooter and put a bullet in him as soon as possible, and you'd probably admire them for it if you didn't know what douchebags they were. The cops got to practice that new template plenty, because after Columbine, it kept happening over and over again. The crazies had a new template to follow, too.

Destin liked the word 'template'.

Destin said: *Templates are dangerous. Templates teach you not to think. History does not repeat itself, Rob. Every second is a new thing.*

Destin said: *If you're someone who sees the truth, you have to try to educate. You show people how limited they are, then maybe they try to get past those limits.*

Robby liked that idea. He wanted to show the others how limited they were.

They worked it all out. Robby and Mark would come into the zoo quietly, weapons stored away, not giving anyone a reason to notice them. Destin would come in separately, guns out from the beginning, playing the part of a nutjob. He was a good actor. He'd take out a few people right away and then make a show of grabbing hostages and herding them into one of the front offices. Robby and Mark would stay back from the entrance gate so that if anyone did make it out, they wouldn't have seen the two of them. Destin would convince the police that they were following a certain script, but there actually would be a totally different script.

Robby and Mark were in charge of that part. While Destin was playing out a hostage situation and keeping all the cops away, Robby and Mark would go hunting. They would have the whole zoo as a playground. They could kill anybody they wanted, however they wanted. No rules. No limits.

And by the end, the police would see how they had been fooled. They would see how they had sat around and let the slaughter happen. Everyone in front of a laptop or a television would see how the police had been sheep. The entire world would realize, too, that they were all sheep. That they lived their lives like poor dumb animals, never thinking for themselves, and that Destin and Robby and Mark had given them a flash of salvation. A flash of genius. That was the right word for when someone had a vision no one had ever had before.

Destin was right about every second being a new thing, because here Robby is and he knew this was coming, but he still can hardly make himself believe it. He is still here, and Destin is gone. This was the plan, but it feels different now in this second.

The smoke is drifting through the air like fog. Robby can smell it.

The body armor wasn't to save Destin, of course. It was only to make things last longer. Destin said anything worth anything took sacrifice, just look at Jesus. Just look at Galileo and Lincoln. *Yes*, Robby thought. *Yes.* The rest of it was all good and fine, and Destin talked about façades and reality and he talked about a single point of entry and exit and perimeters, but Robby did not care much about the ins and outs of it. It was such an honor to be chosen, and Destin knew everything, and Mark is his best friend, sure. But it was the ending that sold him.

He will finish this, and it will be the one thing he has done right. Even if he has not been perfect, he will finish this.

What will it be like? he wonders, and he wonders what it is like for Destin now. He knows people talk about angels and streets of gold, and his mother has said she would like death to feel like sleep, warm in bed, only with people she loves pressed around her, spine to spine, like when he was a baby and slept with her. He wonders if she thinks of his father, the prick, or whether she wants him out of her heaven. Robby does not want to feel anyone around him, though, and he does not want to feel warm or loved or filled with light or any crap like that. He does not want to feel anything. He hopes it is like being in a bathtub, when everything but your nose is underwater and you can't hear anything or see anything, and you cannot even tell you have a body anymore.

He hopes what comes next is nothing. That is the most beautiful thing.

There are people who will miss him. The old man who always remembers his name when he comes to the CVS counter, but Robby wouldn't see him anymore anyway, thanks to his dick boss. The checkout lady at the liquor store always smiles at him. His grandmother doesn't have any other grandchildren, so that counts for something. Mark, but Mark will not be able to miss him, because he will be gone, too. His mother, who forever ago would take him to go get doughnuts on Saturday mornings when his dad was sleeping in and after doughnuts they would come here to the zoo. She always wanted to see the birds even though the birds were the most boring thing, and she could never remember the difference between sea lions and seals.

Seals, she would say.

Sea lions, he would correct, every time.

It is better not to think of her.

Mark is saying something. They are at the railroad track, and Mark has been yammering for ages about how they need to follow the stupid track around and get over to whatever street – Cherry? Dogwood?

None of it matters. It is such a relief that none of it matters. Because despite Mark's delusional escape plan, the beautiful ending is nearly here, and it will find them, no matter where they go. All Robby has to do is keep the gun in his hand. All he has to do is play his part.

7:53 p.m.

A sharp-edged rock slides into Joan's sandal, and she loses her rhythm for a moment. The pond is behind them now, and a thick wall of bamboo has sprung up along the narrow creek to her left, so she can no longer see the water.

Kailynn is a few feet behind her. Mrs Powell is a good ten feet behind the girl. It is clear that the teacher is struggling, even before she calls out, 'Go on without me.'

Joan slows down. She is not that much faster than the teacher, not with Lincoln pulling on every muscle.

'You're doing fine,' she calls back.

She is not sure whether she says it because she wants to encourage the teacher or because she wants to avoid more interminable conversation.

But the teacher slows to a walk, and Kailynn jogs to a stop. Joan has no choice but to pause.

'I can't,' says the teacher. 'My knee's not going to cooperate. I'll find a spot around here and wait it out.'

Joan nods and turns.

'We can't just leave you,' says Kailynn, unmoving.

This is the problem. They do not have time for

consideration and politeness, and they do not have time for talking. It will kill them all – haven't they learned that already?

Joan has learned it, and she has learned it well. She will leave them. She is done considering her options. She has covered a few yards of track, has managed not to look back and see if the others are following her, when she hears a gunshot. It makes her jump after the long seconds – minutes? – of quiet. Above her head, one of the looping white lights explodes, and her first ridiculous thought is that the bulb has blown. But then she puts the sound and the broken glass together, and she fits in the fact that she heard wood splinter and that a crape myrtle branch over her head is tipping down.

Robby Montgomery was only playing with them.

Or Mark and Destin the killing machine are hunting them down.

The specifics do not particularly matter right now.

There is another sound of wood cracking, and leaves flutter down around them all. She looks behind her. For once, thank God, no one wants to talk – they all know the sound of bullets now, and they are all running again, even Mrs Powell, whose teeth are digging into her bottom lip. There is pain in every line of the teacher's face, and there is nothing to be done about it. Joan tries to look beyond Kailynn and the teacher, but the track swerves left and right, and she cannot see very far.

No more bullets come. She thinks she can hear feet, though.

In twenty or thirty steps they are coming up to the playground, with its massive rocks and rope bridge. Then the frog and turtle statues that Medusa left behind in her wake. *I'm a turtle, I'm a turtle,* Lincoln will say when he's on the toilet, making the toilet seat his shell. Or he will wiggle under an ottoman or put a pillow on his back – *I'm a turtle.*

Joan runs faster. Her breath wheezes out, and her lungs burn. The teacher is keeping up, barely. Now they are past the playground, and here comes the splash pad with the fountains still arcing in the air.

The merry-go-round, animals mid-prance.

Even over her own harsh breaths, Joan can hear the teacher grunting with each step. She looks behind her again and can see no sign of the gunmen. But, still, there is the far-off grind of gravel. She does not think she is imagining it.

'Get off the track!' she calls over her shoulder to the teacher. 'Go behind the merry-go-round. Stay down.'

'What?' says the teacher.

'Go on, Mrs Powell!' she hisses, because she cannot think of the woman's first name. 'Just keep behind the merry-go-round and they won't see you.'

There is no time to explain – she cannot see anyone, so hopefully Robby Montgomery or his friend or the killing machine cannot see them, either. But she can hear their feet, so maybe the men will be guided by sound, too, and they will just keep coming down the track, and she owes this teacher something, doesn't she? Also it will simplify things – it will be one less person slowing her down. Mrs Powell has stepped off the track, limping and then disappearing behind the rows of wooden horses and giraffes and antelopes.

The teacher is gone.

Kailynn is still behind her. Joan rounds a bend and can no longer see the merry-go-round, and then the track curves again and she is beyond everything that she knows, entering the other world of the zoo, the one you only see on the train, and she cannot hear anyone behind them, but she is not sure.

If you shaved a tiger, the train conductor said one time, *you'd find out that their skin is striped, too.*

Everything is blessedly dark. Not the complete dark of the countryside on her childhood camping trips but city dark. Mostly dark. They are on the back side of the exhibits. More bamboo blocks whatever the zebras and ostriches might be doing, and the woods are thick all around her, with occasional light-up decorations hanging from the trees – a glowing ghost, a string of blinking black bats, a laughing skeleton.

There is no need to stay close to the track anymore. The woods are all shadows and moonlight. They can disappear into the trees.

'Do you think they—?' she hears Kailynn begin, but the rest of it is lost on the breeze.

Joan hops off the rails, landing heavily, sandal twisting crookedly on the chunks of gravel, but she catches herself and is off through the weeds and pinecones and rotting chunks of wood. Drifts of dry leaves come halfway up her calves. She cannot see where her feet land.

There up ahead, closer than she expected, she can see what must be the outer fence of the zoo, almost invisible – not substantial at all – nothing but chain link. It is maybe six feet high, and she could climb it no problem with her shoes off. As she hears Kailynn come to a stop behind her, Joan jogs closer, putting one finger against the fence, not positive that it is not electric – she should put Lincoln down, but there is no time and she touches it so lightly – and the risk pays off. There is no shock.

They can do this.

She will boost Lincoln onto the fence and help him wedge his feet into the gaps, getting a good grip with his fingers, and she will climb behind him, and she can hold on with one hand while she helps him climb higher, and it might be slow, but they can do it.

Then she sees it. At the bottom of the fence, on the outside, there is a ditch at least five feet deep. She cannot make out the bottom of it. And there is no way she can navigate it with Lincoln, not even if she could figure out how to get him over the fence. Her fantasy of climbing with him is deeply flawed, even with Kailynn helping. They would be so easy to shoot, stretched out defenseless on a fence.

She turns and runs in the other direction, back over the railroad track and toward the animals.

She vaults over a dead log, grunting, and she will not try that again, not with a forty-pound weight on her hip. There are unexpected dips in the ground, and Lincoln cries out when his chin bangs against her shoulder. There are logs everywhere, dead trees decaying into mulch, and the leaves are still thick and deep, and there are more light-up bats dangling. She sees the silhouette of giraffes off to their left, inside fences that are surely eight feet tall.

She feels Kailynn's hand tangled in the back of her shirt

again, pulling the material tight. She can hear the girl breathing. She has not heard more gunshots, and that bodes well for Mrs Powell. But there are other sounds: now that she and Kailynn are awash in leaves, their steps brittle and snapping, she can distinguish the grinding of other shoes on rocks. And if she can hear the men, they can probably hear her.

If she slows down, her footsteps will be softer. But if she slows down, they will only catch her faster.

'They're behind us,' she wheezes to Kailynn, turning her head.

Her shirt loosens as the girl lets go of her. And then, without a word, Kailynn is sprinting off to the left, taking an angle toward the giraffes, and it is a good idea for the girl to try a different direction, because they are a bigger target together. There is no safety in numbers at all. In fact, she has wanted to get rid of Kailynn, hasn't she? The teacher and the girl were both more trouble than they were worth.

It is simpler when it is only her and Lincoln. It is safer.

So Joan does not say a word as the distance between them widens. She can still make out the girl's zigzagging shape at the moment when her own foot catches – maybe her sandal finally breaks and the ruined shoe causes her to trip, or maybe the strap snaps as she falls, she will never know – but there is a long moment of falling, of panic, of feeling Lincoln slipping from her arms and hearing her own high-pitched yelp. She tightens one arm around him even as she tries to twist so that she won't land on him. *Don't drop him don't drop him don't drop him*, she is thinking all the way down. She somehow manages to turn enough that he is half on her back when she hits the ground, but her elbow slams down hard, and the impact makes her arms fly up, and he is flying up, too, no matter what she has told herself, and she watches him fall, his head bouncing against the leaves.

She has landed entirely on her left shoulder and elbow, hand bent back against her side – and she's sunk her teeth into her lip. She licks off blood. She tries to make her arm work as she reaches for her son, and her arm does what she wants it to do, but her hand does not.

He is not crying. This panics her. She cannot see his face in the darkness, only the outline of him. But then he is moving, pushing himself up, stuck on his back like a turtle for a moment.

'Lincoln,' she whispers.

'We fell,' he says.

'You okay?' she asks, crawling toward him, scooping him toward her with her good arm.

'I'm okay,' he says, reaching out one hand, touching her. 'Your face is wet.'

She wipes at her bloody mouth, listening.

Voices.

Not too close but close enough.

Her right shoe is gone, as vanished as the girl. Her knee is bleeding, and her hand is still just hanging limp, although it doesn't hurt much. Could she have sprained her wrist?

She cannot carry him if her hand doesn't work.

She hears something else in the trees behind them. A branch moving. The crackling of pine straw or leaves. Small movements, maybe only the wind, only none is blowing now. A squirrel, possibly.

She pushes herself to her knees, stifling a gasp as her weight hits her injured knee, and then she gets to her feet. The ground is cold and not quite solid. She wiggles her toes and considers kicking off her left shoe, too, but the ground is full of sharp things, and she thinks it is better to have one foot protected. She steps toward Lincoln, bracing herself, and still her knee buckles and she nearly hits the ground again.

The sounds behind her change: there is not a crackling anymore. There are steps, slow and cautious.

The men are coming, and she has no idea if they are ten steps behind her or an acre away, and the police still do not actually exist here. Her knee will barely hold her weight, and her wrist is not working, and she cannot move fast enough. Prickly edges stab into the sole of her bare foot.

They are about to die, she thinks, and she hates herself for the thought.

No. She is not an animal. She has more in her than fight or flight. She takes Lincoln's hand and whispers that the men with guns are coming, and he is running with her, only he is so loud, crashing through the leaves, and he is slow. They cannot do this.

They cannot outrun the killers.

Footsteps, footsteps.

She hears the creek again, somewhere close, water against rocks, splashing. Lincoln missteps, nearly falling, and she lifts him by his one hand, swinging him forward, easing him down lightly onto both feet as she keeps them going.

She looks up, considering the trees. They could climb – more than one of these oaks have spreading branches and forks that lead up to the dark sky. But if she is wrong, if they are spotted, there is no escape, and she is not sure she can lift him, and she does not have time to think about this, but lifting him – lifting him. She thinks of it, of placing him somewhere safe.

Not the trees. She swerves, still keeping their momentum but studying the landscape, all shadows and moonlight and occasional dangling decorations. There is a shrub ahead, as high as her shoulder, and it is thick with leaves. She leads him to it, and she runs a hand through the branches to feel for thorns before she lifts the lower branches and makes a space underneath.

'Stay here,' she tells him, her limp hand pressing lightly against his back, steering him. 'Get down on your belly and crawl in. Be completely quiet. Do not call my name. Do not say a word. I will be right back, but if you make any noise, they'll kill you.'

He whimpers, although he is also crawling, and she does not want to give him a chance to argue with her and she does not want to give herself a chance to consider what she is doing.

'Make yourself disappear,' she says, already standing, taking an extra second to put her hand on his head – the precious curve of it – as she lets the branches fall. He disappears except for his feet, so she reaches under and bends his legs slightly.

Then she is jogging, a staggering kind of run that makes her feel like a pathetic heroine in a horror movie. She pushes back the pain and makes her strides longer and faster and her knee is irrelevant and there is a beach-ball-sized spider with a lightbulb inside it, hanging from a tree, floppy-legged, incomprehensible. It is smiling through fangs dripping red.

She thinks Lincoln will stay there, both because she has told him to do so and because it is dark outside and he does not know where he is. He is not prone to wandering, especially when he is nervous. He will stay. But noise – that is another issue. She does not trust him to be quiet.

She smashes her feet with as much force as possible. Leaves explode under her feet, turning to dust. She grabs at a passing branch and snaps it in half. She suspects she sounds more elephant than woman. When she thinks she is a long way away from Lincoln, she cries out, a short staccato *Ah!* that she thinks will carry for a distance. She exhales, long and loud. She holds her hurt hand tight against her belly. She goes back to stomping loudly, moving as quickly as she can, because although she wants to draw them to her, she does not have a death wish.

She can hear the men moving behind her, steadily, making plenty of noise themselves. She feels a rush of satisfaction and bloodlust and fear.

She is past the elephant habitat, and to her left is a nondescript, multistory building with LARGE ANIMAL RESEARCH FACILITY in big letters. The silver gutters and tin roof are shining in the moonlight. She pushes forward, leaves and twigs slapping against her skin. She passes a low-hanging string of pumpkin lights. Her knee throbs, and she thinks of the teacher, of her hobbling movements, and she imagines her safe behind the merry-go-round. She thinks of Kailynn's hands tugging at her, and she misses the girl's warmth, and she would not even mind her mindless chatter, and the girl's hair is so lovely, like red ribbons blowing.

If Lincoln sees a shining light and he is curious – would he move? Or if a bug crawls near him and he runs from it or if he imagines he hears her voice? She is unraveling, the panic catching up to her, and so she runs faster. She thinks of trash cans, solid and safe, and she thinks of how he was an easy baby, good at eating and good at sleeping, but every now and then there would be a spell where he would cry unremittingly and she could not stop it, and she remembers the waves of savage frustration that left her imagining – so briefly – what if I shut him in the closet and left him there? What if the baby's mother felt that, a thousand times multiplied, terror and exhaustion and frustration, and in one weak second she left the baby and ran, and can't Joan understand that?

No. She cannot.

But what if the men were coming close, as they are now? What if that other mother put down her baby and tried to draw the men away? What if that? Joan can see the woman running, hair in her face, arms empty.

She has not been fair to that woman.

There is a give to the ground under her feet. Leaves and mulch and pine straw, she assumes, and then – with her shoed foot – she steps on something different, something that makes her throat close up. It is soft and substantial – the unmistakable feel of flesh and muscle. She jerks back, then realizes that, whatever it is, it is far too small to be human. She peers down, and in the dim light she sees the triangular point of a wing and a rounded head.

A bird. A dead bird.

They have a library book about the ancient Greeks and their sports, and Lincoln has told her that hockey back then was played with a dead bird, and when a team scored a goal, the bird came back to life and flew away.

Lincoln. She forces her feet to move again.

She can hear wind chimes.

Once when her uncle was driving her to the country, she realized the turn signal ticked out the exact tune of a tongue twister she'd just learned – *Rub-ber ba-by bug-gy bum-pers / Rub-ber ba-by bug-gy bum-pers* – the blinker sang the rhythm of it every time, and it was so clear, so obvious, that the blinker was calling out the words, and now the jingling chimes are ringing out Lincoln's name, and so are the leaves under her feet – *Lin-coln Lin-coln Lin-coln.*

She has succeeded – the men are far away from Lincoln now – but she has not thought about this part: how can she get rid of them? She cannot lead them back to Lincoln. And she is not even sure they are still following her. She cannot hear them anymore, actually, not over the sound of her own footsteps and panting breath. She stops.

Nothing. Nothing but leaves and wind chimes.

She does not pause for long. Maybe she has lost the men, but maybe they are still tracking her. Regardless, she has been away from Lincoln for too long. She needs to work her way back toward him, and she can change course if she sees any sign of the men.

It is difficult to make plans while dodging tree trunks and brambles. It is difficult to orient herself – which way should she be going? The trees are all the same. But then she hears the creek as she scrapes her shoulder on the scaly bark of a huge pine tree. She is disoriented enough that she does not know which way leads to the outer fence or which way leads back to Lincoln, but she knows that the creek will take her in the right direction. The sound of the water will help mask her footsteps, and when she spots that hanging spider, she'll know that he is close by.

The darkness is more complete in this section of the woods. She can no longer make out the ground, and she slows, because she cannot afford to turn her ankle.

She realizes that she does not feel her arm at all anymore, nothing from shoulder to hand, and maybe it should worry her, but it is a pure blessing at the moment. She keeps following the sound of the water, and in the darkness she almost steps into the creek before she sees it. She skids slightly in the leaves and squints down at the water – only a gash in the forest floor. She could easily leap across the entire width of it if both her legs were working properly.

Despite the creek's narrowness, the bank is several feet high, and it is steep. She cannot tell how deep the water is. It is a shiny black nothing. She thinks she sees a small footbridge farther downstream or upstream or whatever, and she has no idea who would be using a bridge out here, but it is the way toward Lincoln. Then again, does she need to cross the creek? Is Lincoln on this side of the water or the far side? She rubs at her forehead, infuriated with herself, because she needs all her sharpness, all her focus—

She hears feet moving through the woods again, even though she has been so sure that they have lost track of her.

She can hear them coming, and she thinks again of her father – his hands were huge – popping heads off doves.

Lincoln, Lincoln, Lincoln. Their feet in the leaves sing out his name, too.

And then she sees them, two shadows walking. They are closer than she expected. She cannot take her time to see if Robby Montgomery is one of them. Instead she drops to the ground, flat-bellied.

Soon their boots will mash her like a dead bird. She lays her palms flat on the ground and pushes, rolling herself down the creek bank, angling herself so that her feet slide into the water first, slowing her.

She goes under the water without a sound.

The cold takes her breath, and she's squeezed her eyes shut because if she loses a contact lens, she won't be able to see a thing. But she swipes at her eyes, blinks them open, then she gets her bearings. The water would barely come past her knees if she were standing, but she is stretched out nearly horizontal, almost submerged. She cannot see past the rise of the creek bank. The shadows are dark and safe. She eases her hands into the water, the creek bed squishing between her fingers, and then she is walking on her hands, seal-like, her body floating behind her.

She assumes there would be bullets if the men had seen her.

The cold water has sharpened her. She is aware of each handprint she is leaving in the creek bottom, each rock against her knee, each spray of water on her cheek, each bit closer she comes to the bridge. She thinks that – if she does not die – she might have been brilliant without realizing it. She can get back to Lincoln like this – floating, not making a sound. She only needs to let the men move past her, and then she can head downstream and find Lincoln.

She gets to the bridge in a few seconds, and then she flips over and backs into the alcove. Her head brushes the bottom of the wooden planks. She is not getting warmer, and she wraps her arms around her knees. There are soft chunks of something – algae? – brushing against her arm, and she does not like that she cannot see what's under the surface, but that means the men cannot see anything, either.

There is no sound except the rushing of the water. She squats lower. It is warmer to be in the water than to be in the air. The bridge is arched, and she looks out through the semicircle gap between wood and water.

Here they come: she sees two sets of feet on the creek bank. She can see nothing above their knees, because the bridge cuts off her view. One pair of feet leaps over the creek, a long, easy jump, one foot landing and then the other. She is glad that he either did not notice the bridge or thought it was beneath him to bother using it. She waits for the second pair of legs to make the leap, but those legs do not move.

Go on, she thinks. *Go on.*

But the second man does not cross the creek. Instead the first man vaults back over the water – did he get called back? – and he steps close to the second man, as if they might be talking.

She does not think they would be standing there if they had spotted her. Unless it is still about the game. Trying to flush her out. She slides down deeper, turning her head so that her cheek dips into the water, and she gets a better view of them both. They are facing away from her, and one of them has the thick shape and baggy jacket of Robby Montgomery. The other one is smaller and thin-shouldered. Robby's friend, she assumes.

So here they are, she thinks. The three of them.

Somewhere out there is the teacher and the girl and Lincoln and the faceless monster in armor and, she supposes, the police. Somewhere out there is a screaming infant in a trash can and a missing mother. Joan thinks about her son and his piles of plastic people and about how sometimes those people are not where you expect them to be. Sometimes Thor has fallen behind a couch cushion and Iron Man becomes the star of your show. Sometimes an arm breaks off the Joker, so you use Poison Ivy as your villain. You recast. You rethink.

The men are maybe two dozen feet away. It occurs to her that she has left her purse somewhere. She is beginning to worry about hypothermia. She thinks of her uncle's story about how, as teenagers, he and his best friend, Larry, were driving across a bridge over the Tennessee River and a woman going in the opposite direction veered into their lane. Their car crashed through the guardrails of the bridge, and both boys were thrown through the windshield into the river. *Did it hurt when you went through the glass?* she'd ask. *Did it hurt when you hit the water? Did you touch the bottom?* Her uncle couldn't answer all her questions. He couldn't remember anything from when his head hit the dashboard at the first slam on the brakes until he was stepping up onto the riverbank, his shoes gone. *Did you kick them off when you were swimming? Did they get knocked off when you were flying through the air?* She was fascinated by what he could tell her – the feel of the slime between his toes and the fact that the woman driving the other car had white hair – but it was the parts he couldn't tell her that she daydreamed about. She imagined herself there, and she saw all the things that he didn't remember.

Did you save Larry? she would ask him. *Did you yell for help?*

I lay there, he would tell her. *I just lay there in the mud and I watched.*

Her thoughts are drifting again. Her brain is going numb. And her feet are numb, too, numb enough that she is concerned she will not be able to stand, much less walk. She is no good to Lincoln if she can't walk.

And still the men are only standing there.

No. They are shifting, separating. The thin one is heading away from the water, and Robby Montgomery is grabbing hold of his arm. But the smaller one breaks loose, and there is some other kind of movement that is not clear in the darkness, and then she loses sight of the small guy.

Robby stands for a moment, and she is about to take her chances heading downstream, but then she sees someone else coming. A pair of feet and legs, moving carefully, and Joan recognizes those skinny legs and tight jeans even before she sees the thick mass of hair.

She sees the moment when Kailynn notices Robby in front of her – the girl's entire body goes stiff. She sees the moment when Kailynn notices that the other gunman is there, too – the girl spins, a quarter-turn. She is holding something in her arms.

Joan cannot hear anything that they're saying. If she backs a little farther under the bridge, she will be unable to see anything.

Maybe it is better that way.

She sinks deeper into the water.

Kailynn nearly screams when the animal darts across the ground in front of her, rattling pine straw, but when it freezes, front paws in the air, she recognizes it. A groundhog. She does not think there's such a thing as wild groundhogs around here. But there is a whole family of them in the petting zoo, and she guesses that the men have smashed and bashed that building like they did the others, so maybe there are sheep and goats and Shetland ponies running around, too. Now the groundhog is creeping toward her, and she stays still, letting it nudge at her leg. She has never seen the ones in the children's area do anything but cower against the back wall of their pen, because all the animals in the petting zoo hate children.

Maybe this one is traumatized. Maybe it wants some comfort.

She reaches down very slowly. You're supposed to hold out your hand to a dog and let it come to you, and she thinks sometimes little kids are the same way and this groundhog is the same way, too. She gets a good grip on it, careful, and the groundhog likes being picked up. It snuggles closer to her as she makes her way through the trees, its little claws catching the ends of her hair. Her little sister does this, too, pressing close and tight when she is scared. Kailynn takes a few steps forward – she has not been running for a while. There's no point. She doesn't know where she is, and she doesn't know where she should be going.

That's not true. She should be looking for Lincoln and his mother. She should have stopped running five minutes ago when she saw them fall, but she couldn't make her legs slow down, and when she finally got herself under control, she was all alone. They are probably dead now – that Lincoln had such pretty hair, and he had smiled at her – and maybe they wouldn't be if she had never brought them into the storeroom. She thought that it was a good thing. She told herself she was doing it to help people, but maybe that is not true. Maybe she only wanted to keep herself from being alone. Her little sister begged Kailynn not to move into her own room, because her little sister sometimes gets scared in the middle of the night and she likes to snuggle – like a groundhog – but Kailynn is not sure that the begging is why she stayed. How is she supposed to know if she did it for herself or for her sister? Because one makes her good and one makes her selfish, and if she is selfish, then she has probably killed that boy and his mother.

She strokes the groundhog's head.

She sees a light ahead, and at first she thinks maybe she has found her way back to the main part of the zoo, but then she realizes the light is coming from a wide shape in the middle of the trees, and she slows down as she comes to an army-style tent big enough for ten people. Next to it is a broken-down jeep. The tent is lit from within, and she can see the silhouettes of three men inside sitting in a circle, and she is terrified for a moment before she realizes that they are mannequins. Another Halloween display.

She backs away, changing course slightly, getting away from the light.

She wishes she had more animal crackers. Maybe Oreos or Famous Amos. She is hating the feel of her own mouth. Her father would laugh at her for thinking of cookies – she knows he would – and she remembers the time she and her sister were at home by themselves and she was pouring a glass of tea when they heard a loud noise in the den and then a creepy laugh. She and her sister ran to the bathroom, but as soon as they had locked themselves inside, Kailynn realized she'd forgotten her phone, which she'd need if they were going to call the police, so she inched open the bathroom door a tiny bit. There was a man right in front of her – she screamed in that second before she recognized her father, who was laughing and laughing.

He loves to play tricks on them. She thinks it reminds him of when he was a kid, back before he wore suits and sat through teacher conferences and cleaned up cat throw-up. He was a preacher's son, and he wrecked the car twice before he turned sixteen. He threw baseballs at windows on purpose. He once caught twenty-three cats in one afternoon and swung them by their tails onto a roof.

A hellion. That's the word he calls his old self. The other kids were terrified of him. The grown-ups were terrified of him.

People say she is a nice girl. She makes mostly As and Bs.

Hardly ever Cs. She saves her money in the bank. But now she wishes that she were the kind of girl who set things on fire instead of the kind of girl who proofreads her work. She wishes she knew how to scare people. She wishes she had worked yesterday instead of today, and she wishes she carried pepper spray like her mother has told her she should, and she wishes she had an Almond Joy, cold, and she wishes she were home in bed and her pillows were fluffed, and she wishes she had grabbed that little boy Lincoln and run with him and saved him, and she wishes she were a woman in a video game with pistols on her hips and a cleavage. She wishes her father could still pick her up and carry her, but she is too heavy.

The groundhog trembles in her arms, and every sound she hears seems like footsteps. She stops, listens, and decides she only hears leaves.

Her father was the sort of boy who should have turned into a psychopath – that's what people say, isn't it? That when you torture animals, it means you will be a serial killer? But he turned into her father instead, and there is no meanness in him. She has seen him cry at commercials.

She hears water up ahead, and she thinks again that there are footsteps. She creeps closer to see if she can spot anything moving through the trees.

She sees the creek, and she thinks she hears a voice, but when she stops to listen, she doesn't hear anything. She steps behind a tree, and she waits and watches. She stands for what feels like a long time, and then she strokes the groundhog and walks carefully until she is right at the water's edge, and she thinks about whether she should cross the water and then – her teachers have told her that she has a problem with focusing, that she sometimes drifts off – and then she is looking up and staring at Robby.

'Hey,' she says, like he has come up next to her at school as she's stuffing books into her locker, like he is not standing there with his gun and what she thinks might be bullets looped over his shoulder. She is embarrassed about saying hello and thinks that it is idiotic, too, to be embarrassed, but she can't take it back.

And then she feels someone behind her, and when she turns around, there is another man.

He is smaller than Robby, and if he is the same one who came into the restaurant earlier, he seemed bigger to her then. Now she looks at him and thinks that he doesn't look any stronger than she is, the kind of boy she could beat at arm-wrestling, but he has a gun in each hand, a big one and a little one. He grins at her, a friendly smile that makes her mouth dry out more.

'You been making friends?' he asks, and he is clearly talking to Robby.

Robby doesn't say anything. He hasn't said a word.

Kailynn angles herself so that she can keep an eye on both of them. She takes two steps backward, turning so she won't fall into the creek. She is holding the groundhog too tightly, and it squirms against her. She hopes they will not hurt the groundhog. She takes a third step and a fourth, and a branch breaks under her foot and makes her jump.

They just watch her. The trees make shadows move across their faces, and the shadows are so thick that she can't tell anything about their expressions.

'One for the road?' says the one she doesn't know. At first she is relieved, because he tosses both his guns to the ground. Then he comes at her so fast that she can't even get her hands up before he is spinning her around, her back pressed against his chest, which is hard like metal.

'What about your big escape?' says Robby, and she keeps her eyes on him. She will not look away from him. She does not know why, but this seems important.

'She's even got hair like a damn squab!' says the one who is holding her. 'Didn't you ever wonder if you could break someone's neck with just your hands? My cousin said that's only in the movies, that we have too much muscle in our necks, but I don't think she's got much muscle.'

Kailynn cannot see the one talking because of the way he is holding her. He twists his hands in her hair, grabbing her braids, and he yanks her head back, hard, and she feels some of her extensions pull free, her scalp stinging. He keeps on pulling until her face is pointed toward the trees and her throat is bent back. She still keeps her eyes on Robby, barely.

She wants to say something brave. She wants to spit at the man holding her or bite him or tell him that he is not strong enough to do anything to her with those toothpick arms, but she cannot talk, because he has his fingers on her throat now, pressing so that she thinks he will leave bruises.

She looks at Robby. He still has his gun in his hand. She cannot tell anything from his face.

'Help,' she tries to say.

'I told you to go to the sea lions,' Robby says, or she thinks he says it.

Kailynn kicks, and she thinks she hits the small man's shin, but it doesn't seem to matter.

The clouds are moving over the trees. She has both hands around the man's wrists, nails clawing into his skin, and she has dropped the groundhog.

She thinks of her father. She thinks of him swinging cats onto roofs. He said he swung each one like a discus, and he felt so satisfied when he let loose and it sailed through the air.

She has skin under her fingernails. Blood on her fingers. The man grunts in her ear, and all she can feel now is this man wrapped around her. He is actually turning her head now, with both hands, and one of his fingers is digging into a soft part of her ear. She gulps for air. It hurts.

Robby says something.

'Nearly there,' breathes the voice next to her ear.

Someone is yelling. She cannot hear well, and she is not sure the voice is even real, but the hands around her throat loosen. She catches herself with her hands as she falls. Leaves stick to her bloody fingers.

When she takes a long breath, it does not sound human.

She looks for the groundhog in the leaves, and she can't see it. Then she looks up at Robby and he is still just standing there, and she is angrier at him than at the man who has been trying to tear her head off her body.

Robby is looking past her, though. Kailynn turns, and her breathing is still terrible, and she sees a woman wading through the creek like some swamp monster.

'Robby Montgomery!' is what the woman yells, just once, or maybe she has said it plenty of other times and this is the first time Kailynn's ears have worked right.

It is Lincoln's mother, soaking wet. She does not have Lincoln with her, and this panics Kailynn.

The groundhog is by her foot. She scoops it up, warm. Everyone but her is moving.

Lincoln's mother is climbing out of the water.

The man who was choking Kailynn is lunging toward where he dropped his guns.

Robby is lifting his own gun toward the woman.

'Mrs Powell told me to tell you—' starts Lincoln's mother, close enough that Kailynn can hear water dripping on the leaves.

The choker has his hand around his pistol, but he grabbed it by the wrong end, and he is shifting it in his hands as he tries to turn himself toward the woman. Robby has jerked his gun up so that it points toward the sky, but he has not loosened his grip on it. Kailynn thinks something is smashed inside her throat.

'Mrs Powell said that she wants to talk to you,' says the mother. 'Mrs Powell says that she wants to talk to you one more time.'

Lincoln's mother is trying to get in front of her, it occurs to Kailynn. The woman is slowly edging closer. Now the creek water from her hair is splattering across Kailynn's shoes and thighs.

Robby Montgomery is watching them both.

'It doesn't matter,' he says, and his gun lowers toward them, and Kailynn thinks, *Well, it mattered a little bit, just about three seconds' worth*, and now the choker is lining up his pistol, and she thinks of her father and his cats.

She throws the groundhog.

Her aim is not good – she does not hit the choker or Robby. But the groundhog passes close to the choker's face, and he jerks back so that he loses his balance and falls into the weeds. Robby Montgomery is looking down at his friend, and then Kailynn cannot see anything else because Lincoln's mother is on top of her, heavy and wet. She is stronger than she looks. She is lifting Kailynn, dragging her, screaming in her ear, shoving her over the bank of the creek and into the water.

Kailynn falls in face-first, swallowing water, and by then the guns are shooting.

8:05 p.m.

Joan hears the bullets, but she doesn't feel them. They are spaced out, the shots, and she keeps her head low, mouth skimming the water, as her hands and feet sink into mud and algae, and she wonders whether Robby Montgomery and the other one can see them clearly. She can barely see her own hands cutting through the water, so surely the men cannot see any better than she can, and that explains why she is not dead yet.

She feels a stone dig into her thigh, a burst of pain. Kailynn is gagging on water, possibly vomiting, but the girl is also crawling toward the bridge as fast as Joan can push her.

And they are under the bridge now. Not safe but safer, for a few seconds, at least. The bullets have stopped.

'Keep going,' she whispers to Kailynn, and already the two sets of feet are coming toward the bridge, because, of course, where else would she and Kailynn have gone but the bridge?

She shoves the girl backward again, and then they are out from under the bridge, scuttling backward, and for a moment the wooden planks completely block her view of the men. Then she can see the vague outline of their heads, and they are not moving anymore. There is some sort of tugging going on between them – one of them trying to pull the other one in a different direction? If it is an argument, it does not last long, because soon they are both vaulting across the creek, heading into the woods on the other side.

She finds herself wondering if Robby Montgomery ever fired his gun – he did not kill her when she was coming up out of the water, all soft and helpless – but there is no time to consider it.

'It's okay,' she says to Kailynn, who has stumbled and gone underwater and come up sputtering. She works an arm under the girl's back and lifts her, swiping at the water pouring from her face, and the girl's hair is heavy on her arm, and her neck is so fragile-feeling, but they cannot stop, so she keeps pushing the girl forward.

They are moving again as Joan watches Robby Montgomery and the other one jog away from the creek and farther into the trees. She can't trust that, though, because she can't trust anything.

Her leg is throbbing now, and she is beginning to wonder if it was something other than a rock that hurt her. She focuses on the cold of the water and the slime on her hands and on how, during his first trip to the lake, Lincoln stared at the water, suspicious, and he asked her, *Do we have hippos in America?* There is nothing in the world she wants like she wants the weight of him.

She and Kailynn are a good distance past the bridge now, still belly-up in the black water. Joan can scarcely make out the two shooters: they have turned into only shadows. As she makes her hands and feet move faster, one of the men lifts an arm toward the creek, and then someone skips a stone across the water.

Joan knows immediately that this cannot be right, but that is the sound – a rock hitting the water, three or four times. A half a second after the sound of the splashes, she hears four cracks in the air, one after the other. Then one of the men falls to his knees with a loud grunt.

She understands then.

There are bullets hitting not only the water but the ground, too, kicking up the leaves – not a firestorm of bullets, nothing like what she has seen in movies, but a series of shots, delineated. More like what she remembers from dove hunting – a crack from the gun and then her father reloading and then another crack.

She looks toward the men, and now she can tell that it is Robby Montgomery who has fallen to his knees on the ground. She can make out the wide line of his shoulders and the flapping of his jacket. The other man is running.

Someone is shooting at the shooters.

There are fireflies that must have been flushed out by the gunfire. They flash through the trees. Robby Montgomery drops to his elbows, and then he is not moving at all. She cannot recognize him as a person anymore – he is a dark shape in the dirt. A pile of leaves. A log.

The other one is still running.

Joan turns her head to the other side of the creek and now, finally, she can see the police coming. There are two groups of them, and they move in triangles: one man in front, one behind him on each side, and it reminds her of geese, only there is one at the back, too.

There is a third group coming through the trees, saviors coming from everywhere, only they are half formed, clumped together so that they are a mass of raised arms and weapons, padded around the middle so that their angles are alien, and they are so silent. The bullets keep coming – she can hear them, she thinks, one by one, a whooshing sound in the air, a separate sound from the crack of gunfire – and it is only getting louder. More guns. More bullets sailing over her, landing a few feet away from her. No more have hit the water since that first burst of fire, but they are still too close.

She sinks down as far as she can.

The running man is yelling, but she cannot make out any words.

The fireflies flare, rhythmic.

She manages to coordinate her hands and feet enough to push herself backward, farther away, but her bad wrist collapses and she goes under. Now it is Kailynn who is helping her up, and there is algae tangling around her arm – no, it is the girl's fingers circling her wrist, wrapping around the bandage that the girl made herself. Joan blows water from her nose.

Go, go, go, she tells herself.

They do not tell you it is like this.

They do not tell you that you cannot tell the good guys from the bad guys, that the noise is so much that it not only deafens you but blinds you, because you cannot help but close your eyes, and that sound and movement is coming from everywhere so that you don't know which way to go.

She is not sure why there is so much smoke.

One of the men – good guy? – is nearly at the creek, only a few steps away, and he seems very tall. He is the point of the triangle, and he is not quite running or walking but some combination, fast and smooth. He comes close enough that she can tell he is wearing something like earmuffs over his ears, but she cannot see his face – she would like to see his face. She does not want to jump up and startle him, because she would only be one more shape in the dark, and who knows what he would do if he was surprised?

His gun is raised, and she actually sees a flash when he pulls the trigger. She didn't know you could see the bullet leave the gun.

There are no fireflies, she realizes.

She sees the man who is not Robby Montgomery fall to the ground, but he is still shooting. He pulls himself behind a pine tree, and he is almost invisible behind it from her angle—

Move, she reminds herself.

There is a rush through the air in front of her. She felt a streak of heat that time, warming the air by her cheek.

Lincoln could be wandering through the woods, she thinks, and what if he walks straight into this or into some other group of shooting men – there could be God knows how many policemen here now, descending, and apparently when they finally decided to save the day, they did not mess around – and Lincoln would have no idea what the sound of bullets might mean. He would not know anything, and they would kill him in a heartbeat. He is so small, so hard to see, surely, in this rush of smoke and bodies.

There is another splash in the water near her feet. She is on her hands and knees now, still staying low, but picking up speed, and Kailynn is next to her. Joan tells herself that if the gunfire stops, she will call out for help and she will trust that the police will recognize a woman's voice and that they will not shoot her. But the gunfire is not stopping. She and Kailynn settle into the movement of hands and knees, moving like paddles on a canoe – in and out – and she ignores the cold and she ignores her entire body, unsteady wrists and deadened feet and all the weak, faithless parts of it. When she looks over her shoulder, she cannot make out any human shapes. Maybe the policemen are chasing the gunman farther into the woods. Now there are only trees and the fading sound of bullets.

They stay in the water for a short while – miles, it feels like, but she imagines it is no more than a hundred yards.

'Let's get out here,' she whispers to Kailynn, and for the first time it occurs to her that the girl has not said a word. 'Are you okay?'

'Where's Lincoln?' asks the girl as they heave themselves up the muddy bank.

Joan loses her balance and has to catch herself.

'I hid him under a bush. We have to get him. The bullets,' she says, and she has run out of breath.

She gets to her feet. Her skirt is clinging, somehow still in one piece, and Kailynn is pushing herself to her feet, too. Joan helps the girl up by one arm and thinks of how she is the opposite of Lincoln, who is so dense and solid. This girl's bones feel like china, like blown glass, like handles on teacups.

The girl feels like all kinds of precious things. Joan does not know why she was so slow to see it. She surely couldn't see anything at all if she couldn't see this girl in front of her, this girl with red ribbons for hair and legs like origami, who makes fried chicken and whose father bleeds for her.

'You hid him?' Kailynn repeats.

'They were coming,' Joan says, and her vision blurs slightly.

She steadies herself. She grabs her skirt in her fists and lifts it above her knees. She looks down, and there is pine straw under her feet, but she can no longer feel the difference in the foot with a shoe and the foot without one. That is good. That is helpful, the lack of feeling. She runs, and it feels good, like how she feels after nine or ten miles, bodiless, her mind disconnected. Only she keeps stumbling, catching herself on the trees. She must still be attached to her body, because it is faulty.

'We'll find him,' she says to Kailynn.

'We'll find him,' Kailynn says back to her, and the girl's hair is lifting and falling as she runs, and Joan thinks what a terrible plan it was to run up to gunmen with no idea what to say other than Mrs Powell's name, like it was some talisman, some magic sword that would conquer Robby Montgomery. She is lucky that she and Kailynn aren't both dead, but they aren't, so maybe it was not such a flawed plan.

Joan cannot feel any other parts of herself, but she can feel her leg, the pain shooting up to her hip, and she keeps tripping. Still she runs, and nothing looks familiar, but just as the panic is making itself known, she sees the hanging spider through the trees – only a formless, glowing blob – and she makes her way to it. She calls Lincoln's name, softly, slowing. She is ten feet away. Five feet away, calling his name again.

No one answers.

'He was here?' says Kailynn.

'He's here,' Joan says.

She comes to the spider and reaches out, tapping one of its legs, making it swing. She is sure that it is the same spider. She scans the woods – the shrub, which one was it?

There. She thinks it is there.

The gunfire is slowing in the distance, like popcorn nearly done.

She runs to the bush, but somehow she is crawling, and by the time she can touch the branches, her head is on the ground and her knees are digging into the dirt. She lifts the branches and peers underneath.

He is not there.

'Lincoln? Lincoln?' she calls anyway, not able to look away from the empty dirt and the empty branches, the space where he is not.

'Lincoln?'

She means to say it louder, but her voice is not working. Back on her feet, she starts in one direction, stops, and tries a different one.

She cannot think of how to look for him. She has no pattern to follow. He never wanders off. He always holds her hand. She lost track of him only once, at the fair, and she found him in thirty seconds.

'Lincoln?' she whispers, getting softer instead of louder.

'Lincoln!'

She screams it. Suddenly her voice is working, and his name rings out loud and long, and she does not care if anyone hears her. Kailynn is calling for him, too.

Her boy has listened to her too well. Wherever he is, he is not making a sound. She was so sure that he was too scared to venture out, but she has misjudged him and now what?

There are possibilities she will not consider.

She does not have to consider them as long as she keeps moving.

She settles on running in circles, wider and wider, around the shrub where she left him. She falls forward and lands hard on her hands. She picks herself up.

Joan looks under bushes and reaches toward every waving branch, and she passes the spider again, dangling, and she passes twenty trees that look just alike, and there is a stump, hollowed out, and there is a long shroud of ivy draped over a sapling. There is a hanging plastic ghost, unlit, bell-shaped.

She stops, shifting her feet, and she can tell something is not right. She reaches down and realizes that blood is covering her toes. But she does not feel it, so it doesn't matter.

Kailynn is still somewhere nearby, calling his name.

Joan focuses on the ground, which once seemed like it was the same patch of leaves and dead wood repeating itself endlessly, but now that she is staring at it, she can see the details separate themselves. There is enough moonlight to see mushrooms and a swathe of monkey grass. A popped balloon with the string still attached. A plastic witch's cauldron, overturned, crooked. A lone string of white lights cutting through the darkness. She avoids the light and lifts the branches of a willow tree. She passes the ivy-covered sapling again, and she pulls the ivy apart. It is dense – impenetrable – no sign of him.

There is no word for what she feels pushing up through her rib cage, pulsing. It is like a scream but with fists and claws. She will not let it out.

She sees the glowing spider again, now only a vague shape in the trees. She looks back over all that she has passed, and there is the pointless string of white lights, and she sees a clump of what might be dead wisteria. She steps toward the wisteria, which is wide enough to conceal him. Off to her left is the witch's cauldron again, and this time she sees what she did not see the first time.

She yanks herself to a stop.

The cauldron is crooked in a way that means it might have something underneath it. In a way that might mean it is caught on a small ankle or foot.

I'm a turtle, I'm a turtle, I'm a turtle.

She thinks of him hiding under an ottoman, his head peeking out.

She knows she is right even before she lifts the cauldron – she knows she has followed some pale thread from her brain to his. There are a million of these threads between them, brain to brain, and the threads tell her when he is getting hungry and when he is about to cry, and they tell her that he will like the idea of using marshmallows for a tiny astronaut's boots. Sometimes the threads get twisted: after all, they told her he would stay under the bush. But this is a perfect thread, soft and warm like Sarge's fur and silver like Thor's helmet – and the thread leads her to him.

She holds up the cheap plastic cauldron with one hand, and underneath it he is curled into a ball like a roly-poly. It is the same position she remembers from tornado drills when she was a girl. He has his arms tucked around his head, and he does not look up.

She tosses the cauldron to the side. She drops to her knees. 'Lincoln?'

'Mommy,' he says, looking up at her, smiling, and again her body is not working. She cannot even reach for him, and then he is moving, and that lets her move, too. She grabs him under his arms and drags him through the leaves, and he is against her, so warm. So solid and heavy.

The scream-like thing inside her evaporates at the feel of him, dissolving back into air and blood and bone. She runs a hand over her son – he sounds calm enough, but his face is damp.

'Do you know what I was?' he asks against her ear.

She cannot say it at first. She swallows.

'A turtle,' she answers.

'Yes!' he whispers, ecstatically, burying his hands in her hair. 'Why are you so wet?'

He pulls his hands from her soaking hair. She captures his hand in hers, and she wraps herself around him, and she is cold to the bone and she has maybe never been so relieved.

'I fell in the creek,' she says.

'Oh. What are those noises? Guns? More guns?'

She has almost stopped hearing the guns.

'The police are here,' she whispers. 'Why didn't you answer me when I was calling?'

'I didn't hear you. I was disappeared.'

She pushes herself to her feet, and she holds his hands because she is not sure she can pick him up. They should go back to the front of the zoo, maybe – surely whatever was happening there has finished.

'He's okay?' says Kailynn, coming up behind them, out of breath.

'Yeah,' Joan says, taking a step. 'He's fine. Come on.'

She notices the leaves in Kailynn's hair as the girl falls into step beside her.

'What's wrong?' Kailynn says.

Joan doesn't know why the girl is asking, but then she notices that she is on her knees again. She is confused, at first, by the damp feel of the ground.

She hurts.

She has heard people say they do not feel getting shot – who has said it? Someone real or pretend? She can feel it now. It reminds her of when her father accidentally slammed her hand in the back door when she was small – he didn't know she was behind him – and the pain was so big that she could not feel where it started.

Kailynn is grabbing at her hand, pulling. Joan looks down and sees that the blood is coming so fast from her leg that she can watch it pool on the ground.

Kailynn stops pulling at her.

'Oh,' the girl says, her face so close. Her fingers turn gentle. 'Oh.'

Joan touches her side, and her side is wet, too, and she cannot make her legs move. But she can also hear that there are still footsteps in the woods, not distant enough, and she is not sure if the gunfire has really stopped.

It is not safe to stay here.

'Take him,' she says to Kailynn, nodding at Lincoln. 'Head back toward the exhibits. Sit somewhere and wait until the police come to help you.'

She likes that image. Not the shadowy policemen in the woods but a solid, safe wall of uniformed men and women, guns disappeared. They will tell her son this is over. They will make him safe. They will find Mrs Powell and tend to her knee, and they will check every nook and cranny and trash can. They will lift up a baby and find a mother, and of course the baby and the mother will be together again. Of course that must be the ending.

Lincoln is holding tight to her with both hands.

'No,' he says, shaking his head, wide-eyed. 'No.'

'Go on,' she says to him, and she shoves him away from her. Then she pulls him back because she can't help it, can't just let him go without holding him again first. She is on one knee, with the other leg stretched behind her. She wraps her arms around him and presses her face to his temple, and she breathes in the scent of him, which is always changing and the same and now is something like bread. She tries hard to make every cell in her body remember this – his hand in her hair, soft skin stretched over cheekbone, *Mommy* – so that if she can keep anything with her for always, it will be the feel of him like this.

'You're my boy. Go with Kailynn.' No, she realizes, that is not fair. He needs more than that. He needs to understand. 'I need to wait here, sweet. For now. Until there are doctors.'

He is crying.

She makes herself let go of her son's fingers, makes herself let go of him entirely, even though she cannot stand the moment when his skin is a separate thing from her skin.

'I want to stay with you,' he says. Kailynn is reaching for him, taking his hand, threading their fingers together. He goes with her, saying 'Okay' in that trembling way he has, but her head goes wavy. She loses track of things for a long blink, and then her eyes are open again.

The lights strung through the trees are beautiful to her now. She does not know how she didn't see it before. They are long ropes of white, like pearls or moons, and there is a ball of bright orange in the distance and red and blue lights flashing somewhere, reflecting off the trees.

She is still on her knees. No, on her stomach. She will get up soon, but for a moment she watches Lincoln run, holding Kailynn's hand. He is moving more quickly than she expected, his usual graceless run that she loves, his feet flying up sideways. He is not fast, not linear, but every part of him is moving – shoulders and feet and hands and elbows, heading off in every direction. He is not built for aerodynamics, her boy.

She tastes blood. Maybe she has bitten her lip again.

He looks bigger the farther away he gets, and she is aware enough to realize that this is not right. But he is filling up the screen in front of her, blotting out the swooping branches of the pines. There is only him. And the lights. Bright lights spreading through the sky like ribbons on the Maypole when she was in sixth grade in her lavender dress and she looked up at the ribbon she was holding, long and winding – *Pay attention, girls*, said Mrs Manning, who was in charge of the whole ordeal, *this is tricky* – and she wove her ribbon together with the others, in and out, and the sherbet-colored ribbons filled up the sky, and at the end of every ribbon, a pair of hands holding tight – Kailynn's fingers twisting in her shirt, Kailynn's hand in Lincoln's, ribbons winding – and that is what the lights are like now. Beautiful.

There are beautiful things. Pay attention.

Her hair has fallen into her mouth, and she jerks her head. The ground under her is damp.

Lincoln. She doesn't know where he is. She needs to lift her head.

She loses track again, and then, when she turns her head, she catches a glimpse of him from a distance, his messy curls, and he is surrounded by people in dark clothes, down on their knees. It is nice when grown-ups make an effort not to tower over him. But she is not positive whether he is actually standing there talking to policemen or whether her thoughts have gotten syrupy.

This is a story about a little boy named Steve who would grow up to be Horseman.

This is a story about robots and lasers.

This is a story about when I get married, Mommy. I'm going to have a wife. Her name will be Lucy. I'm going to have five boys and five girls. But they'll grow in my belly, not hers, like seahorses do.

She wants to hear his story. She will close her eyes and hear him better.

She needs to keep her eyes closed, because the ribbons of light are too bright.

Not ribbons. One light.

272

A man is holding a flashlight and leaning over her.

'Ma'am?' he says, and he is kneeling, and the light is gone. 'You're all right.' She feels something pressing hard on her leg. 'You hold on a second. We've got help coming.'

He is wearing a dark shirt, and there is the glare of something bright on his chest. She thinks he might be Mr Simmons, a teacher she had in fifth grade, who read an essay she wrote and told her she was going to be somebody one day.

'Lincoln,' she says.

'Your boy?'

The man pushes her hair back from her face, and he is so gentle about it.

'Little dark-headed guy?' he asks her.

Her eyes are closed. She is going to open them.

'Lincoln,' she says.

She thinks she says it.

She thinks time passes. She feels herself lifted, raised up. There are voices, but they are not saying real words. There are more lights. There are shapes moving around her.

She feels the touch of small fingers on her hand.

She shifts slightly, and Lincoln's hand fits into hers. She thinks that he says her name. She thinks that she can feel his breath, warm. She feels his skin against hers, and his fingertips are flickering across her palm, telling her every story she's ever heard.

ACKNOWLEDGMENTS

To Laura Tisdel, my friend, who renewed my ridiculous dream that I might one day discover an editor who was brilliant and would also be fun at a slumber party. That is what this entire process has been like – one brilliant, long-distance slumber party. Both Frankie Gray and Anne Collins have helped to sculpt the book into a sleeker, better version of itself. I'm immensely grateful to Kim Witherspoon for telling me to make things more complicated and for, in general, managing an impressive combination of competence and charm. William Callahan helped me out with a smart and thoughtful read that made the book forever richer. Thank you, Jason Weekley, for your knowledge of guns and your helpful early fact-checking. Likewise, thank you to my brother Dabney for explaining what happens when you shoot various objects (and thank you for the goats).

Thank you to my mother, Gina Kaye Phillips, for all the stories that come with more than four decades of teaching. Thanks to Hannah Wolfson for a helpful early conversation and to Donny Phillips for his cat escapades. I'd also like to

ACKNOWLEDGMENTS

acknowledge the references in this text to *Goodnight Moon* by Margaret Wise Brown, *The Highwayman* by Alfred Noyes, and 'That Hell-Bound Train' by Robert Bloch.

Finally, thank you to Fred, best of husbands and best of readers.

READING GROUP GUIDE

1) *Fierce* is set over the course of three hours. Why do you think Gin Phillips chose such a condensed timeline?

2) At one point, Joan says 'The rules are different today.' Throughout the novel, she has to make some questionable choices that, under normal circumstances, no one would ever do. Can you pinpoint what these were? Did you agree with the decision she made? Would you have done the same in a similar situation?

3) What did you find to be the most important element of this novel – the tense situation they find themselves in, or the tender depiction of the relationship between Lincoln and Joan? How does Gin Phillips use one to highlight the other?

4) *Fierce* features chapters from the points of view of different characters throughout the novel. How did this structure affect your reading experience?

5) Why do you think the author chose to set this novel in a zoo? How does the setting relate to the action on the page?

6) What do you think the overall message of the novel is?